OUR
KIND
OF
CRUELTY

OUR KIND OF CRUELTY

ARAMINTA HALL

MCD · FARRAR, STRAUS AND GIROUX   NEW YORK

MCD
Farrar, Straus and Giroux
175 Varick Street, New York 10014

Library of Congress Cataloging-in-Publication Data
Names: Hall, Araminta, author.
Title: Our kind of cruelty / Araminta Hall.
Description: First edition. | New York : MCD / Farrar, Straus and Giroux, 2018.
Identifiers: LCCN 2017038361 | ISBN 9780374228194 (hardcover) |
    ISBN 9780374717995 (ebook)
Subjects: LCSH: Stalkers—Fiction. | Psychological fiction. | GSAFD: Suspense fiction.
Classification: LCC PR6108.A458 O94 2018 | DDC 823/.92—dc23
LC record available at https://lccn.loc.gov/2017038361

Open market edition ISBN: 978-0-374-90567-5

Designed by Abby Kagan

Our books may be purchased in bulk for promotional, educational, or business use.
Please contact your local bookseller or the Macmillan Corporate and Premium
Sales Department at 1-800-221-7945, extension 5442, or by e-mail at
MacmillanSpecialMarkets@macmillan.com.

www.mcdbooks.com • www.fsgbooks.com
Follow us on Twitter, Facebook, and Instagram at @mcdbooks

1 3 5 7 9 10 8 6 4 2

*To
Jamie,
Oscar,
Violet,
and
Edith,
as always*

One can be too ingenious in trying to search out
the truth. Sometimes one must simply respect
its veiled face. Of course this is a love story.

—IRIS MURDOCH, *The Sea, the Sea*

PART

ONE

The rules of the Crave were simple. V and I went to a nightclub in a predetermined place a good way from where we lived. We traveled there together but entered separately. We made our way to the bar and stood far enough apart for it to seem like we weren't together but close enough that I could always keep her in my vision. Then we waited. It never took long, but why would it when V shone as brightly as she did? Some hapless man would approach and offer to buy her a drink or ask her to dance. She would begin a mild flirt. And I would wait, my eyes never leaving her, my body ready to pounce at all times. We have a signal: As soon as she raises her hand and pulls on the silver eagle she always wears around her neck, I must act. In those dark throbbing rooms I would push through the mass of people, pulling at the useless man drooling over her, and ask him what he thought he was doing talking to my girlfriend. And because I am useful-looking in that tall, broad way, and because V likes me to lift weights and start all my days with a run, they would invariably back off with their hands in front of their faces, looking scared and timid. Sometimes we couldn't wait to start kissing, sometimes we went to the loo and fucked in the stalls, V calling out so anyone could hear. Sometimes we made it home. Either way, our kisses tasted of Southern Comfort, V's favorite drink.

It was V who named our game on one of those dark, freezing nights where the rain looks like grease on your windows. V was wearing a black T-shirt that felt like velvet to touch. It skimmed over her round breasts and I knew she wasn't wearing a bra. My body responded to her as it always did. She laughed as I stood up and put her hand against my hot chest. "That's all any of us are ever doing, you know, Mikey. Everyone out there. All craving something."

It is true to say that the Crave always belonged to V.

Part of me doesn't want to write it all down like this, but my barrister says I must because he needs to get a clear handle on the situation. He says my story feels like something he can't grab hold of. He also thinks it might do me good, so I better understand where we are. I think he's an idiot. But I have nothing else to do all day as I sit in this godforsaken cell with only the company of Fat Terry, a man with a neck bigger than most people's thighs, listening to him masturbating to pictures of celebrities I don't recognize. "Cat still got your tongue? My banter not good enough for you?" he says to me most mornings, as I lie silently on my bunk, the words like unexploded bombs on his tongue. I don't reply, but it never goes further than that because in here, when you've killed someone, you appear to get a grudging respect.

It is hard to believe that it isn't even a year since I returned from America. It feels more like a lifetime, two lifetimes even. But the fact is I arrived home at the end of May and as I sit here now writing in this tiny, dark cell it is December. December can be warm and full of goodness, but this one is cold and flat, with days that never seem to brighten and a fog that never seems to lift. The papers talk of a smog blanketing London, returned from the dead as if a million Victorian souls were floating over the Thames. But really we all know it is a trillion tiny chemical particles polluting our air and our bodies, mutating and changing the very essence of who we are.

I think America might have been the beginning of the mess. V and I were never meant to be apart and yet we were seduced by the promise of money and speeding up time. I remember her encouraging me to go; how she said it would take me five years in London to earn what I could in two in New York. She was right of course, but I'm not sure now that the money was worth it. It feels like we lost something of ourselves in those years. Like we stretched ourselves so thin we stopped being real.

But our house is real and maybe that is the point? The equation could make me feel dizzy: two years in hell equals a four-bedroom house in Clapham. It sounds like a joke when you put it like that. Sounds like nothing anyone sane would sell their soul for. But the fact remains that it exists. It will wait for us without judgment. It will remain.

I employed a house hunter when I knew I was coming home, whom I always pictured stalking the streets of London with a gun in one hand and a few houses slung over her shoulder, blood dripping from their wounds. She sent me endless photos and details as I sat at my desk in New York, which I would scroll through until the images blurred before my eyes. I found I didn't much care what I bought, but I was very specific in my requests because I knew that was what V would want. I was careful with the location and also the orientation. I remembered that the garden had to be southeast-facing and I insisted on the house being double-fronted because V always thought they were much friendlier looking.

There are rooms on either side of the hall, rooms that as a child I simply didn't know existed, but that V taught me have peculiar names: a drawing room and library. Although I've yet to fill the bookcases and I have no plans to become an artist. The eat-in kitchen, as estate agents love to refer to any large room containing cooking equipment, runs the entire back length of the house. The previous owners pushed the whole house out into the garden by five feet and encased the addition in glass, with massive bifold doors that you can open and shut as easily as running your hand through water.

Under-floor heated Yorkshire stone runs throughout this room and into the garden, so when the doors are open you can step from inside to out without a change in texture. "Bringing the outside in," Toby the estate agent said, making my hands itch with the desire to punch him. "And really, they've extended the floor space by the whole garden area," he said, meaninglessly pointing to the sunken fire pit and hot tub, the built-in barbecue, the tasteful water feature. He was lucky that I could already imagine V loving all those details, otherwise I would have turned and walked out of the house there and then.

And that would have been a shame, as upstairs is the part I like best. I've had all the back rooms knocked together and then repartitioned so we have what Toby would no doubt call a master suite but is actually a large bedroom, a walk-in wardrobe, and a luxurious bathroom. I chose sumptuous materials for all the fittings: silks and velvets, marbles and flints, the most beggingly tactile of all the elements. I have heavy curtains at the windows and clever lighting, so it's dark and sensuous and bright and light in all the right places. At the front of the house are two smaller bedrooms and in the attic is another bedroom and en suite, leading to a roof terrace at the back. Fantastic for guests, as Toby said.

I've also taken great care over the furnishings. A tasteful mix of modern and antique, I think you'd say. Modern for the useful things like the kitchen and bathroom and sound system and lighting and all that. Antique for the decorations. I have become a bit of an expert at trawling shops and sounding like I know what I'm talking about. And I found a field in Sussex, which four or five times a year is transformed into a giant antiques market. People from eastern Europe drive over huge trucks filled with pieces from their past and laugh at all of us prepared to part with hundreds of pounds for things that would be burned in their country. You're meant to bargain with them, but often I can't be bothered, often I get swept away with it. Because there is something amazing about running your hand along the back of a chair and finding grooves and ridges and realizing that yours is only one of so many hands that must have done exactly this.

I bought a cupboard last time and when I got it home and opened it there were loads of telephone numbers written in pencil inside the door. Marta 03201, Cossi 98231, and so on and so on. It felt like a story without a beginning, middle, or end. They struck me as the possible workings of a private investigator, or even clues in a murder case. I had imagined having it stripped and painted a dark gray, but after I found the numbers I left it exactly as it was, with flaking green paint and an internal drawer that sticks whenever you try to open it. I've become attached to the rootlessness of the numbers. I like the thought that none of us will ever know what really happened to these women or to the person who wrote down their numbers. But I'm not sure what V will think about the cupboard. Perhaps she will want to smooth the numbers away.

The colors on the walls all belong to V. Lots of navy blues and dark grays, even black in places, which the interior designer assured me wasn't depressing anymore. She encouraged me to have the outside of the cupboards in the walk-in wardrobe painted a shining black and the insides a deep scarlet. She told me it was opulent, but I'm not sure she was right because all I see when I walk into the room is leather and dried blood.

Almost the first piece of mail I received after I moved in was an invitation to V's wedding. It came in a cream-colored envelope and felt heavy in my hand, my not yet familiar address calligraphied in a fine ink. The same flowery hand had emblazoned my name across the top of the card, which was thick and soft, the black lettering raised and tactile. I stared at my name for a long time, so long I could imagine the hand holding the pen, see the delicate strokes used. There was a slight smudge against the *i*, but apart from that it was perfect. I took the invitation into the drawing room and rested it on the mantelpiece, underneath the gilt mirror, behind the tall silver candlesticks. My hand, I noticed, was shaking slightly and I knew I was hotter than the day allowed. I kept my hand against the cool marble of the fireplace surround and concentrated on the intricate curls holding up the perfect flatness of the shelf. It reminded me that pure, flawless marble is one of the most desired materials known to man, but also one of the hardest to find. If it's easy it's probably not worth having, V said to me once, and that made me smile, standing in my drawing room with my hand against the marble.

I knew what she was doing, it was all fine.

I had e-mailed V from New York to let her know I was coming home. That was when she replied to say she was getting married. It was the first piece of correspondence we'd had since Christmas and it shook me very badly. I had only stopped trying to contact her in February and I e-mailed with my news at the end of April, which meant she'd only had a couple of months to meet someone and agree to marry him. "I know you'll be surprised," she wrote, "but also I think your silence these past few months means you've accepted that we are over and want to move on as much as me. Who knows, perhaps you already have! And I know it seems quick, but I also know I'm doing the right thing. I feel like I owe you an apology for the way I reacted to what happened at Christmas. Perhaps you just realized before I did that we were over and I shouldn't have behaved as I did, I should have sat down and spoken properly to you. I hope you'll be happy for me and I also hope that we'll be able to be friends. You were and are very special to me and I couldn't bear the thought of not having you in my life."

For a few days I felt simply numb, as if an explosion had gone off next to me and shattered my body. But I quickly realized how pedestrian this reaction was. Apart from all the love she clearly still had for me, V seemed to be under the impression that I had wanted the relationship to end. Her breezy tone was so far removed from the V whom I knew that I wondered for a moment if she had been kidnapped and someone else was writing her e-mails, although the much more plausible explanations were that V was not herself, or that she was using her tone to send me a covert message. There were two options at play: Either she had lost her mind with the distress I had caused her at Christmas and jumped into the arms of the nearest fool, or she needed me to pay for what I'd done. This seemed by far the most likely; this was V after all and she would need me to witness my own remorse. It was as if the lines of her e-mail dissolved and behind them were her true words. This was a game, our favorite game. It was obvious that we were beginning a new, more intricate Crave.

I waited a couple days before replying to V's e-mail and then I chose my words carefully. I adopted her upbeat tone and told her I was very happy for her and of course we would still be friends. I also told her I would be in touch with my address when I got back to London, but after the invitation landed on my mat I knew I needn't bother. It meant she had called Elaine and that in itself meant something. It also meant that she probably wasn't as angry as she had been. I quickly came to see the invitation for what it was: the first hand in an elaborate apology, a dance only V and I could ever master. I even felt sorry for Angus Metcalf, as the ridiculous invitation revealed him to be.

MR. & MRS. COLIN WALTON

REQUEST THE PLEASURE OF

YOUR COMPANY AT THE MARRIAGE

OF THEIR DAUGHTER

VERITY

TO

MR. ANGUS METCALF

AT STEEPLE CHAPEL, SUSSEX

ON SATURDAY, 14TH SEPTEMBER

AT 3:00 O'CLOCK

AND AFTERWARD AT

STEEPLE HOUSE

I woke sometimes with the invitation lying next to me in bed, not that I ever remembered taking it up with me. Once it was under my cheek and when I peeled it from me I felt the indentations it had left. In the mirror I could see the words, branded onto my skin.

I left it a few days and then sent a short note to V's mother saying I would be delighted to attend. Not, I knew, that she would share my delight.

I have spent a lot of time with Colin and Suzi over the years and there was a time when I imagined them coming to see me as a sort of son. Sometimes at Christmas it was hard to shake the feeling that V and

I were siblings sitting with our parents over a turkey carcass. "We make a funny pair," she said to me once, "you with no parents, me with no siblings. There's so little of us to go around. We have to keep a tight hold of each other to stop the other from floating away." Which was fine by me. I loved nothing more than encircling V's tiny waist and pulling her toward me in bed, feeling her buttocks slip like a jigsaw into my groin, as our legs mirrored each other in a perfect outline, her head resting neatly under my chin.

Sometimes I think I liked V best when she slept. When I felt her go heavy in my arms and her breath thicken and slow. I would open my mouth so that my jaw was able to run along the top of her head and I could feel all the ridges and markings on her skull. It didn't feel like it would be hard to go farther than the bone, to delve into the pulpy mixture protecting the gray mass of twisted ropes that formed her brain. To feel the electric currents surging, which kept her alive and alert. Often I would feel jealous of those currents and all the information they held. I would want to wrap them around myself so she would only dream of me, so that I filled her as much as she filled me.

I wonder if V had to argue with her mother to invite me, or if Suzi thought it would serve me right to see her daughter happily married to someone else. I wonder if she planned to look at me during the ceremony and smile.

But in retrospect Suzi always was a stupid woman, always pretending she wanted to be different when really she wanted to be exactly like the people who had surrounded her all her life. I should have realized this sooner, as soon really as I heard her name.

"I'm Susanne," she said to me on our first meeting, "but call me Suzi," which wasn't too bad until I discovered she spelled it with an *i*. A *y* would have been too cozy for Suzi, too normal, too close to who she actually is. And you should never trust people who yearn to be something other than who they are.

Y

It wasn't even vaguely hard to get a job in the City when I arrived back in London. I had glowing references from the American bank and my performance there spoke for itself. My new salary was large and my bonus promised even more. I didn't mind the journey to the office each day and I even liked the tall, glinting building where I worked, high in the clouds. I spent my days shouting about numbers and watching them ping and jump on the screens on my desk. It was so easy I couldn't understand why everyone didn't do it.

V had always said we should aim for retirement at forty-five and it was a target that looked easily within my grasp. I presumed she hadn't completely changed her life since February and was still at the Calthorpe Centre, working in her sterile basement on her computer programs that, she said, would render humans useless one day. She claimed not to know why she did it, why she persevered so steadily to make machines cleverer than we are, but I think she loved the idea of inventing something artificial that was better than the real thing. I think she loved the idea of seeing if she could outsmart human emotion.

It occurs to me now that if V hadn't gotten her job we might have gone to America together. We might still be there. But I don't like to think this way, it leads you down too many dangerous paths, into worlds of temptation that can never be yours. And I indulged too much in that sort of thinking as a child: That woman kissing her child in the park could be your mother, your key could let you into the house down the road with roses around the door, the smell of frying onions could be someone preparing your dinner.

And anyway, that is what happened. I got the job in America and she got the job in London. We were both riding the crest of a wave, me offered a salary so high I couldn't take it seriously and V the youngest person ever to have been taken on as a director at the Calthorpe Centre, only five years out of university.

"How clever of them to make it sound so innocent, like a medical foundation or something," she said after she took the call.

I wrapped her in my arms and whispered my congratulations. "But I'm going to New York in three months," I said.

She pulled away from me and her face tightened around her words. "I can't turn this down, Mikey."

Something rose through me that I thought might tip me off-balance. "I won't go then. I can get another job here."

"No. You've got to go. It's an amazing opportunity for you. You can do a couple of years and earn lots of money and then we can start our proper life when you get back."

"You make it sound so easy."

"That's because it *is*. We'll talk every day and it's not that far. We can fly over for weekends. It will be romantic." She laughed. "You'll be even more like my eagle, flying across the Atlantic in your silver bullet."

But that thought jolted me. I reached out and took her by the shoulders. "You have to promise that you won't ever Crave without me, V."

She shook herself free and rubbed where my hands had held her. "Don't be ridiculous."

Her tone cut at me and I turned away, trying to hide my hurt. But she followed me, twisting her body around mine. "Mike, I would never do that, you must know that."

She stood on tiptoe so that her mouth was against my ear. "I love seeing how scared they are of you," she whispered. I held myself still, until she said, "Let's Crave."

I think we both knew it would be our last time. We went to a nightclub in Piccadilly Circus. We'd been there before, but not for at least six months.

It was always filled with foreign students and tourists and gangs of boys up from the provinces. And the odd prostitute or escort. No one there looked like they were having a good time and the music was a hard, steady thump that reverberated through your body and felt like you were giving yourself CPR. The lights strobed, making everyone's skin take on a sickly, alien pallor. And something fluorescent in the air made the whites of everyone's eyes glint and lint show up on everyone's clothes.

V was wearing a gray silk dress that revealed the milky whiteness of her shoulders and her long, thin neck that curled into the base of her skull. She had piled her dark hair on top of her head, but tendrils had escaped to caress her neck, in a promise of what your lips could do. Black liner flicked over her eyes, stretching and elongating them, and she licked at her full lips that had never needed any lipstick. There was a blush high on her cheekbones, but I didn't know if it was real or false. She smiled as the barman handed her a tall, brown drink and I saw her nails were painted black.

My own drink was too sweet and it coated my throat so it felt tight and sore. My head was filled with the knowledge of the time we were going to have to spend apart, which was causing an ache to build in my temples. A drunk man swayed into me, his girlfriend giggling on his arm. We were right next to the bar and it would have been very easy to take his head in my hands and bash it against the hard wood. The blood would have come quickly, his head contorted and broken, before anyone could have stopped me.

I looked back at V and she was still alone, still leaning against the bar, her drink making frequent trips to her mouth. It was possible she looked too perfect for this place and I thought about telling her we should leave. It was like putting an exotic butterfly in a roomful of flies, all buzzing around their own shit. I pushed myself off the bar to go to her, but as I did a man approached her. He wasn't much taller than she was; stocky, his large muscles bulging like Popeye's from a pristine white T-shirt. His skin was swarthy and even from where I stood I could see it was covered in a film of sweat. A heavy silver chain with some sort of round coin encircled his neck and his black hair was slicked off his face. He wasn't ugly, but something about him was grotesque, almost like his features were too large for his face.

I stopped myself from moving, my eyes locked on the encounter. I imagined, as I always did at this moment, what it was like to be that close to V, to feel the heat from her body and to imagine your hands at work there; to look at her lips as she spoke, to catch glimpses of her tongue as she laughed and wonder what that mouth was capable of. He leaned forward as he spoke, craning close to her ear, his hand poised in the air just by her arm, as if summoning up the courage to touch her. She laughed. He dropped his hand to her hip, where it finally connected with her body through the silk. She was still leaning against the bar, but she tilted her hips forward slightly so he could slide his hand behind her, against her buttocks. He closed the gap between them, extinguishing all the air, his groin pushing against her hips, no doubt already advertising whatever it was he had. I kept my eyes on V's hands, but they stayed on her drink and the eagle hung untouched around her neck.

My breathing had deepened and my body felt weak and useless. A mist was drawing down and I worried that soon I wouldn't be able to see at all. Soon I would miss V's sign and she would be swallowed by the night and the man. I turned my head and saw the neon exit sign above the door. I imagined walking toward it and into the open, returning alone to our flat, getting into bed, and waiting for her to come home. I imagined letting go and not caring, the idea like tiny pins in my brain.

I looked back and even though the man's face was against V's neck, I could see her hand on the bird. The woman in front of me yelped as I pushed her out of the way. "Watch out," she called after me, pointlessly. But even in the seconds it took for me to reach her, I saw that V's expression had changed by the time I came upon them. She wasn't laughing anymore and was pushing slightly against the man's chest as he lowered his face toward hers. I took him by the shoulder, yanking him backward, so his drink made a stain down the front of his T-shirt.

"What the fuck are you doing to my girlfriend?" I asked, feeling the people around us melting into the background.

"What the fuck?" he said, straightening up. We stared at each other for a minute, but I had height and muscle on him and he had felt my strength when I'd pulled him back. He waved his hands in the air. "Nice fucking girlfriend," he said to me. Then he looked at V. "Cocktease," he said, turning away.

I felt V's hand on my arm as it tensed and drew back, ready to lay waste to his stupid, oversized face. She turned me toward her and pulled me closer and I leaned down and kissed her, putting my hands where his had been, laying my claim. Her tongue was quick and fast and I wanted her so much I thought I would sweep the drinks off the bar and lay her in the spilled liquor. But she pulled me away, past the round tables and chairs, past the writhing bodies on the dance floor, past the booming speakers, past the merging couples to a dark corner. She backed herself into it, pulling me toward her. She opened my fly and pulled me out, wrapping her legs around me. The silk of her dress slithered upward too easily and she wasn't wearing underwear, so I was inside her quickly and she was biting the side of my neck and moaning and it was like all the other people had gone and we were the only ones there, the only ones who mattered.

Afterward, in the cold night air, with drunken people bustling along their sad, forlorn ways to terrible encounters, V said, "For a second I thought you'd abandoned me."

I took her hand. "How can you say that?"

"Because I touched the bird and it took you a while to come."

I realized I must have spent longer looking at the exit sign than I'd meant to. "I'd never abandon you," I said.

"Promise?" she said, and I looked over and saw she wasn't giggling anymore and she looked smaller, the black lines smudged around her eyes.

I stopped, even though the streets were so full that people immediately walked into us. I lifted the delicate silver bird that lived on the chain around her neck and she stepped toward me. "I'm your eagle," I said. "You know that."

I didn't give V the necklace. In fact, she told me she bought it for herself with her first ever paycheck from a waitressing job when she was sixteen. She told me she'd been walking past a shop and it had glinted at her from a window and she'd felt a deep desire to possess it. I had always presumed it to be a dainty bird, like a swift or even a clichéd lovebird, and I was surprised when she first told me it was an eagle. But when I looked properly I saw the length of the wings and the curved beak.

"Eagles are magnificent," V had said. "They are the only birds that get excited by a storm, then they fly straight into it and use the wind currents to lift them above it, so they can look down on all the chaos. But also," she said, putting her hands over mine, "they are very loyal. They mate for life."

I'd leaned down and kissed her mouth. "I'm your eagle," I'd said.

I thought it expedient to make friends in my new City job, even though the same plan hadn't gone that well in New York. I would be fine if it were just V and me forever, but I've learned that people find you strange if you're happy like that. So, I've learned their ways. I understand now that people do not always mean what they say. That they enjoy hours of meaningless chat in crowded bars without a reason like the Crave for being there. That they are happy to share their bodies with others and then act as if they barely know them.

If someone says something like "I could fucking kill him" or "I'm feeling so depressed" or "My legs are about to literally drop off," they don't actually mean any of those things. They don't even mean anything close to those things. When a woman puts her hand on your leg she does not expect you to reciprocate. When a man calls you mate, it doesn't mean he likes you. When someone says "We must get together soon," you shouldn't ask them when or text them the next day.

When I was in primary school I pushed another boy in my class, Billy Sheffield, and he fell and grazed his knee. My teacher, whose name I forget, told me I had to say sorry, but I refused because I wasn't. He had called me some name, again I forget what but it would have been something along the lines of Two Stripe or Fleabag, in reference to my market-stall trainers and unwashed clothes. Either way, I wasn't sorry. So they took me to the little office where rumor had it they sent the crazy kids. A rosy-cheeked woman smiled at me and told me to sit in a comfy chair while she offered me sweets. It made me wonder if being crazy was all that bad after all.

"Why aren't you sorry?" she finally asked me, after I'd stuffed myself with candy.

"Because I'm not," I said.

"But when you saw the blood on Billy's knee, didn't you feel bad that you'd done it?" she said.

I thought back to the moment, standing over Billy and looking down at his raw knee, the skin scraped back and drops of blood popping onto the skin. I knew how it would sting and burn, how a bit of gravel might get trapped inside and how the nurse would right now probably be spreading foul-smelling iodine across the graze, wrapping it in a white bandage that he would wear like a medal of honor. "I thought he deserved it," I said.

"No one ever deserves to be hurt," she said, still smiling.

"He called me a bad name."

"Yes and that was very mean. He'll be punished for that. But you still have to say sorry for hurting him." I must have looked blank because she went on. "Sometimes, Michael, it's worth saying sorry even if you don't completely mean it. Just to keep the peace and make the other person feel better."

I still often wish I'd asked her if that applies to all emotion, or only contrition.

But I have learned enough lessons over the years to better understand what is and is not expected in life. I knew, for example, that when George, who worked in the office next to mine, asked if I'd like to come out for a drink soon after I started in the City, I should arrange my face into a smile and say yes.

I had by then established a successful routine, and that made me feel confident about being able to adapt to a social situation. I rose every day at five, ran for forty minutes, the same route, which was an acceptable 9k, came home and showered and dressed, and left the house at six ten in order to be at my desk by six forty-five. The office had its own gym, as all those offices do, and so I also worked out during my lunch hour on Monday, Wednesday, and Friday. I would have done it every day, but I knew there would soon be client lunches to attend and times when it was necessary to look as if I were so busy I was working through lunch. This setup meant I had a bit of flexibility and could switch my days around if need be. I also bought a bench press and weights for home. For now they were in the bare library, but I knew V would never agree to this arrangement so I had already looked into the costs and feasibility of excavating the basement to make way for a gym. V always loved the heat, so I thought a sauna would work down there as well.

There were eleven of us out that evening, although only two are worth mentioning: George and Kaitlyn. George was loud and good-looking, but he drank too much and wasn't very bright. His godfather ran the firm or something and his father was a lord, so he never had to worry about things like performance. You'd be amazed how many people there are like that in the City. How hard the rest of us have to work to carry them. And you could hate them, but what's the point. The world, as I learned at a young age, is hardly fair and there's nothing anyone can do about that.

Kaitlyn worked in another office along my corridor, so we'd waved and said hello before. She was thin and tall and always dressed in some sort of dark-colored suit and wore amazingly high heels. I would watch her stride past my windows and wonder how on earth she didn't trip and break her ankle. And yet she moved so effortlessly in them I came to conclude that she must have been wearing them for so long they had become an extension of her legs. Kaitlyn was very pale, with the lankest, blondest hair I'd ever seen. She was so blond the shade extended to her eyelashes and eyebrows, which gave her an otherworldly quality. And her eyes were very blue, almost like looking at ice. I thought she'd be stern and severe, but in fact she was the exact opposite.

"So how are you finding us all?" she asked when we found ourselves at the bar together, her accent a beautiful, soft Irish.

"So far, so good."

"I hear you made a killing at Schwartz's. I'd love to work there one day. My dream is to live in an apartment overlooking Central Park."

"My apartment overlooked Central Park." I glanced back at the rest of our table as I spoke, wondering when I could leave. We had been there for two hours and they were all getting sweaty and red-faced, with a few of them making frequent trips to the toilets.

"Oh wow," she said. "Why did you come back?"

"I did my two years. London's my home. The plan was never to go for more than two years."

"Yes, but *New York*. And Schwartz's."

Neither of us seemed to want to go back to our table, so I sipped my drink at the bar. "My girlfriend has a job here she couldn't leave."

"Oh, right. It must be impressive if it tops Schwartz's."

"She's not a banker. She works in artificial intelligence."

Kaitlyn whistled through her teeth, an odd sound, not unlike one you'd use to call a dog. "Wow, what a power couple."

"Not really." I noticed that Kaitlyn wasn't drinking her wine and the glass was tilting over the bar. "Careful, you might spill that."

She looked down and laughed, taking a small sip. "So where do you live now?"

"Clapham."

"Oh, near me then. Are you by the Common?"

I nodded. "Yes, Verity was very particular about being near the Common. She's a runner."

"I'm a walker," Kaitlyn said. "I've got a little dog and I walk him there every weekend. It's the closest I get to home."

"Where's home?"

"A tiny village in the south of Ireland, you won't have heard of it."

"Is your family still there?"

She nodded, and I was struck suddenly by the thought of her flying across the sea to this harsh London life, away from the coast and the hills.

"What brought you here?"

She shrugged. "Oh, you know, life. Ireland's beautiful but it's not the easiest place." For a terrible moment I thought she was going to cry, but she laughed instead. "I bet you have one of those gorgeous double-fronted houses on Windsor Terrace."

"How on earth did you know that?" I asked too quickly, wondering if she'd been looking through my personnel file or something.

But she laughed again. "Because that road is just one long line of bankers, that's why!"

I tried to picture some of my neighbors, but realized I couldn't. I hoped she was exaggerating. Because if there is one thing V hates it's unoriginality. And what could be more unoriginal than working in the City and living on a road of bankers. I could feel Kaitlyn looking at me but I refused to return her stare, feeling my cheek color under her scrutiny. I hated her at that moment, with a deep, horrible passion. Because how dare she come along and piss on my bonfire? My beautifully laid, perfectly proportioned bonfire.

It took me all the evening until my walk home from the Tube to realize that what Kaitlyn had said didn't matter anyway. V wasn't a banker, so she wouldn't know if all her neighbors were bankers. I breathed more easily as I walked, but still I peered into all the windows with undrawn curtains. And it didn't make me feel much better, because I saw a lot of similar rooms, not just to each other but to my own. A lot of dark walls, industrial lighting, expensive modern art on the walls, sleek corner sofas, state-of-the-art media systems, stripped floors. I also saw a lot of bloated middle-aged men in half-discarded suits and thin blond women in pale cashmere, holding glasses full of what would undoubtedly be the finest red wine.

I poured myself a glass of my own fine red when I got in, loosening my tie and throwing my jacket over a chair, kicking my shoes into the corner. I knew V would hate that, but I also knew she wasn't there to see and I would never behave like that once she moved in. I wandered into the drawing room and put Oasis on the media system. Oasis is V's favorite band, mine too. Before I met her I only listened to bands like the Clash and Nirvana and Hole. I liked to lock myself away with music and let it thunder into my ears while I beat a frantic imaginary drum on my bed. V said I should listen more to the lyrics because that was where the beauty lay. She allowed Nirvana, but she couldn't believe I didn't own any Beatles or Bowie, any Lloyd Cole or Prince, any Joni Mitchell or the Carpenters. But mostly she couldn't believe I didn't own any

Oasis. Noel Gallagher writes the best love songs in the world, she said, which made me feel jealous of him, that he could make her feel something I couldn't.

V's wedding invitation taunted me from the mantelpiece and I felt an overwhelming urge to break the rules and contact her. I got my laptop out of the cupboard and sat with it on the sofa. First I googled her name, but as usual nothing came up. Her Facebook profile was still deleted and she had never been on public social media sites like Twitter or LinkedIn. She had, of course, changed her phone number after the American incident and I didn't even know her address. The only access I still had to her was by e-mail. In January and February I had e-mailed her every day, sometimes more than once a day, but she never replied, not until the one I'd sent in April about coming home. Which meant that my breaking off contact had been the right thing to do.

I realized as I sat there that I had partly stopped e-mailing her to make sure she didn't delete that account as well. Because if she had, then I would have had very little link left to her and that thought was too terrifying to contemplate. Naturally I had also recognized that I needed to get myself together and set up back in London before I could present myself as a realistic proposal to her again. I glanced back up at the shiny, cream-colored invitation and the rage I felt was so pure and intense I was surprised the paper didn't combust. It had taken her only a couple of months to meet and agree to marry this man. It was possible she had fallen so in love she had been, what they call, swept off her feet.

I stood at this thought, knocking my laptop to the floor, and paced the length of my drawing room once, twice, three times. I had to stop then and bend double, placing my hands on my knees and retching. I stood and leaned my head against the wall, knocking it slightly as I did, although that felt good, so I did it again, then again, the thump reverberating pleasantly through my body. When I stood back I saw some blood on the newly painted walls, so I went into the kitchen to get a cloth. The half-finished bottle of red was on its side so I picked that up as well. But as I was crossing the hall back to the drawing room there was a ring on the doorbell. It was past midnight and V was the only person I could imagine calling at this time. She was practically the only person who knew where I lived.

I rushed to the door and threw it open, but it wasn't V, just a small, slightly overweight woman, dressed in what looked like pajamas.

She took a small step back as I opened the door.

"Oh sorry. Are you okay?" she asked, gesturing to my forehead.

"Yes, yes, it's nothing," I said, realizing as I spoke that I was still holding the bottle of wine and the cloth. "Walked into a door."

"Oh, okay. I live next door."

"Yes," I said, although I couldn't remember ever having seen her before.

She held out her hand. "Lottie."

I nodded. "Mike."

She smiled awkwardly. "Yes, I know. We work together."

"Oh," I said, trying to arrange my face into a look of recognition, although really my brain was scrambling for who she might be. "Oh, sorry, yes of course."

She laughed. "I'm at the other end of the trading floor, so, well."

"No, no, I was just being stupid." Her features meant nothing to me.

"Although I think I might be moving over to your team in the near future."

I vaguely remembered an e-mail I'd received in the week about a change in personnel. The idea of living next door to a colleague was terrible, but I smiled. "Oh, great."

"Anyway. I'm really sorry to ask. It's just I'm doing a 10k tomorrow and have to be up really early and, well, the music, I just wondered."

I turned as she spoke, aware suddenly of Liam Gallagher shouting behind me about champagne supernovas, the noise spilling out into the street. "Oh I'm so sorry. I didn't think."

"No, no, it's fine. Normally I wouldn't be such a party pooper, but you know." Lottie was backing down the path as she spoke, her hand raised in a gesture of farewell.

"I'll turn it down right now," I called after her.

I shut the door and went into the drawing room where the noise hit me like a wall. I snapped off the stereo, the silence immediately pressing around me, my eardrums still beating.

I sat on the sofa and poured myself a final glass. In the silence it was much easier to think clearly. Of course V hadn't fallen in love that quickly. Of course she hadn't fallen in love at all. She was still in love with me and I knew that to be true for two reasons: First, V wasn't the sort of person to be swept off her feet, and second, she would never have been so angry about the American incident if she hadn't loved me. I had to keep reminding myself what I had already worked out: This was all part of our game. This was our ultimate Crave and only I would understand that.

I picked my laptop off the floor and rested it on my knees. Perhaps it would be stranger to simply turn up at her wedding without contacting her first. The rules of any game dictate that a move by one player is followed by the move of the other. She had made the first move, I must make the second.

To: missverityw@hotmail.com
From: mikehayes86@hotmail.com
Subject: Hi

Dear V,

I just wanted to let you know I'm back now. Thanks for the invite to your wedding, I've let your mum know I'm coming.

I've got myself a job at Bartleby's and I've bought a house in Clapham, although you must know that, as how else would I have received the invitation! I really think you'd love it. You should come round some time. It would be good to meet Angus as well.

Where are you living now? Are you still at Calthorpe? I hope all is good there.

I'm still very sorry for all that happened and I can't pretend I wasn't surprised when you told me you were getting married. But I know life moves on. I understand a lot of what you said to me now.

It would be really good to see you.

Much love,

Mike (Eagle)

I debated for a while about putting in the eagle bit, but V had often called me her eagle and I needed to start reminding her of who we were. I wanted her to know that I got it, that I knew we'd started playing again.

I woke a few hours later with a pounding head and stiff limbs, the sun streaming through the window, revealing all the particles in the air before my face. I pushed myself up and saw another patch of blood where I had been lying. I reached my hand to my temple, but it was tender to the touch, so I stood and looked in the mirror above the fireplace. I was shocked to see a mean red lump protruding above my eyebrow. It looked like a tiny volcano on my face, rising to a dark peak, from which a thin line of dried, almost black blood was encrusted down one side.

I showered and brushed my teeth and drank a pint of water to rid my mouth of the taste of rotting meat, which removed the desire to die. But still all I felt capable of was putting on a tracksuit and dragging a blanket to the sofa. If V were here I knew she would make me some hot tea and feel my forehead, she would tuck in the covers and ruffle my hair. I checked my e-mail, but my in-box was empty.

The day was very long. I ordered in food and watched the sort of television programs that had punctuated my childhood, but which V had taught me to despise. Where once these types of shows had soothed me, sometimes even made me laugh, now I could only see them through her eyes, could only see fat, stupid people competing for nonexistent prizes, as if humiliating yourself in public was the point.

I checked my e-mail every ten or so minutes. At one point I unplugged and then reset my broadband. But I was worried this had done something to it, so I called my provider, who assured me there was nothing wrong with my connection. I asked Google how long undeliverable mail takes to be returned and was told the postmaster should inform you of a difficulty almost immediately, but confirmation could take up to three days.

The day drifted into the evening and the television got worse, but I knew I couldn't concentrate on books or music. I had my laptop open next to me, my in-box forever on the screen, my finger constantly refreshing the page.

I slept fitfully, on the sofa again, although this time I did have the foresight to close the curtains. I dreamed of V, trapped in an electronic world of her own creation, stuck behind a million passwords that no human would ever be clever enough to decipher. She was being attacked by a massive eagle and screamed my name constantly. I woke with a start, my heart pinning me to the sofa like a butterfly in a box, my body covered in sweat, and my mouth painfully dry. I lay very still and regulated my breathing, first into my toes, then up my legs, through my belly, my chest, neck, and out of the top of my head. I felt better when I'd done that and I could see light creeping around the edges of the curtains, which gave me some hope. And I remembered all was not lost, Suzi and Colin were still at Steeple House, just as they always would be, and I knew that place as well as anywhere in the world.

I left it until ten a.m. and then ten minutes more. By then I had run and showered and dressed and cleaned the house and opened the doors into the garden and made myself a pot of coffee. I would walk across the Common in a bit and buy a paper, maybe even have lunch in a pub. Normal Sunday pursuits.

Steeple House's number was still stored in my phone, although it wouldn't have mattered if it had been lost. Suzi took a while to answer, but I knew better than to ring off, knew she would be in the garden on a fine summer morning with her daughter's wedding looming and all the guests to impress.

"Mike?" she said, failing to hide her surprise behind her over-accentuated vowels.

"How are you, Suzi?" I asked, keeping my voice light.

"Well, we're fine, thank you," she replied, recovering herself. "Thank you for replying to the invitation so swiftly."

I was worried when she said that. I thought I'd left an adequate amount of time, but maybe I was wrong, maybe I looked too keen. "It will be lovely to see you and Colin."

"Yes. How long have you been back in England?"

I could hear the radio spluttering on in the background and I knew it would be Radio 4, which was never turned off in Steeple House. V and I always listened to Radio 4 as well and I do miss it, but it's one of the things I still find too painful. "A couple of months. I've bought a house in Clapham and got a job at another bank."

"Well, yes. Verity told me." It was good to know they had dis-cussed me.

"Fantastic news about Verity's promotion," I said, which was a gamble, but not that big a one, if you knew V.

"Oh, you heard?" I could hear the pride in her voice. "Have you two been in touch then?"

"Just by e-mail." I let the conversation rest for a minute. "In fact, that's why I was ringing. I wanted to send her and Angus an engagement gift and I haven't got their address."

I felt Suzi's hesitation down the line, as large as a bear. "Oh, well, that's very sweet of you, Mike. But you don't need to do that, surely. And anyway, why don't you ask Verity for it?"

I half laughed, trying to sound casual. "I was going to, but then I thought that might ruin the surprise."

"Well, yes, I suppose it might," Suzi said, but still I could feel the hesitation.

"Oh, don't worry," I said cheerfully. "I should have thought it's a bit of an odd thing to ring and ask after all this time. I'll just e-mail her, don't worry."

"No, no. Sorry, I'm being silly. It's 24 Elizabeth Road, W8. I don't know the whole postcode, but I could get my address book."

"No, postcodes are easy to find." I looked at the words I had written on the pad in front of me. I knew W8 meant Kensington and I had a feeling I knew Elizabeth Road. Large, grand houses. "How about a flat number?"

"Oh no, they have the whole house." Again I heard the swell of pride in her voice. "Anyway, I'm glad you're feeling, well, better, Mike. It'll be good to see you at the wedding."

"Yes," I said, heat rising through my body. "Thanks."

"I think it's a good idea to put all that nastiness behind us. And Verity's very happy now. It's good of you to understand that."

"Yes." I wanted to say something more significant but my voice felt caught inside me.

"Anyway, take care," she said, ringing off before I could say goodbye.

I stayed sitting at the long table that runs across the back of the kitchen, by the bifold doors. I could imagine V holding lunches and dinners at the table, the doors open, me manning a barbecue. The day felt like it had darkened, but there wasn't a cloud in the sky.

"Oh no, they have the whole house," I said out loud, mimicking Suzi's entitled voice. "We don't say toilet," she said to me on my second or third visit to Steeple House. They were having a lunch party and she took me to one side before it started. "Or pardon, for that matter," she'd added. "And please don't hold your knife like a pen."

She'd walked away from me after that, leaving me to wonder at all the other things I did wrong without realizing. I found V in the garden and told her what her mother had said, but she told me not to worry, that her mother was a stupid snob. "Please, please promise me you'll say at least one of those words during the meal and you'll definitely hold your knife like a pen," she said. At first I refused, but she put her hand down my trousers and stroked me until I would have agreed to learn Chinese, if that's what it took.

The guests did flinch when I said both words, Suzi's color rising up from her shirt to her taut, chicken-like neck. But V just smiled and winked at me when nobody was looking.

I must have sat at the table for longer than I realized after speaking to Suzi, because it was two o'clock by the time I set off on my paper errand. There was a newsagent close by, but I thought a walk across the Common would do me good and there was a pub on the other side, which appeared to be nice. I bought *The Observer* and a pint and sat outside at a table overlooking the road. I checked my e-mail on my phone, but my in-box was still empty. Instead I did what I'd been avoiding all morning and typed 24 Elizabeth Road, W8, into Google Maps. The house was just what I had expected—grand, white, imposing. I expanded the image, but I couldn't make out anything beyond white shutters and dark rooms behind.

Next I googled V's fiancé, Angus Metcalf, my hands shaking slightly against the keys, so I had to retype his name a few times. There were quite a few results, but I knew immediately which one he was. Angus Metcalf of Metcalf, Blake, apparently the preeminent advertising company of our age, which had embraced the more cynical, ever connected world we live in to come up with the most innovative, exciting, and successful campaigns of the past decade. On the staff page was a black-and-white photograph of a rugged-looking man. He was smiling at the camera, his eyes creased and his hair graying slightly at the temples. I suppose some people would have called him attractive, but I thought he was very simian-looking and I had to tear my mind away from imagining his apelike hands on V's body. His smile was too full, as if he were laughing at you rather than with you. I estimated him to be quite a bit older than us, early forties perhaps, which made me feel a bit better because he hadn't retired yet and he must be approaching V's magical number of forty-five, which would suggest she wasn't that serious about him.

"Mike."

I looked up and Kaitlyn was standing in front of me on the street, a disgusting little dog in her arms. The thing was yapping at me and I would have dearly loved to kick it across the road. V said anyone who kept pets was mad and this seemed to prove the point.

"Hello," I said. "What are you doing here?"

"I've just been walking Snowdrop." She laughed. "Remember, I live here."

"Sorry, of course you do," I said, remembering our conversation from Friday evening.

"God, what happened?" She motioned to my eyebrow.

I reached up to the sore area of skin. "Oh, nothing. I walked into a door."

Her forehead creased into a frown. "Are you here alone?"

"Yes. Just reading the paper."

"Where's Verity?"

I was slightly shocked to hear V's name in Kaitlyn's mouth and it took me a minute to remember everything I'd said to her. "At home. Making lunch."

"Oh, how nice." But she stayed standing where she was.

I stood up and drained my pint. "Anyway, better be off. I was only meant to be getting the paper." I held it up like an exhibit.

"Oh yes, well. See you tomorrow." She put Snowdrop down and they moved away, all their long spindly legs marching on the pavement. I was relieved to see Kaitlyn was wearing trainers today and giving her poor feet some time off from the vertiginous heels.

V says it is unfeminist to wear shoes in which you can't run. Naturally she made an exception when we were Craving, but then she said it didn't count because she had me. Strong body, strong mind, V always said, and she is totally and completely right.

I went home and changed again into my running gear, setting off almost immediately back across the Common, although I ended up going much farther, getting lost in my movement, feeling my body move through the pain, and feeding off the adrenaline leaching into my muscles. It reminded me just how strong I am. Just how capable.

When I got home I made myself shower before checking my e-mail. V doesn't like workout sweat. She says it's different from sex sweat and she used to scream if I came anywhere near her after a run. She definitely wouldn't want me dripping on the sofa. And all in all it was the right thing to do, all of it, because when I finally sat with the laptop there was a reply from her, writ bold in my in-box.

To: mikehayes86@hotmail.com
From: missverityw@hotmail.com
Subject: Re: Hi

Mike,

Lovely to hear from you. I've been meaning to get in touch. Actually I was going to write before we sent out the invites, but time spun away from me, as usual. I rang Elaine to get your address. She says she hasn't seen you or your new house since you got back. She sounded a bit wistful actually, you know the way she does. You should ask her over.

I'm so glad you're coming to the wedding. I was worried you might feel a bit put out by it all, but it sounds like things are good with you. (Do feel free to bring someone, by the way, if there is someone, that is.) I'm so happy that we can be friends. It got a bit silly back there and we both said things we probably shouldn't have. I definitely acted a bit like a spoiled brat. Meeting Angus has put everything into perspective for me and has made me grow up quite a lot.

I would love to come and see your new house sometime and you must come here for dinner. I am still at Calthorpe, still trying to override humans!

It's all a bit manic at the moment, as you can imagine, but after the wedding we'll set a date.

Take care,

Love V xx

I read the e-mail many times, until I had absorbed it and let it become part of me. It was impossible not to see the implied meaning behind everything V said. When she said "time spun away from me, as usual," and "you know the way she does," she was clearly asking me to remember how well we knew each other. Even telling me to invite Elaine over was like her laying a hand on my arm, the way she used to do when dispensing advice, letting me know she still had the power to make me do things. And then the line in parentheses saying I could bring someone, a line marked out in its ridiculousness. "If there is someone" she had written, knowing full well there never would be anyone apart from her. "We both said things we probably shouldn't have" was an apology, and "meeting Angus has put everything into perspective" was like telling me that she was using Angus as a way of understanding our relationship. She would "love" to see my house and promised a "date," two cleverly chosen words.

But of course the most significant phrase was "still trying to override humans." We will be masters of our own world, she used to say to me. Don't worry, Mike, she'd said, I'll invent a chip that makes you and me cleverer than even the machines and we can ride off into the sunset together while everything else goes to shit. Those words told me that V and I were still on course to do that.

I felt significantly better by the time I looked up and realized dusk was settling over the day. I decided not to reply. We had both shown a tiny part of our hands, keeping most of our cards close to our chests for the fun that lay ahead. The Crave, I felt, had picked up pace.

Everyone at work commented on my lump and for some reason found my walking-into-a-door story hilarious. "You were definitely a bit the worse for wear," George said with a wink, making me stuff my hands into my pockets. He, as I remembered, had fallen on leaving the pub so there was no way he could have noticed what I was doing. I shut myself in my office, counting down the time until lunch when I could forget it all by concentrating on the weights I would have suspended above my head.

Kaitlyn knocked on my door at midday and I motioned for her to come in, which she did gingerly, which irritated me. "Just wondering how the head is?" she said, with a wide smile.

I was genuinely perplexed. "Everyone seems very interested in my head. Has no one ever come into work with a bump before?"

She laughed lightly. "Well, I can't think of anyone. And I suppose they just find it amusing because of Friday night."

"What about Friday night?" I asked, leaning forward over my desk.

"Oh nothing. Just, you know, you were quite drunk. Not that it matters."

I tried to piece together the events of the evening but I couldn't remember much until getting off the Tube and walking home down my road. Which meant I couldn't have been that drunk or I'd never have been able to do that.

"Anyway," she said. "I hear you live next door to Lottie."

My mind blanked, but then I remembered. "Oh, yes. How do you know that?"

She cocked her head to one side but I could see a blush washing her transparent cheeks. "She mentioned it."

"Well, yes." I just wanted her to leave, but she stayed standing in my doorway.

"I go round to hers sometimes. Next time I'll look over the fence and say hi."

I couldn't think of many things I would like less. "Okay."

She looked at her watch. "God, I'm starving. What are you doing for lunch?"

"Going to the gym."

She looked at my arms and laughed. "Guess you don't get those by magic. Have fun," she said as she left the room.

Since V got her hands on me women have always found me attractive. I never used to notice, but V taught me how to look for the signs. She used to say we should reverse Crave, but I never saw the appeal in that. V sculpted me into what she jokingly called the perfect man and she wasn't happy until every part of me was as defined as a road map.

If I stood naked in front of you, you could trace every muscle in my body, you can see how I am put together and how I work. And I can't deny that I enjoy the feeling that gives me; I like the sense of dedication that has gone into creating me.

V would sometimes moan when she touched me, tracing her finger along all my dips and ridges, down shimmering veins and into forests of hair. I've done too good a job, she'd say sometimes, you're like Frankenstein's monster. You'll run off and leave me and I'll regret what I've done. And in a way she was right, as the American incident proved. I did become a monster.

The stupid thing was I never found Carly attractive. I didn't even particularly like her. She chewed gum and spoke with a deep nasal drawl that grated inside my head. She laughed too loudly and wore her skirts too short. She also was unashamed in her pursuit of me. She marked me out like a big-game hunter and everyone in the office knew I was her prize.

But I was so fucking lonely over there. I begged V to let me come home all through the first year, but she kept on saying I was doing so well and making a future for us and how important that was to her and how much she loved me for the sacrifice I was making. We were both very busy at work and as the second year progressed we saw each other less and less, although we still Skyped and e-mailed and texted all the time. V would even sometimes sleep with the computer next to her all night so I could watch her through the day. I'd lock myself in the toilets at work and will myself down the wires and into the bed. Once or twice I even masturbated like that with the computer resting on the back of the toilet while my work colleague was taking a shit in the stall next to me.

Carly just caught me on a bad night. We'd gone out to celebrate a deal I'd landed, not that I wanted to go, but the boss made it clear it was what was expected. And everyone bought me drinks all night and before long the room was spinning and all the women there looked like V. I think I ended up crying because I remember a huddle of people around me and cold water being splashed on my face. I remember being lifted under the arms and the shock of the cold night air. I remember someone calling me honey and telling me it was going to be all right. I remember puking against a building and feeling like a monkey had stuck his arm down my throat.

Then we were in a strange flat and there was loud music and we were dancing with all the lights off and I realized it was just me and Carly. We were passing a joint between us and Carly was taking off her top and her breasts reminded me of V's. All I wanted at that moment was to sink into a body, to stop the droning in my head and the aching, miserable loneliness eating its way through me. And ultimately, like V said, I am a weak person. I succumbed, and once I had, I felt like a man who hasn't eaten in days being given a steak. I couldn't stop, even when Carly squeaked, even when she pushed at my hands, even when dawn started to crack open the sky. But I must have stopped because I woke the next day on the living-room rug, a blanket thrown over me.

I knew before I opened my eyes that the moment I did, my head was going to split into lots of tiny pieces. The rug was sticky beneath me, its synthetic fibers making my body itch. My vision was blurred at first and the pain across my shoulders and shooting up my neck was like a knife scraping out my veins. And it was hard to believe that my throat wasn't coated in poison as with every breath it felt like tiny pins were shooting through my sinuses.

I lay on my back, wondering how I was going to move again, taking in my surroundings. The room was small and dirty, the walls painted a depressing baby blue, with photographs stuck like a collage opposite the window. An Indian-looking throw with thousands of tiny mirrors covered a sofa that looked like it could have been pulled from a dump. The view from the window and the tight air told me I was in a damp basement, which was probably damaging the health of whoever lived there.

Although of course I knew who lived there, and the thought wrenched at me as if it were piercing my skin.

I sat up and the room lurched, my vision jagging at the edges. My stomach followed and I ran into the hall to find my way to the bathroom where I covered the toilet and the walls in a lurid pink vomit. I was shaking when I finished but I made myself stand so I could face myself in the mirror. My dick was purple and sore and we hadn't used a condom. I was going home for Christmas in a week and I knew there were many sexually transmitted diseases that take months to show up.

I became aware of my smell: a musty, animal stench that rose from my groin and my armpits and made me gag again. I stepped into the shower, with its chipped, blackened tiles, and stood with my face turned into the jets.

The water was hot but I was still shivering. There was something terrifying about this flat, so that it dragged over my skin like a bad dream. I looked out at the toilet with the cracked seat, containing the streaks of shit I had seen smeared inside as I'd vomited. There was a blunt razor on the side of the sink still holding someone else's hair. A spattering of black spores chased themselves up the windowless walls and the mirror ran with condensation.

I turned my face to the wall and leaned my forehead against the cold tiles, but my brain boiled with a knowledge that ran through me like death—this disgusting, degrading, awful place felt like home. It reached out to me and wanted to take me in its shriveled arms. This, I realized, was where I was meant to end up. Carly was the woman most suited to me and, like a dog, I had followed my nose home.

I was sick over my feet, into the base of the shower, the smell harsh and acrid. I chased it down the drain with my feet, knowing it was going to cause a blockage. Surely I had worked too hard for this to be where I ended up.

When I came out of the bathroom Carly was in the lounge wearing a tracksuit, her hair scraped into a ponytail and her face scrubbed clean of makeup. I went to fetch my clothes from the floor and she flinched as I passed. She watched me with her arms folded across her chest as I stepped into my crumpled suit, now soaked in the stench of the flat.

When I had finished dressing I forced myself to look at her and was at once so disgusted I thought about holding one of the couch pillows over her face and hiding her body in the wardrobe. I couldn't imagine anyone missing her.

"You should go," she said.

Her words surprised me but they were also a relief as I had imagined some dreadful scene in which she thought what we had done the night before meant something. A muscle twitched in the corner of her mouth and I felt the need to make things clear before I left.

"Last night was a terrible mistake," I said. "I have a girlfriend in England whom I love very much."

She snorted. "You're telling *me* it was a mistake."

It felt as if the terrible flat had swallowed all meaning. "I don't want you to try and contact her or anything."

"For God's sake. Don't worry, your mystical girlfriend won't be hearing from me." She motioned to the door. "Please, just go."

I let myself out, hearing her rasp the lock into place behind me as I shut the door. When I reached the street I saw it had snowed overnight and I wasn't wearing the right shoes, which seemed like an insurmountable problem. I started crying with my first step, the tears quickly becoming sobs, so that soon passersby were avoiding me as I lurched down the street.

In the days it took for the lump on my head to disappear I felt the need to prove myself at work, so I inadvertently stayed late most nights. On Tuesday I didn't leave until ten. The night was warm, and there were people all over the streets, spilling out of pubs and restaurants, their arms wrapped around each other. And all at once I missed V with a sharp, stabbing pain, as if someone had stuck a knife between my ribs. I wanted to go to her house and knock on the door and tell her I didn't want to play anymore. I wanted to cut to the end of the Crave, to the part where we're together in bed and laughing at the rest of the world. I wanted to fall at her feet and tell her I understood, that I deserved my punishment, but it was enough now, I would never do anything remotely like that again, I would never even leave her side.

I found myself walking toward Kensington, a journey my iPhone told me was 4.8 miles and would take me eighty-nine minutes. It wasn't a ludicrous distance. It was almost on the way home. I hummed through Oasis's *Definitely Maybe* as I walked, filling my head with the noise. It only took me seventy-three minutes to get to Elizabeth Road, but I am a fast walker. Number 24 was about halfway down and as grand and imposing as I had feared, with newly refreshed paint and gleaming black-and-white tiles on the pathway and up the steps. A large black lantern hung on the porch, switched on and shining brightly out of the spotless glass.

Angus, I realized, must be extremely rich, far richer than me, a thought that made me want to sit down in the street. I crossed the road to a darker corner in case anyone looked out of the window and fished out my phone. Zoopla told me the house had been bought five years ago for £3.2 million; its estimated worth now £8.1 million.

Lights were on in the front room, although the white shutters were closed, so there was nothing to see. I had the very strong sense that V was in there, moving around in the rooms beyond, maybe even thinking of me. Maybe she was unhappy, maybe she too was regretting starting this game. It was entirely possible that her unhappiness had drawn me here because our connection was so strong. It seemed absurd that I could simply cross the road and knock on the door and she would be revealed to me. I hesitated on the curb, my feet half on, half off, rocking with the thought. But the likelihood was that Angus would be home and, although his part in the Crave wasn't entirely clear to me yet, I didn't think it involved a doorstep argument. V had other plans for him, of that I felt sure.

A light flicked on in an upstairs room and I saw a figure pull some heavy curtains across the window. My heart jumped into my mouth and my hand reached uselessly upward, as if to wave. Even though I'd only gotten a shadowy glimpse of the person, I knew it was V. "I'm here, my darling," I whispered into the night. "I'm coming to save you." She had felt me, I knew that then. She might not have known for certain I was standing on the street outside her door, but something had pulled her upstairs and to the window. Something had compelled her to give me that sign.

I don't remember getting home that night or how I broke the wineglasses. I went into the kitchen after my run the next morning to get a glass of water and there was a pile of glass in the corner by the bifold doors. I turned and there were three glasses missing from my open shelves. I reached out for one and realized if I had turned and thrown it immediately it would have landed right where the pile of glass now was. There was something familiar in the movement and there was a certain pleasure to be found in imagining myself being so reckless. But the actual memory was absent.

"I know, I know, sorry, V," I said, as I got the dustpan and brush from under the sink. "Don't worry, I'll hoover afterward. I don't want you getting any glass in your feet."

After that I showered, shutting my eyes against the water, but still I couldn't shake an uncomfortable feeling of dislocation. I toweled off my body and felt a bit better because my muscles reminded me that I am strong and in control. But the house still felt so empty when I came onto the landing, dressed for the day. I knew I only had to walk down the stairs, put on my coat, pick up my phone and briefcase, and leave, but still it felt scary. As if my only actions could be ones I knew by heart. Actions I would repeat again and again and again, meaninglessly. My mind jumped forward to the winter and I saw myself doing all these same tasks in the dark. Without V anchoring me, I realized suddenly, it didn't matter how strong I was, I was still very capable of floating clean away.

"See you later," I shouted as I shut the door behind me, which made me feel somewhat better. An image followed me all the way to work of V asleep in our huge bed, with the linen sheets she liked and the mohair blanket on the end. I had even invested in those pointless pillows you see on beds in magazines, which I simply threw onto the floor every night and replaced every morning. But V'd had them on our bed in our flat and she always seemed to judge hotels by the number of extra pillows they provided.

V didn't have to be at work until nine thirty, so it was entirely feasible that when she moved in she would be able to have an extra half hour in bed after I left. Or maybe she would go to the kitchen and use the coffee machine to make one of her beloved espressos, which she would take back to bed. I was glad I had hoovered, in case she wanted to stand by the back doors and look out over the garden while she sipped her coffee.

I hadn't, I realized, cooked properly since I'd moved in, and that was a shame as I liked cooking. I resolved to buy some ingredients on my way home that evening and christen the kitchen with a proper meal. I reasoned that might make it feel more like home.

Work was busy that day. We were in the middle of the Hector deal and the chairman had put me in charge. It should have been relatively simple, but some of their figures didn't add up and no one was answering my questions in a way I thought to be adequate. I felt myself coming close to losing my temper a few times during the day, as I heard one excuse after another. And not just from the people at Hector but also from my own team. I think I might have spoken a bit harshly and I felt people glancing in at me as they passed my office. But I can't believe I wasn't fair. If people do a competent job and give me the right answers, then all is good. I can't stand incompetence. V says I expect too much from other people, which always used to make me laugh, as I was brought up to expect nothing at all.

I stopped at the deli on the High Street on my walk home from the Tube. I had loaded up with wine and salads and was standing looking at the ridiculously priced vacuum-packed steaks when Kaitlyn walked in. I raised a hand in greeting, but inside my heart sank. She seemed to be behind me wherever I went and the feeling was unnerving. I turned back to the red meat, hoping she'd get what she needed and leave, but she came straight over.

"What are you having?" she asked, her own empty basket hanging off her arm. "I'm starving but don't know what I fancy eating."

"Steak," I said, keeping my eyes on the meat. "It's Verity's favorite."

"Oh," she said. "I'm vegetarian."

I turned to look at her and her deathlike appearance made a bit more sense. But I also realized something else. I couldn't very well buy just one steak now that I'd said that. I reached up and deposited two large steaks in my basket, trying hard not to hear Elaine's voice telling me how she could feed five people for a week on what they cost. When you are brought up in a foster home, excess never comes very easily, however much money you accrue.

Kaitlyn moved toward the next fridge and picked up some gourmet hummus and a fresh pasta sauce. Her hand hesitated over the wild mushroom or the spinach-and-ricotta tortellini, but the wild mushroom won. "I wish someone was cooking for me tonight." She sighed.

"V and I take it in turns," I said. "Whichever one of us is back first."

"That's nice," she said. "It's a bit lonely buying all these sort of ready meals and eating them in front of the telly. It doesn't make it any better just because you've paid ten times what you would in Tesco."

I tried to smile, but an image of Kaitlyn doing just that almost knocked me off-balance. I expected that she changed into a tracksuit and pulled her hair back off her face as soon as she got home. She probably let her dog eat the leftovers from her plate.

We stood in the queue next to each other, which took an annoyingly long time because a woman at the front was going through every ingredient of her vegan lasagna. Kaitlyn smiled wearily and I pretended to be interested in a nonexistent message on my phone. We emerged into the evening together and walked up the hill until it was my turnoff, where we said an awkward good night. I realized as I walked down my road that I would be seeing Kaitlyn again in eight hours and that it was perfectly possible that neither of us would speak to anyone else in the meantime.

I got changed myself when I got in, but not into a tracksuit, just some chinos and a T-shirt. I put on Oasis and turned on the oven. My plan was to flash-fry one of the steaks in garlic and salt and then give it ten minutes in the oven while I made a good dressing for the salad. But as I got the packets out of the bag I saw both steaks had a sell-by date within the next twenty-four hours, which meant I would have to cook them or waste one. I was hungry anyway, so I released them into the air, rubbing them with garlic. Once they were in the oven I opened the bag of organic baby greens and chopped an avocado and some baby plum tomatoes and made a mustardy dressing.

I had overestimated and there was enough salad for two people. I put the bowl on the table and lit the candles that lived in glass hurricane lamps. They reflected nicely in the bifold doors and I saw the kitchen was well designed for supper parties or romantic dinners. V loved a nicely laid table and so I got two white napkins out along with the cutlery. Then I took down two wineglasses and put the bottle of red between the place settings. The steaks smelled ready and so I served them up. Two would have taken a whole plate and looked ridiculous. I carried both plates to the table and put them into their places. The meat was succulent and cooked to perfection, the hard brown skin yielding to the red, earthy flesh. And the salad was a perfect complement, crisp and light and benefiting from the blood on the plate. The wine had also been a good choice, full-bodied and fruity, real coat-your-throat stuff.

As I sat Liam began his mournful rendition of "Wonderwall" and I had to put down my knife and fork for a minute to stop myself from choking. Because nobody feels the way I do, V said, as the lyric sounded out, and I heard her words so clearly I had to remind myself that she wasn't actually sitting opposite me.

"Your favorite song, V," I said, raising a glass and catching sight of my reflection in the door.

For the record, I didn't actually think V was sitting with me that night. But it gave me a wonderful glimpse of what our future held, of how we would be when she did finally come home to live with me.

If she had been there I would have spoken to her about the time we were in Ireland and I arranged for her to hold an eagle. At least, *hold* is the wrong word. She had to put on a long, thick leather glove that reached right up to her shoulder and stand very still, while the eagle's handler attracted the bird with a dead mouse. We were standing in the grounds of an old castle, the sea whipping against the shore and the trees and grasses of the garden bent almost double by the wind. V's hair was flying around her head, as if it were alive, and her eyes were fixed upward, into the sky. I followed her gaze and saw a speck of a bird high up in the slate-gray sky above our heads. It hovered for a few minutes, surveying us, and in those moments I wanted to rush to V and rip the glove off her hand, to pull her away and cover her with my body. Because as the eagle started to descend it was obvious it saw only the prey, obvious it cared nothing for us and our petty concerns. It whizzed over my head, so close I could feel the wind from its wings, and as it glided toward V, I could see the meanness of its talons, the damage they could do. Don't touch her, I wanted to shout, but it was landing before I could move, with a weight that made V's arm buckle so the handler had to grab it and hold it upright and she laughed. The eagle picked at the mouse in her hand and V stared at it like it was the most beautiful thing she had ever seen. But then the handler moved behind the bird and put a tiny black mask over the eagle's eyes, making it look like an executioner. He then transferred the bird onto his own gloved hand and V dropped her arm, reaching out to stroke the top of the eagle's head. Thank you so much, she was saying by the time I reached them.

She turned to me and her eyes were sparkling. "That's the best present anyone's ever given me," she said.

Angus might be able to buy her more diamonds than I could, but I doubted very much he was as thoughtful as I am. I doubted very much that he even knew her well enough to be as thoughtful as I am.

The next day at work was no better than the last and I felt like we were wading through mud toward the finish line. Not completing the deal simply wasn't an option and I made sure everyone on my team knew as much. Kaitlyn put her head around the door at the end of the day and I looked up and realized most people had gone home already. I glanced at the clock on the computer and was surprised to see it was nearly eight.

"I'm just about to head off," Kaitlyn said. "Wondered if you fancied a drink on the way home?"

I opened my mouth to deliver a ready excuse, but was struck by the length of the evening ahead of me. All I would do if I went straight home was stop again at the deli and eat on my own, and the thought seemed suddenly desolate. And Kaitlyn was fine, nice even. "Okay. Give me ten minutes."

We took the Tube to Clapham and went into a pub on the High Street. It was loud for a Tuesday night, but not unpleasantly so. Kaitlyn sat at a table and I went to the bar to get us both a pint.

"Thanks," she said, as I sat back down opposite her. I raised my glass to her in mock salute. "So how's Hector going?"

I rubbed my hands across my face. "Slower than I expected."

"Yes, I heard you weren't happy."

I looked up at her. "What do you mean you heard?"

She colored. "Oh, nothing. You've just looked quite stressed."

"Have I? I haven't felt that stressed."

She raised an eyebrow. "It's okay not to be Mr. Super Cool all the time, you know."

I gulped at my drink and felt the alcohol releasing into my bloodstream.

"Where are you from, Mike?" Kaitlyn's eyes were fixed on me.

"You mean where was I brought up?" She nodded. "Well, all over really." I nearly stopped myself from saying more, but Kaitlyn was smiling and sometimes it felt good to talk, as the adverts always say. "I was born in Luton, but I was taken into care at ten and I didn't get a permanent home until I was twelve. That was in Aylesbury."

Kaitlyn's smile had fallen. "Oh, I'm sorry. I didn't know."

I shrugged. "Why would you?"

"Why were you taken into care?"

I drained my glass. "Usual story. Alcoholic mother, abusive boyfriend, absent father."

"That's awful. I had no idea."

I laughed because why on earth would she have any idea. I am not the sort of person you would look at and think they had been in care. "Would you like another?" I held up my empty glass.

Hers was half full but she stood up. "My turn, let me." I watched her go to the bar and order our drinks. I noticed that she took one of her feet out of the killer heels and let it rest on the cool metal footrest.

When she came back she had recovered her smile. "So you were adopted at twelve. By whom?"

I shook my head. "Not adopted. But I went into permanent foster care. A really nice couple called Elaine and Barry. They were great." And as I said Elaine's name I could have been sitting at the kitchen table with one of her stews in front of me. It was funny to think of her like that, out of context, and it made me feel like I had a hole in my stomach.

"So do you still see them then?"

"Yes."

"And what about your mum?"

"Oh God, no, not for years."

"Well, they must have done a pretty good job, your foster parents. I mean, you've turned out well, haven't you." She laughed lightly.

I knew my hand was tight around my pint. "It was Elaine who made me realize I was good with numbers," I said. "I was really struggling before I went to live with her but she put everything into perspective for me." The atmosphere in the pub had become very close, almost like we were under water and running out of air. I knew I had heard that phrase "put everything into perspective" before, but I couldn't quite place it and I couldn't work out why it made me feel so uneasy. And I also couldn't quite remember what Elaine had done or what I had struggled with before. I have always had pockets of unsettling memories that I can't be entirely sure are connected to me—the open mouths of shouting adults near my face, kicking heels, blood on the ground, pain in my chest. I pulled a breath into my stomach and concentrated instead on the feel of Elaine's hand on top of my own, Barry's cheer as I scored a garden goal, the warmth of the fire in their front room. I heard her say to me as if she was right by my ear again, "You just need to channel it, Mike. You're good with numbers, why not see what you can do with them."

"Are you okay?" Kaitlyn asked, and I was almost surprised to see her sitting opposite me.

"Yes, fine." I checked my watch. "But I should probably get going."

"I'm sorry if I asked too much," she said, her face as pale as the moon.

"No, no, not at all."

"We're quite alike actually, Mike. I mean, I wasn't adopted or fostered or anything. But we're both outsiders."

"Outsiders?" The word felt hot in my head.

"Yes. Haven't you noticed what an old boys' club it still is at work? How it's all don't you know so-and-so and where did you go to school? People like you and I need to stick together. They don't naturally like us."

"Don't they?" The thought was both ghastly and new to me.

But she just laughed. "It's not as bad as it used to be, but we still have to watch our backs."

I resisted the urge to turn around. "Thanks for the advice," I said, standing up. "But I really should be going. Verity will be wondering where I am."

She stood up with me. "Oh yes, of course."

Kaitlyn went to the toilet and said I should go on without her, so I strode up the hill to my road with her words turning inside me. I hadn't realized I was an outsider at work and it made me wonder what else I hadn't noticed. V would have warned me about that. She knew all the codes and what everything meant. She could have even told me what to say, or at least why I shouldn't care about it.

I turned onto my street and the loneliness hit me again like a gust of wind. I had nowhere else to go other than back to my dark, empty house, and at that moment it was about the most unappealing place in the world to me.

I took to walking home from work most nights, especially as the days were long and the warmth stayed late in the air. The Hector deal went through and the chairman said I could expect a large bonus. I wondered how much houses were in Sussex—for weekends of course. Walking via Kensington wasn't that much of a detour, in fact it was pleasant, looking at the palace and the park, crossing over the Serpentine and looking at the birds and the boats. I didn't walk down Elizabeth Road every evening, only sometimes, only when I felt like V wanted me to.

It was a few weeks before the wedding when a taxi pulled up outside number 24 and V and Angus got out. She was wearing a pair of loose white trousers and a pale blue shirt, with white, low-heeled sandals. Her hair was tied in a loose bun at the nape of her neck and she had a gray bag slung across her body. Her skin looked tanned and I thought she had lost a little bit of weight; her collarbone certainly looked more defined than when I'd last seen her. She waited on the pavement while Angus paid the driver, checking something on her phone, which made her smile. When he turned to her she held the phone out to him and he looked and laughed, putting his arm around her and kissing the side of her head. Angus was dressed more smartly, in a crumpled blue suit with an open-neck shirt. I tried to work out what they'd been doing as I watched them climb the steps to their front door. It was nine thirty, maybe they'd met after work for an early supper. Or been to the cinema.

V unlocked the front door and they went inside, closing the door behind them. I waited, but no one went into the drawing room. I thought it likely that the kitchen was in the basement and so I crossed the road and walked toward the black railings, taking hold of them and looking down. I had no idea what I would say if V saw me, but at that moment it didn't matter either. I could see a sink in the window and the lights were on, but the view was infuriatingly oblique.

There were some old stone steps running from the road to the well in front of the basement, which was dark and in shadow. I pushed the gate at the top of the stairs and it yielded. I checked the street, which was empty, and then walked inside. I kept my body flat against the wall, sliding down the mossy bricks. I didn't look into the window until I was at the bottom of the stairs, tucked behind a bend in the wall. And then I wished I hadn't.

The room was illuminated like a screen, bright and inviting, a huge kitchen stretching out into a dining area with a large table. V was sitting at an island in the center of the room on a high stool, sipping from a glass of wine. Angus was cutting something on a board on the opposite side of the island and whatever he was saying was making her laugh. Occasionally he would hold out a piece of cheese or meat, or whatever it was, and she would take it and nod and lick her fingers. But then he stopped chopping and leaned back against the wall of ovens behind him. He said something else and she looked up at him and I thought I might be sick because her eyes were wide and shining and trained only on him. And I knew that feeling too well, knew what it was to have V look only at you.

She stood then and circled the island, walking toward him, where he pulled her into him so there was no air at all between their bodies. She laid her head against his chest with her face turned out toward me, a generous smile on her lips.

I wanted to run up the stairs and into the evening, but of course that was impossible. I had to watch V turn her face to Angus and the long, slow kiss they gave each other. I had to watch him take her by the hand and lead her from the room. They switched off the light as they left the room and so I was able to stumble up the stairs without worrying too much about being seen. I felt woozy when I reached the street and slightly unconnected to what I was doing, so I kept on having to remind myself that it was necessary for me to get myself home.

I hailed a taxi when I got to Kensington High Street and lay back against the soft seats, refusing to answer any of the cabbie's inane questions. My head felt like it had a vise around it, which was being slowly but surely tightened. I thought I might be sick and remembered I hadn't eaten anything since an overpriced sandwich at lunch.

But when I got into the house the thought of walking through the empty space to the kitchen was too much and I went instead straight up the stairs to my bedroom, where I undressed in the dark and crawled into bed, my body shaking. I pulled some of the pillows into me, shaping my body around them, clinging to their soft surfaces.

"I'm so sorry, V," I said into the night, my face wet with my own tears and my whole chest as raw and ripped as if I had been mauled by a bear.

If I could have told V about Carly anywhere other than Steeple House I would have, but she had been ill with flu and so was already there when I arrived home for Christmas.

I had booked a car to take me from the airport and I arrived in the early evening, on an unseasonably warm December night, pitted with fitful rain. Suzi and Colin were pleased to see me and led me in front of an unnecessarily warm fire, where they asked me lots of questions and accepted their gifts and looked at photos on my phone. V, they told me, was asleep and that was for the best as her temperature had only just come down and they'd had to call the doctor the previous night. But before long she emerged in the doorway, her hair messy and her body wrapped in a large blanket. Suzi told her to come and sit by the fire, which she did.

We hadn't seen each other for eleven weeks and all I wanted to do was take her in my arms, but it was impossible with her parents gazing down on us. I couldn't understand why they didn't leave us alone.

"How are you feeling?" I asked, and it sounded stilted.

"Much better," she said. "Another good night's sleep and I'll be fine."

"I always forget how you young are in constant communication with each other," Suzi said. "In my day you had to write letters and everything took forever."

"I don't know," V said. "A bit of mystery. That sounds quite romantic."

"Anyway, Mike," Suzi said, "I've put you in the blue room." She stood as she spoke and Colin followed her, as he always did. "Night, you two," she said as they left. "And don't let Verity stay up too late, Mike. We don't want her relapsing."

V rolled her eyes at me. "It's like I'm ten again."

I smiled. "They just care."

She sighed. "Sometimes you can care too much."

I slid onto the floor and sat next to her, putting my arm around her shoulder. But she moved away. "Sorry, ow, I'm still quite achy." She looked fine, though; there was even a bloom of pink on her cheeks.

The knowledge of what I had to tell V weighed heavily inside me. Because the sex I'd had with Carly had been unprotected I'd already had all the necessary tests. The HIV test had come back with an initial negative but, as I had suspected, the definitive results for that and all the other tests would take up to three months. I would have told V anyway because there has and will never be any point in us keeping secrets from each other, but there was no way I would have put her in any sort of physical danger.

"What's wrong?" V asked.

"Nothing. Just tired after the flight."

"No, there's something else, I can tell."

So I told her, as we sat by the fire. Probably I was wrong to do it there and then. Maybe her brain was still slightly addled from her fever. Almost definitely I said the wrong things, even though I had gone over and over my lines on the plane. I told her I'd made a terrible mistake, I would do anything not to have done it, it was only because I was so lonely and missed her so much, I wanted to come home, I would do anything to make it better, she, V, was the only person in the world I cared about, she was all I had, she was everything.

V sat very still while I spoke, her gaze focused on her hands, which were twined in her blanket. When she finally looked up her eyes were rimmed in red and her mouth was set into a small line.

"Are you fucking joking?" she said finally, and I started to cry. "What sort of man are you?"

"I don't know," I said, which was true.

"And how dare you say you did it because you were lonely," she spat out. "As if it was all my fault. You talk like I made you go to America, like it was my idea. Don't you think I missed you as well?"

"I'm sorry." My tears were now so violent I could taste them.

"I thought you were different."

"I am."

She snorted.

"Nothing like this will ever happen again, I promise," I pleaded.

"You're so weak. Sometimes you remind me of a piece of modeling clay, like you could be anything. You disgust me."

"Please." I clamped my hands over my ears. "Don't."

"Don't!" she shouted. "Maybe you should have thought of that before you fucked some secretary because you felt a bit lonely."

"Oh God, V," I sobbed, "please. It was nothing. This doesn't have to change us."

She laughed at that, but it was not a happy sound. "It changes everything. It completely alters my perception of who you are. I thought we understood each other, but evidently we don't at all."

"But I do, I do understand you. I love you more than anything, anyone. I will never stop loving you."

"Just fuck off out of my sight."

"No, not until you tell me you love me too."

"I hate you."

"V, stop, I love you."

"I hate you."

"I crave you."

She had stood up by then and I was down on my knees, my arms wrapped around her legs. "I fucking crave you, V," I shouted.

She slapped me on the face, which made me let go of her legs, and she was gone from the room in an instant, the blanket pooled by the fire. I stood and followed her as quickly as I could, but by the time I reached her door it was locked tight against me. I knocked a few times, but the noise simply echoed around the still house and so I went to the blue room, where I lay fully clothed on top of the sheets.

The next morning V's door was still locked and so I simply sat outside it, calling through the wood from time to time. Eventually Suzi came up the stairs.

"I think you should go, Mike," she said.

"I can't go until V speaks to me," I replied.

"She's very upset. She doesn't want to speak to you today." Her face was quivering slightly as she spoke and her hands were clasped in front of her. I was aware of the presence of Colin at the foot of the stairs.

"It's all a terrible misunderstanding," I said.

She frowned. "It sounds like a bit more than that."

"How do you know?" I sounded harsher than I meant to.

"I spoke to her last night." I couldn't quite imagine that happening and wondered if Suzi was lying, because V would never tell her about our life. And what had I been doing at the time? Surely I hadn't slept?

"Please, if I could just speak to her I'm sure we could work it out."

Suzi shook her head. "I really think you should go now, Mike. See how the land lies in a few days."

"But it's Christmas tomorrow."

Suzi looked down. "I'm sorry, Mike."

I ordered a taxi to take me back to our flat in London and sat and waited for it on my own in the kitchen. I couldn't quite believe that V wasn't going to come down the stairs and ask me to walk around the garden with her. I left her Christmas present, a pair of diamond studs, on the kitchen table and wrote a hurried note on the Christmas-tree label. I am still your eagle, was all I said, all I needed to say.

I looked back as we drove away down the gravel drive, the tires crunching like a welcome, but the house looked stern and empty and there were no faces at the window.

I could have called Elaine and spent Christmas with her and Barry and whatever kids they had with them at the time, but the thought was simply too awful. Just the anticipation of the explanations involved was exhausting and besides, I had already sent them lots of expensive gifts from New York, so I felt I had done my duty. Instead I sat in my and V's empty flat and ate stale bread and cold baked beans because I couldn't bear to let myself have anything nice. I looked out the window at fathers pushing new bikes down the road and felt like breaking something.

I called V every hour and sent her too many text messages to count. But she never picked up and never answered. She didn't come back to our flat between Christmas and New Year's and there were no messages telling me what she was doing. We had arranged to spend New Year's in New York and I went to the airport on the 30th to see if she turned up to catch our flight, but she didn't show and the plane took off without either of us. I called her from the airport, saying that I hadn't gotten on the flight without her, that I could meet her anywhere, but that we mustn't spend New Year's apart.

She sent me a text an hour later: I'm not going to see you, Mike.

I went back to our flat and had some flowers sent to Steeple House.

She sent another text that evening: I am not at Mum and Dad's.

Where are you? I texted back immediately, but she didn't answer.

I rang Steeple House and Suzi answered. "Can I speak to Verity, please," I said.

"She's not here, Mike. I'm afraid she didn't see the flowers, although I told her about them."

I tried to keep my voice even. "Where is she?"

"She's gone away with friends."

My mind spun at this information. "What friends?"

I felt Suzi hesitate. "I'm not sure who. Some people she met at work, I think."

"She's gone away with people you don't know to somewhere you don't know?"

Suzi coughed. "She's an adult, Mike. She can do what she likes."

I knew she was lying. "Please, Suzi. We have to talk."

"I'm sorry, Mike. It's not up to me. I suppose Verity will contact you when she's ready."

"Yes, but when might that be?" I asked hopelessly.

"Sometimes things just run their natural course. You've got a good life over there in New York, Mike, and Verity has one here. You were both very young when you met, it's hardly surprising that things change. That doesn't have to be scary, you know." Her tone was soft and it sounded like the sort of thing mothers told their children. But it made my head feel hot and I put the phone down on the stupid woman because certainly I would have said something unforgivable if I had stayed on the line.

I rang V next and shouted down the line into the echoey silence. I called her a few bad names. I told her she couldn't just walk away like that. I said we needed each other. I told her again I craved her.

Later that day I received an e-mail:

Mike,

I am changing my number, so there is no point in trying to call me again. Your behavior has been appalling and I don't just mean with that girl, I mean in how you told me and how you tried to blame me in some way for what happened. Making money has always been unnaturally important to you, but I went along with it because of your background and all you've been through and I could understand how you wanted to create a better life for yourself. But sometimes you scare me and, to be honest, I haven't felt particularly comfortable in our relationship for some time now. You need to find your own happiness within yourself. I don't want to be craved, it's too much. Go back to New York. I won't be returning to our flat until you have left the country.

Verity

I knew immediately that she didn't mean a word of the e-mail, but I also knew her forgiveness was going to be hard-won. I had to start by doing as I was told, so I booked the next flight out to New York.

God, those first few weeks were awful. Mind-blowingly, gut-wrenchingly awful. I remember them like an illness; my whole body ached, my mind was dislocated, the world felt cold, and everything took longer than necessary. I made the mistake of writing V e-mails, daily at first. I said the same things in all of them, a list of pathetic apologies and admonitions. Lines of promises and hopes, dreams and failures. I begged and pleaded, I prostrated myself. I agreed to anything and everything. But she never replied, not once, not one single word. In the end I understood that there was nothing I could say to make it better. That actions were all that counted and I simply had to show V the kind of man I was capable of being.

After my trip into the basement at Elizabeth Road I became obsessed with the need to see V on her own, without Angus. I realized that the first time I saw her simply couldn't be at the wedding, with him. But I knew better than to request a meeting. She had laid out the rules in her last e-mail and I couldn't possibly risk moving backward. The only way I could think of orchestrating it was to "bump into her." All it took was a bit of patience and, for V, I would wait till the end of time. I loitered a lot where the top of her road met Kensington High Street, reasoning that it was a perfectly understandable place for anyone to be walking at any time.

In the end I got my reward. Two Saturdays before her wedding, V rounded the corner dressed in black Lycra leggings, trainers on her feet, and her hair pulled into a sharp ponytail. My heart actually jolted at her so close, as if she physically occupied a hole inside me. She jogged on the spot as she waited to cross the road and I knew she was going to run around Kensington Gardens.

I acted quickly, maybe too quickly, raising my arm and shouting her name from where I stood, by the bus stop. She turned, looking around for what she thought she had heard, only realizing it was me as I walked toward her. Her mouth formed an O as I approached and her jogging stopped. I reached her quickly and we stood for a few seconds just looking at each other. She was wearing a black top that zipped up under her chin so I couldn't see if she was wearing the eagle.

"My God, Mike," she said finally, and her voice was a little hoarse.

I leaned down and kissed her cheek, inhaling her scent of musky roses, which I was pleased hadn't changed. "V."

"What are you doing here?"

"Oh, just a bit of shopping. How about you?"

She motioned down the street I knew so well. "I live here."

I looked where she was pointing and feigned surprise. "Do you? How nice."

She blushed. "Well, it's Angus's house really, but you know."

I nodded. "You must be excited about the wedding."

She flapped her hands in front of her face. "Well, weddings seem to be mostly about planning."

"I'm sure Suzi has it covered."

She laughed. "So, anyway, you look well." She looked at my chest as she spoke, hardly hidden by the light cotton shirt I was wearing. I could feel her hands on me and I had to shake away the memory.

"So do you." A statement that was never a lie, but especially not that day.

"Just trying to run off those last few wedding-dress pounds." She laughed.

There was an absurdity to the conversation. What we both really wanted to do was rip each other's clothes off and fuck right there on the side of the road. V licked her lips and her breathing was heavy. I could have reached out and taken her hand, there was nothing stopping me.

"I'm glad you're happy, V." I lingered over the letter that had always meant something to us both.

"Thank you. Are you?" Her gaze was deep and penetrating and I knew there was so much more she wanted to say.

"Yes, I'm fine. Work's going well and I'm getting my house sorted. I've just had some quotes to put a gym and sauna in the basement."

"Oh, fancy."

"Well, you know how I love to work out." I kept my eyes fixed on hers.

"Anyway," she said, tearing her eyes away from me and facing back to the road. "It was lovely to see you, but I should get running. Angus and I have a tasting in a couple of hours. The caterer has had to change an ingredient in the starter, something to do with suppliers—"

"Where did you meet him?"

"What?" She looked back at me and her eyes flickered.

"Angus, where did you meet him?" I hadn't planned on asking about him, but she had brought him up and I didn't want her to think I was intimidated by him.

"Oh, a work thing."

"It's been very quick."

She nodded. But then she looked down. "Don't, Mike. I can't do this, it's too hard."

I smiled my best smile. "Sorry, I didn't mean to upset you."

"No, it's fine. It's lovely to see you," she said, but her voice quivered.

"And you." I turned from her as I spoke and walked off, glancing back after a few moments, to see her still waiting on the curb for the traffic to clear.

I wonder if that's what alcoholics feel like when they have a drink after a long time sober. As if every nerve ending has been smoothed, all your blood warmed, your mind stroked. I walked like I was on a cloud, I'm surprised I didn't glide, didn't rise into the sky and float above the hordes of people on the pavement. I thought up heroic deeds and noble sacrifices. I made speeches that made others cry, I solved tensions, stopped wars, made peace. It was like my heart was a balloon that someone had finally filled with air and the only possible expression I could hold was that of a smile.

But of course the peace didn't last very long, not even into the evening. And just like an alcoholic I craved my next fix. I searched my brain for reasons to call V and wondered how odd it would be to "bump into" her again. I let my mind play with me and thought that maybe the mere sight of me would have been enough to make her too want to forget the Crave and cut to the end. At any moment of any day I thought it was possible she was telling Angus it had all been a terrible mistake and that really she loved someone else. I strained to hear the ringing phone or doorbell I knew was coming.

After a few days of living in this state of constant anticipation I realized I must have done something wrong. V always had very strict rules and guidelines and clearly I hadn't behaved entirely properly. She had as good as told me that she still loved me when she had stopped me from talking about Angus because "it's too hard," but there was clearly something more she wanted from me, some ultimate proof that would make me worthy of her love. But, like a fool, I couldn't yet work out what it was.

Naturally I knew the location of her office; I'd met her outside Calthorpe's discreet entrance enough times and it wasn't actually that far from where I worked. There was a bar opposite and I took to leaving work early and sitting at a table by the window. I saw V on only my second night, which was like a sign that I was meant to be there. She emerged from the large, revolving doors just before half past seven, before I'd even had time to sit with my pint at the table in the window. She was wearing a pale blue dress and white trainers with the gray bag slung across her body. Her hair was in a loose ponytail at the base of her neck and she was reading something on her phone, which made her mouth turn downward. Perhaps Angus was being annoying about some aspect of the wedding. Or perhaps she was wondering how to get out of the whole thing. After she had finished reading she stood for a minute, looking tired and distracted. I sipped at my beer and wondered if it would be possible to get a decent shot of her on my iPhone, because even the sight of her, just the knowledge that she was so close, had slowed my heart for the first time since our too brief encounter a few days ago.

A man approached her, holding an open map in front of him, a small backpack sitting between his shoulders. He asked her something and she replied, leaning over the map and pointing. My body tensed as I watched, knowing that with his height advantage and the angle of her body he was probably able to see down the front of her dress. She finished talking and stood back but he was still standing too close. He said something else and she took a step back, shaking her head, her smile now fixed and closed. He reached forward, but she pulled back her hand and her smile dropped. I stood, my hands clenched at my sides.

It seemed suddenly obvious that V knew I was here watching and that she had engineered this Crave for me to see.

I went and stood in the door of the bar and as I did so I saw her hand shoot to her neck, saw it grab the silver charm that could only have been her eagle. She was calling me as clear as day and I was here, right where I could save her. I stepped into the road, but the man shrugged and began walking away. V stepped forward and raised her hand and a taxi pulled up almost immediately. I watched her get in and speak to the driver, sitting back gratefully against the seat as they drove away. And then I found my breath hard to catch because there was no way that could have been a coincidence. She had been talking directly to me.

The man with the map had stopped again, but now he turned the corner and so I ran across the road and fell into step behind him. He walked annoyingly slowly, stopping often to either look at his map or up at the sky. I slowed my pace and slunk into doorways or leaned against walls when he stopped. It was quite interesting actually; it made me realize I rarely look up in cities, but that there are some amazing sights to be seen if you do. London, it appears, is watched over by gargoyles.

They sit above windows and doors, snarling and laughing at us, casting evil spells.

I had no real plan as I walked, but I couldn't stop following him. I alternated between wanting to ask him if V had paid him to enact that scene and wanting to mash his face into the ground. He was tall, but he was out of shape and he walked with a lolloping gait that made me think he had a bad knee. I was sure I could pulverize him in minutes. I could have him lying bloodied and broken on the ground quicker than it would take him to lose consciousness. I could take his stupid backpack and go through his phone for messages from V. And the police would put it down to a mugging and he'd go back to wherever he came from and tell the story for the rest of his life. But of course this wasn't possible. It was a balmy summer evening in central London and all the streets were heaving with witnesses. I probably wouldn't even get as far as my first punch before someone called the police.

The man went into an off-license and came out with four bottles of Beck's that he carried with his finger through the top of the box in a very irritating way. I was certain by then that we were heading for St. James's Park, which was odd because we must have walked a long way and I hadn't realized we were even going in that direction. The sun had sunk away and the sky had turned from a deep polluted orange to navy blue. I checked my watch and it was nine fifteen. Once in the park the man sat on one of the first benches and produced a Swiss army knife from his pocket to open the first beer.

"Excuse me," I said, remaining standing in front of him. He looked up at me, a slight smile on his face.

"Yeah," he said, his accent deeply American.

"I saw you approach a young woman. She came out of a building on Chancery Lane and she helped you with something on your map. Directions maybe?"

He smiled. "Oh yeah." But then he scrunched up his face. "How do you know?"

"I saw."

"But that was a while back." Something shifted in his eyes, and he sat forward.

"What did you say to her?" A feeling not unlike electricity was running up my legs.

"What? I asked her directions."

"No, after that." I could tell he was slow-witted.

"I asked her if she wanted to go for a drink." He sipped from the beer as if to prove his point and I thought it would have been easy to ram the bottle in as far as it would go, so he choked on the glass. "What's this about, man? Have you been following me or something?"

"Yes," I replied. "Did she ask you to speak to her?"

"No." He laughed. "Who the fuck are you?"

"She's my girlfriend." I tried to keep my voice even against the still of the night. "We play this game. I just thought you might be part of it. It's okay to tell me. It won't ruin anything."

He looked over his shoulder. "Is this for some TV show or something?"

"No, I'm serious. I'm not going to do anything to you. I just need to know if she paid you to speak to her."

"This is fucked-up shit." He put the empty bottle on the ground and opened another. "D'you want one?"

"No." I could smell the hops from where I stood and I knew how delicious it would taste. "Look, who are you? What do you do?"

"Fuck, man, are you serious?" I could see the glint in his eye, almost as if he was enjoying the game as much as V and me. I nodded. "I'm American," he said pointlessly. "Just traveling through Europe. Working here and there. Nothing serious. I was lost and asked your girl for directions. She's pretty and I thought I'd try my luck. She said no, I went on my way. Nothing more or less."

I breathed into the soles of my feet. "Thanks." I turned and walked away. I could hear him laughing behind me, the sound following me out of the dark park.

He was just the sort of person to enjoy being part of our Crave, or to need the money enough to do it even if he didn't want to. V had no doubt paid him to keep quiet. And of course she would anticipate me following him and talking to him. That would have been part of the deal. I felt like I was starting to understand our situation better, that the rules of our new Crave were becoming clearer. It was obvious this wasn't a game to be played in one night or one moment and it was also clear that the stakes were very much higher. I just had to work out what the end point was and when it was meant to take place. Not surely, I felt, before the wedding, which was now only ten days away.

I woke the next morning with my alarm and pulled myself out of bed and into my Lycra. My head was heavy and my muscles sluggish and only when I returned home from my run did I notice the half-empty bottle of vodka and remember what I'd done when I got home the night before.

My CDs were splayed across the floor of the kitchen by the garden doors, their contents spilled like entrails. I couldn't remember playing any, but it seemed likely I had. I went to the stereo and saw the volume button turned up to max.

I made an effort to say hello to Lottie at work that morning, planning some sort of apology that didn't actually appear when I saw her blush and look at the floor. I found it hard to concentrate on work and sought Kaitlyn with an excuse about some figures I could have worked out in my sleep.

"Are you okay?" she asked as I leaned over her desk while she entered the numbers.

"Yes, fine," I said breezily.

She turned and looked up at me, her bright eyes quivering slightly. "You look a bit rough."

I straightened up. "Really?" When I'd shaved that morning I had noticed a redness around my eyes and thought maybe I'd lost a bit of weight in my face.

"I hope you're not working too hard."

"No, it's fine."

"And last night, Mike, I . . ." She blushed and I desperately tried to search my mind for whether or not I had seen her the previous evening, although I couldn't have.

"What?"

She shook her head. "Nothing. It just looks like you had a rough night."

"I'm fine."

She went back to the numbers, tapping on her keyboard. "Is everything all right at home?"

"Yes. Of course."

She stopped typing and turned to me. "I know we haven't known each other very long, but you can talk to me if you'd like, you know."

I knew I was going to have to say something because Kaitlyn clearly wanted more than I was giving her. "There is something. I get really carried away with my music sometimes and I think I listen to it too loudly. I'm worried I've annoyed Lottie."

But she ignored the statement. "Doesn't it annoy Verity?"

"She's away at the moment. With work."

"Oh." Kaitlyn tapped her finger against the glass of her monitor. "All done. I've e-mailed them to you."

"Thanks." I went back to my desk feeling no better. I wished I hadn't gone to see Kaitlyn; everything about her was irritating. I didn't like the way she looked at me, as if she were peeling back my skin with her eyes.

My cell rang and I saw Elaine's name flashing on the screen. I had ignored so many of her calls, but this one I answered, a rush of need spreading through me at just the thought of her.

"Mike," she said, sounding shocked. "Goodness, is that actually you?"

I laughed. "Sorry, I've been so busy since I got home. I've been meaning to call you."

She snorted. "How are you, love?"

"Really good."

"Are you settling into your new house?"

"You must come and see it." But even as I said the words I cringed against the thought of her and Barry in the space and how they would never understand it.

"Well, I'd love to. But actually I was ringing to see if you'd like to come out for lunch this Sunday."

It felt like I could taste her words and there was something intoxicating about them. "I'd love to."

"Oh super. We've got a new boy just started with us and I'd love you to meet him."

Sundays were a good day to fill as it was hard to watch over V on the weekend.

Y

The journey to Aylesbury was shorter than I had anticipated, so I ended up ringing Elaine and Barry's doorbell at twelve o'clock. Elaine answered in her apron, the house fugged up with the smell of roast dinner behind her. Her face leaped into a smile when she saw me and she pulled me toward her, folding me into her warm, earthy smell. Stepping into the house felt like stepping through time, as if I really could push through space and arrive somewhere different. And yet nothing was different, it was all completely the same. The same worn carpet on the stairs, the same oval table under the mirror loaded down with keys and letters, the same cracked linoleum on the kitchen floor, the same ancient oven that billowed smoke, the same clothesline hanging across the garden, the same wooden table on which we would later eat.

Barry came in from the garden and I saw his roses resplendent behind him. "Mike, my boy," he said, advancing toward me and wrapping me in a hug. He felt fatter, I thought, although Elaine was perhaps slimmer. "Well, well, look at you," he said, standing back.

I looked down at myself and saw my polished brogues, my pressed chinos, my crisp blue shirt. It was almost embarrassing in this house. But Barry got us a beer and we sat in the garden and Elaine tried to sit with us, but kept jumping up to perform another task, making Barry roll his eyes at me. The conversation felt weary as soon as it began and there were times when I didn't know how I was going to answer all their questions. But at the same time I didn't want to leave, at that moment I could have sat in the garden forever.

Just as we were sitting down to lunch the front door slammed and a tall, lanky boy came into the kitchen.

"Oh good," Elaine said, "you're just in time."

He came and sat at the table and I could see his chest moving and the sweat on his skin. It reminded me of all the times I had run home to eat Elaine's food. He kept his eyes fixed on his hands in front of him.

"Mike," Elaine said, "this is Jayden. Jayden, this is Mike—you know I told you about him. Mike was with us for longer than any other child we've ever had."

He nodded over toward me. "All right."

I smiled back. "How long have you been here?"

"A couple of months."

Barry stood up to carve, while Elaine ladled potatoes, carrots, parsnips, and Yorkshire pudding onto our plates. Sunday lunch in Elaine's kitchen never changed, whatever the weather. I wanted to ask Jayden why he was here but knew better. I estimated him to be about thirteen or fourteen and from the hungry way he ate I could probably guess the answer anyway.

"Jayden's mad keen on football," Barry said, which I knew must please him as I had sat and tried to keep my eyes open on plenty of Saturday nights while *Match of the Day* droned away on the television.

"D'you know the scores?" Jayden asked, his mouth disgustingly full of food.

"No, don't tell me," Barry said, holding his hands over his ears and making Jayden laugh, and I wished suddenly I had been able to play this game with him. I knew all at once that Jayden had my room and that he would have put up his own posters and hung his clothes in the wardrobe and that it would already feel like a mini home to him. Elaine and Barry were laughing at something he'd said, which I'd missed, and the chair felt weak and insubstantial beneath me. Things did change and move on, even love.

Elaine reached over and put her hand on mine. "Oh, it's so lovely to have you here, Mikey. We've missed you, haven't we, Barry."

"We certainly have," Barry said. "While you've been off wheeling and dealing."

"Did you really live in New York?" Jayden asked.

"Yes." My throat felt strangely clogged.

"Mega."

"But what else has been going on in your life?" Elaine asked. "Any nice lady I should know about?"

I shook my head and for a terrible moment I thought I was going to cry. Thought I was going to lay my head down between the gravy bowl and my plate and weep. "No, no lady."

Elaine tapped my hand. "I hear Verity's getting married."

"Yes."

"She rang to get your new address. Are you going to the wedding?"

I felt the atmosphere around the table shrink and spiral. Verity had sat where Jayden was on quite a few occasions. I had been embarrassed to bring her at first, but she claimed to love it at Peacock Drive. She said it made her feel cozy, and Elaine and Barry had always marveled over her, like I had brought them an exotic flower to look at. It all felt wrong suddenly. It was too much that she wasn't sitting here now and we weren't talking about our wedding. I wanted to tell Elaine and Barry what a mistake it had been and how V and I loved each other in a way no one else could possibly begin to understand.

"Yes," I said, "it's next Saturday."

"What's he like, her fiancé?"

"I don't know, I haven't met him."

I saw Elaine glance at Barry. Jayden had taken out his phone and was swiping at something on the screen.

"So you're all right about it then, are you?" she asked hopefully.

I smiled like I knew she wanted me to. "Yes, of course."

Her body seemed to relax at that. "Oh good. It's just Barry and I knew how hung up on her you were and we didn't want it to have upset you."

I felt a million miles away from Elaine and Barry at that moment, the gulf of understanding between us so immense it was like we meant nothing to one another.

"She's a lovely girl, but there's plenty of lovely girls out there, especially for a fantastic young man like you." Elaine was looking at me very closely, as if trying to tell me something with her eyes, so I kept my smile rigid.

"It's going to be okay," I said.

She looked at me quizzically. "Well, of course it is."

"No, I mean, between me and V. It'll all work out fine."

"It's nice you can be friends," she said, but I saw her smile had slipped, a bit like a wig on an old man's head. "Maureen's Julie got married last year to a man she met on one of those Internet sites."

I thought of Maureen's Julie and her doughy body, her lank thinning hair, her oversized glasses. I could feel my own muscles tense, even though I was sitting down, and it seemed ridiculous that Elaine could suggest such a thing.

"Hang on there," Barry said. "The poor lad's only just turned thirty, you don't need to go marrying him off."

I felt so tired by the time I left that I wasn't sure how I was going to make it home. My eyes ached with the pressure of keeping them open and my throat felt raw and scratched. By the time I stepped off the Tube I was shivering against the warmth of the day and I felt the sweat popping out on my skin on the short walk back to my house. Once there, all I could do was strip naked and climb beneath the covers, giving in to a restless sleep in which V visited me in so many different forms I found myself unable to keep up. I woke throughout the night to the sounds of foxes mating and people laughing and at one point I reached across the bed and felt V's solid shape. But when I pulled her toward me I realized I was holding a pillow and kicked it away from me in disgust.

Even though I dreamed of her all night, the only one I clearly remember is her standing in her new doorway holding her eagle toward me. She had ripped the chain from her neck and it lay crumpled and pathetic in her hands. Be careful, I said to her, or you'll lose it. It doesn't matter, she answered, you're not coming, are you.

I didn't feel any better when my alarm sounded in the morning, in fact if anything I felt worse, a deep sickness now also lodged in my stomach. I called work and left a message explaining I was ill, something I couldn't ever remember doing before. I slept most of that Monday as well, my dreams not unlike a rough sea. But by evening I knew I was over the worst of the fever. I ordered food on my laptop from my bed, chicken soup and dumplings, with fine noodles. I paid enough for it to be delicious and fresh and for a while I felt better as I ate it slowly, leaning against my pillows, listening to the news on the radio.

But my thoughts have always waited in darkened corners for me, watching for moments in which I am lulled into a false sense of security.

Their favorite torture is to remind me of my solitude. That there is no one to bring me chicken soup or feel my head or even care about my fever. As I lay weakened in bed they dragged up a memory of standing behind the bars of what must be a cot, my diaper so wet I could feel the urine stinging my skin, my throat raw from crying, my hands freezing. I don't know how this memory ends because it is fogged. I don't even know if it is a single memory or something that happened many times.

I have always preferred the ones that feel more concrete. It's easier to cling to the hard facts: My stomach rumbled so much in class other boys used to gurgle at me on the playground; my trousers would often fall to my knees because there was nothing to hold them up; I had to explain in front of the whole class that we didn't have any books in our house; I faked illness whenever we had a school trip because it would have meant bringing a packed lunch; I was never asked to one other child's house or birthday party; I spat at my feet to stop myself crying; cold can penetrate into your marrow in a way that nothing else can; I was very, very good at lying about the origins of my bruises and scratches.

The last time I was properly with my mother she was lying on the sofa in our flat, her body already floppy from drink, her speech slurring. Miss Highland had had me in her office again the day before to remind me I didn't have any duty to protect someone who didn't protect me. I had nodded and smiled and presumed nothing would change. But it must have, because when the familiar knock sounded on our door that evening I let them in. I didn't lie down flat on the floor so they couldn't see me when they looked through the letter box, like Mum had taught me. I didn't even try to wake Mum or bother to formulate a ready lie. I just opened the door and let them walk through into the living room covered with moldy plates and overflowing mugs of cigarettes. I let them gag at the stench in the bathroom and stare openmouthed at the piles of empty beer cans and bottles in the kitchen. I confirmed my name and let them lead me to a car. It was only afterward, on our drive to the home, that I realized I hadn't even asked what was going to happen to Mum. But it was too late by then.

I stayed in bed again on Tuesday, ordering in more food and managing to make it to the kitchen for cups of tea. I noticed that the weather was glorious, with streaming sunshine and clear blue skies, and I thought late summer was the perfect time to be getting married. By the end of the day I felt stronger and after a shower I felt well enough to put on some shorts and sit in the garden for half an hour with the sun on my face. Tomorrow I would have to get back to some serious workouts as I was determined to look as perfect as possible for Saturday.

I woke the next morning with the distinct impression I had forgotten something, but it was only on my run that I realized what it was. I hadn't bought V a wedding present. The thought was so ghastly I had to stop and bend over, pretending I had developed a sudden cramp. I couldn't quite believe I had been so negligent. If I wasn't meant to stop the wedding, then my gift had to be very important.

It was my next move in our new Crave and I felt sure it would be the first present V opened.

It was all I could think of throughout the day. Even when the chairman popped his head around my door and asked me if I was feeling better, I know I didn't give him my full attention. I was even quite dismissive when he said there was a new project he thought would suit me, and he shut my door with a look of vague confusion on his face.

Just before I left for America, V and I were asked to the wedding of an old friend of hers from university. At the bottom of the invitation they had written, "No presents, please, your presence is the only present we need." V had fake retched when she'd read that. What crap, she'd said, everyone wants presents.

It came to me the next morning and so I went at lunchtime to a rare-book shop I found on Google. There were hardly any books of the type I requested, he'd told me over the phone, but naturally he did have one. Its rarity, he warned me, would make it more expensive than the hideously expensive ones all around us in the musty, overcrowded shop, but I had expected that. I waited while he went to fetch it, breathing in the dust of centuries and running my fingers across worn and broken spines, the leather cracked and chipped.

I was pleased by the size of the book that he laid on the wooden table at the back of the shop and, as soon as he turned the first page, I knew I was going to buy it. There were pages and pages of detailed, gorgeous pictures of eagles, each one protected by a thin layer of white tissue paper. The prints were good enough to cut out and frame, something the dealer told me had happened to so many of these types of books. I was lucky, he said, that I had found his shop because he could guarantee he was the only person in London to have such a magnificent item in stock. But I was barely listening, instead marveling at the riches in front of me, the golds and blues, the intricate details, the amazing scenes. He told me he could let it go for £3,500 and I didn't bother to bargain because I would have paid double, maybe even triple, for a gift so perfect.

I had the book professionally wrapped at another place I found on Google, leaving it overnight and collecting it at lunchtime. From there I had it couriered to Steeple House. I could have taken it back to the office to accomplish all these tasks but couldn't bear answering questions about it all afternoon. I didn't want to turn up with it on the day and, more than that, I hoped V would open it before the wedding, I hoped she would get the message.

Y

V once told me that I'm useless at interpreting signs and at the time she was probably right. We were lying on the grass near her home in Sussex and it was one of those blisteringly hot summer days that only really seem to exist in memory. We had taken a picnic to a nearby field and V had laid our rug in the semi-shade of a tree. We had eaten and drunk the bottle of wine, and I was on my back, V resting on my chest, my arm lazily slung around her. I could feel her head rise and fall with my breathing and I remember thinking that this was what bliss felt like. That you could put a picture of us next to the word in the dictionary and everyone would understand. And I also knew it was the first time I had ever truly felt that way. Of course Elaine and Barry had made me feel happy and safe and loved even. But this feeling, which seemed to spread through my blood, from my toes up into my head and along my muscles, this was new. It was also delicious; it was like a drug and I was already addicted.

"Look, there's a swan," V said, pointing upward.

I looked into the sky but there was nothing there. "Can they fly?"

She laughed. "No, not an actual swan. A cloud swan."

"A what?"

"Didn't you ever play that game when you were young? You know, making shapes out of the clouds."

"No. We didn't play any games."

She leaned up on her elbow so she was looking down on me and her hair brushed against my cheek. "Sorry, Mikey. I didn't think."

"It's okay." I reached up and wound a piece of her hair around my finger. "It doesn't matter now."

"Was it very terrible?"

I tried to think of something to say about childhood, but all that came to mind was the color gray and the feeling of cold concrete. It had only been five years since I had last seen my mother by then, but she had already blurred and morphed into more of a feeling than a person and I found I couldn't grab hold of a memory that felt real. "It wasn't all bad," I tried, but that sounded wrong. "Elaine and Barry were great."

"Of course," V said. "But what was your mother like?"

V and I had only known each other for about six months at that point and I had never properly spoken to anyone before about my mother. But with V, I always had the feeling that nothing was ever enough, that we could never do or say or know enough about each other. If I could have turned myself inside out to show her how I worked, I would have done it.

"She was very sad," I said finally, which sounded true as I said it.

"In what way?"

"In every way." I tightened my twist on V's hair and realized how easy it would be to rip it from its roots. "I think she drank as a way of blocking life out." The conversation was starting to make me feel funny, as if there was something I was forgetting.

"What about your dad?"

"I don't have a dad."

"Everyone has a dad," V said, her eyes locked on me.

"No, the space is blank on my birth certificate. My mother said it could have been one of a few men, none of whom she was still in contact with." The words sounded unreal outside of myself, where they had lived for so long. I almost wanted to catch them like butterflies and put them back. I couldn't meet V's eyes in case I had made her hate me.

But she leaned down and kissed me very softly on the side of my mouth. "Oh, poor baby," she said, so gently I could have cried. Then she laid her head back on my chest and we breathed together for a few minutes. "The swan is still there," she said.

I looked back into the sky, but all I saw were wispy clouds against the peacock blue. "I still can't see it."

She laughed. "You're not very good at interpreting things, are you?"

I pulled her closer to me. "I love you," I said, needing to say it so much at that moment I thought it might burst out of me if I didn't.

She was quiet for a moment, but then, "I love you too," she said.

I can't tell you why V loved me as much as she did. I spent the first year of our relationship terrified that she would wake up and realize she had made a stupid mistake, or identify me as the faulty goods I had always presumed myself to be. But it didn't happen and I came to realize that she loved me in spite of who I was, which was not something I had ever imagined happening. At times I even let myself believe that she loved me because of who I was, although that thought never seemed quite real to me.

I thought it was a joke when she came up to me at a party I hadn't wanted to go to in our second year at university. I thought once she had her light she would walk off, but she leaned against the wall and asked me my name and what I was reading and where I was from and all those normal questions. And I was so stunned I didn't ask her any in return, which I only remembered after I got back to my room hours later. I sat at my desk then and wrote out a list of things I wanted to know about her, all the things I would ask her next time, if the phone number she had given me proved to be real. And I also marveled at the fact that I had even been at the party, via a series of odd coincidences, which was the first time I considered the possibility that fate had wanted us to meet.

There's a French film called something like *The Red Bicycle*, I can't remember the exact title. I saw it years ago late at night on BBC Two and I was so mesmerized by it I forgot to check the title until weeks later, by which time I couldn't find any reference to it, to the extent that I sometimes wonder if I dreamed it or if I really watched it.

In the film there is a boy who works in a shop and a girl who cycles past the shop every day on her red bicycle. They nearly meet a hundred times, their paths crossing but never merging. As the film goes on you get the feeling that they need to meet, that it's imperative to humanity, that when they do something magical will happen. But still they never do. Then they both board a ferry on an ordinary day. They sit near each other but still fail to notice each other. Even when the storm rolls in and catastrophe strikes, even when it is obvious the boat is sinking rapidly, even when people are losing hope, still they fail to notice each other. The boat sinks and people are dying, perishing, leaving, but still they are flailing on their own. Then the camera pans out and we are watching the event as news footage. The newscaster is telling us it is the worst maritime disaster in French waters since the war, that it is feared only two people have survived. There is a shaky shot of two people being helped off the upturned hull into a lifeboat. They are the only two people left, and they look at each other, and you know immediately that all it was ever going to take for them was one glance.

And what that means is that sometimes two people need each other so much it is worth sacrificing others to make sure they end up together.

The weather on the morning of V's wedding was perfect. Blue skies and warm sunshine, neither too hot nor too cold. The air felt like a kiss on your skin and there was a sense of anticipation in the atmosphere, almost as if you could feel the plants growing and the flowers blooming. I had bought a new suit for the occasion, a beige linen that I wore with a white shirt and brown tie. I had been careful in my choice, keen not to seem like I wanted to stand out but also making sure that it showed off my body to the best of its advantage. I had also bought some new cuff links, two old silver coins fashioned into a new purpose. In fact, I had bought two pairs, simply because I had been unable to resist a pair of antique engraved cuff links I saw in the window of a shop in Burlington Arcade. The flowing lines were very subtle, but still undeniably in the shape of a V. I had considered wearing them, but decided against it because they were the cuff links I would wear to our wedding.

I left the house at eleven sharp because even though the service was in Sussex at three, I couldn't risk being in any way late. Funnily I was in a good mood.

I knew it wasn't real, I knew it was all part of our Crave and I was determined to enjoy myself. Apart from anything else, I hadn't visited V at either work or home since my illness earlier in the week and I was desperate to see her.

As I walked down my path Lottie's front door opened and Kaitlyn came out. "Oh hello," she said.

She had become like some weird presence in my life and she unnerved me slightly. I almost wondered if she had been watching my house from Lottie's window and had engineered leaving at the same time as me.

"Bye," she called to Lottie who waved and shut the door.

We fell into step together on the pavement. "What are you doing here?" I asked.

"We've just been to LBT." I presumed she meant some sort of exercise class as she was wearing Lycra.

"Oh, I didn't know you and Lottie were so friendly."

She laughed. "Yes, we are." We walked on and then she said, "You look very smart. Where are you going?"

"A wedding."

"No Verity?" I thought I could hear a note of amusement in her voice, which made me want to slap her.

"She's there already. It's her sister who's getting married, at their parents' house in Sussex."

"Oh, how nice."

"Yes, it's an amazing house. It's got its own chapel in the garden, which is where the wedding is taking place. It dates from the Norman times and there's a rumor that there's an underground tunnel running from the house to the chapel."

"Oh right." We'd reached the main road and she was turning in a different direction. "Well, have fun. See you Monday."

I felt myself heat up as I continued on to the Tube. What had I been thinking of, saying something like that? Now, when V came to live with me, I would have to change jobs, maybe even move. Because Kaitlyn would no doubt keep popping up and she was just the sort of annoying person to ask V about her sister or the wedding.

I looked back and watched Kaitlyn cross the road, almost wishing a bus would speed over the hill and drag her under its wheels.

The train journey calmed me somewhat as we left the urban sprawl and started to glide through quintessentially English countryside. It couldn't all happen instantly, which meant I would be able to secure new employment before V did move in. You couldn't just get married and then immediately get divorced and, even when you did, it would no doubt take a bit of time. I let my eyes relax as I stared out the window and the countryside began to blur and merge, until it became a series of soft greens flowing past me.

I still hadn't worked out exactly what V wanted me to do, which bothered me. Usually I knew my role in a Crave and we played by set rules. I understood that the American incident meant V had changed the rules and that she was punishing me by not revealing them to me. I comforted myself with the thought that at least I knew the purpose or the endgame. I knew we were heading toward the inevitability of being together, I just didn't know yet exactly what was expected of me. All I could be sure of was that it was going to be something big, something that undeniably and irrefutably proved my love for V forevermore.

I arrived nearly two hours early, so I went to the village pub I knew so well, before walking up the lane to Steeple Chapel. I ordered a pint and went to sit outside with the paper, even though I knew I wouldn't be able to read a word. There was a group of people dressed for a wedding already there and their voices rose into the soft air. Angus's friends, I thought, looking at their bright clothes and tousled hair.

Over the course of the next hour the pub began to fill with more and more people obviously going to the wedding. Lots of people were kissing and greeting each other and women were squealing in a way that made me wonder how any of them could have been invited by V. I was on my second pint by then and as it hit my stomach I became aware that I hadn't eaten since breakfast. I checked my watch and it was two fifteen, so I stood to begin the five-minute walk to the chapel. But as I did so a woman broke off from one of the groups and came toward me, a broad smile on her face. I knew I knew her, but it took me the whole of her approach to work out she had been one of V's friends at university.

"Mike," she said, "how lovely to see you."

We kissed on both cheeks in that bizarre way people do nowadays, her hat nearly falling off in the process. "Hello," I said, not remembering her name, even though I knew we'd spent a fair proportion of time together over the years. She'd been for dinner at our flat with her boyfriend, whose name I also couldn't remember.

"You look well," she said. "Was America good?"

"Yes, fantastic."

"How long have you been back?"

"Oh, a few months." I shifted my weight, my brain still scrabbling for her name.

"Come over. James would love to say hello."

I let her lead me to a group of people, where a man I recognized as James shook my hand. The other people in the group looked at me expectantly. "You remember Ben and Siobhan, don't you?" James said. "What did you read again?"

"Economics." I smiled at the people I didn't recognize.

"Oh yes," James said. "We were all English."

Louise! It came to me finally. "What are you doing with yourself now, Mike?" James asked.

"I work in the City. How about you?"

"Oh we're all in the media, in various ghastly forms." James laughed, although I could tell he was really pleased with the fact.

"It's lovely that you came," Louise said. "I always think it's so nice when people remain friends, even after tricky breakups."

I looked at her, not entirely sure what she was talking about.

"Have you met Angus?" James asked.

"No, not yet," I said.

"Oh, he's a top bloke. We went to Dorset with them at Easter and it was a real laugh."

I looked between the smiling faces and wondered what they were doing. The thought even occurred to me that V had set this up as well. But I couldn't contemplate that because my mind felt mugged by the thought of Dorset and what that meant. Of the thought of V anywhere other than the house in Kensington, work, or Steeple House. It made me feel quite shaky.

"We should get going," I said, looking at my watch again.

"Oh, there's hours yet," James said. "Brides are always late. Louise kept me waiting twenty minutes, I began to think she wasn't coming."

Everyone laughed except me. "No, there's only twenty-five minutes. I'm going to get going."

I waited a few seconds but nobody moved, so I turned and walked away. "See you there," I heard Louise calling after me.

There were quite a few people at the chapel by the time I arrived, which meant James was wrong and I was right. I told the young boy at the door I was with the bride and was directed to the left-hand side of the chapel, where I sat about five rows back, but near the aisle, so V could see me when she came in. Angus was standing near the front, chatting with another man who had a shock of ginger hair. Angus looked different in the flesh, slightly shorter than I remembered from my brief glimpse of him getting out of the taxi. And maybe also slightly slimmer. He hadn't made much of an effort with his hair, which still looked too long, and there was a hint of stubble on his face, making him look absurd on his wedding day. He rubbed his hands over his chin and even though he was smiling, his eyes looked nervous.

I thought he seemed unsure as to whether or not V was coming. It was entirely possible they'd had a massive row as the day grew closer and she realized what she was doing. It occurred to me that maybe she wanted me to stop the wedding in some way. Maybe I was meant to stand up at that moment when the vicar asks if anyone present knows of any lawful impediment to the marriage. I sat very still for a while, considering this, but in the end I concluded this could not be what was expected of me. V hated scenes; she would especially hate one in front of all her family and friends. No, she had brought me here to bear witness and my role in the destruction of this marriage would be much more subtle.

By the time I looked up the chapel had filled to such an extent that people were standing at the back and the man sitting next to me had his legs pressed right up against mine. There was a clatter of heels on the floor and I turned and saw Suzi rushing in. She was beaming, her face set in an expression of happiness, which didn't look entirely real, especially sitting as it was underneath a large pale yellow hat that did nothing for her complexion. Her dress was the same pale yellow and as she wafted down the aisle I thought she looked like a giant slab of cheese. She caught my eye as she passed; her smile faltered momentarily but then intensified. She too, I realized, wanted me to bear witness.

The music started and the room fell silent. I could feel V in the entrance to the church, like a wire was attached between us, strengthening and tightening. We all stood and I could see from the rapt expression on Angus's face that she was beginning her slow walk. I held myself very still, knowing I could move my head and see V in an approximation of what she would wear to our wedding, because of course she would save the best dress for me.

The people opposite were all smiling and exclaiming and there wasn't much time left, so I turned my head, just at the moment she came level with our pew. She glanced up and our eyes locked for a moment, before she looked away. But I saw the jolt in her. I knew then what it had cost her to put me through this and I wanted in some way to let her know I was okay and I understood.

Her dress was made of very old lace, resting over what looked to be a fitted silk gown that flowed around her body like water. It glistened as she moved, hinting at her perfect body in a tantalizing fashion. It was scooped in the back, revealing her spine and the muscles that held her together, her pale brown flesh a reminder of all the times I had held her. Her hair flowed in loose ringlets, fixed in places by small white flowers. She radiated, purely and simply, and my heart reached out to her as she passed, screaming and weeping in my chest.

I barely heard the service as my blood was rushing through my ears. I stood and sat at the right times and sang the hymns, although I couldn't tell you what they were now. I listened to bloody Louise and Angus's brother read extracts about love from books I didn't recognize. And I tried to avoid looking at V and Angus standing side by side, the quick smiles they gave each other, or the note of joy in his voice when he said, "I do."

The air felt thin and my vision was starting to become pitted, almost as if I were losing sight of something. It had also become unbearably hot in the little chapel and I doubted there was enough air for the number of people there. Finally V and Angus went to sign the register and the people next to me began to chat in a low murmur. I rolled the wedding program into a cylinder, my hands tight against the card. And for the first time, maybe ever, I felt a rising anger at V. This had been a stupid idea of hers, it went above and beyond what had been needed. This was a binding contract, it was going to take pain and time to extricate herself from it and I still wasn't even clear what she expected of me. I looked then at her forehead as she sat in the seat just vacated by Angus, as she steadily signed her name, and I wondered again what was going on beneath her skin, inside her skull.

If I had been standing close enough I think I might have taken the heavy golden cross from the altar and smashed it against her head, in order to delve about in the red mess of her brains to try to understand what she meant by it all.

It was a relief to emerge into the bright sunlight and stand back a bit while everyone shouted and cheered and threw their confetti high into the sky, like colorful acid rain. The air was filled with excited chatter and noise and children ran between the gravestones. But I felt tired and weak and could feel a pain building between my shoulder blades, a reminder of the punishing run I'd done that morning.

A woman had set a tripod up in front of the doors and people were being summoned and posed, until all that were left were V and Angus. He drew her toward him, his arm encircling her waist and she raised her face to meet him and they kissed slowly, like they had done in the kitchen the night I'd watched from the shadows. I readied myself for movement, waiting for her hand to reach for her bird, but as I had the thought I realized she wasn't wearing any jewelry around her neck, nothing at all. Only small pearls on her earlobes. My breathing quickened as I tried to work out this new sign, but for the moment nothing came to me.

We followed the path that led to the field at the bottom of Steeple House and went through the gate into the garden, which had been magically transformed into a land of wonder. A huge white marquee stood on the lawn, bedecked with flowers and garlands, shading lots of round tables on which glass sparkled and shimmered. A long table greeted us, loaded with popping bottles of champagne and fizzing glasses. I was handed one as I walked by and sipped straight at it, even though my head already felt addled and my stomach was as empty as a cave.

Emptiness is such a familiar yet terrifying sensation for me, scorched into my physical memory so deep it drags me backward through time to when it wasn't in my power to feed myself. A time when I had no money to even buy myself a loaf of bread. A time when I was always alone, even when my mother was with me. A time in which I couldn't make myself lovable and I didn't know how to love. A time when it had seemed as if I was never going to fill the deep, all-encompassing void in my soul.

Luckily at the reception there were lots of young girls dressed in black and white holding trays laden with food. Except the food on offer was all one bite and I knew I couldn't take a handful, like I wanted to. I drifted to the edge of the party, pretending to admire Suzi's flower beds, really wishing I could snip the heads off the flowers one by one, leaving them dead or dying in the border.

Everyone else had splintered off into groups and the noise they were making was too loud and close. I circled the outside of the party, looking for V, but I couldn't see her anywhere. It was possible, I supposed, that she and Angus were continuing their argument elsewhere. Or maybe she had broken down and admitted everything to him, maybe seeing me during the ceremony had been too much. I took another glass of champagne as a tray passed by me, even though the bubbles were hurtling themselves against my empty stomach, pressing the void higher and higher, squeezing my heart and blocking my throat.

A line was forming in front of the marquee, so I went to join it, standing between people who were still chatting, as if everyone had so much to say. It took me a minute to realize that V and Angus were standing just by the entrance to the marquee, smiling and shaking hands, kissing cheeks and sometimes exclaiming and hugging. I wiped my palms against my trousers, but they slicked again immediately. I was five people away from them and inching ever closer.

The short, fat woman in front of me kissed Angus dramatically and then held V's face in both her hands and kissed her lips, exclaiming as she did so at her beauty. Angus turned to me, his cheeks high with color and his mouth already smiling. He reached out and shook my hand with a tight grip. "Hello, thanks for coming. Sorry, you are?" Up close his skin was lined and he was definitely older than us, my early-forties estimation had been correct.

V was still being mauled by the fat lady but I could feel her straining toward me. "Mike," I said.

His eyes widened for a moment and his glance flicked my length. "Oh Mike."

"Yes."

"Hello, Mike," V said, now free.

I turned to her. "You look amazing."

She blushed, but I stepped toward her, leaving Angus to deal with the next person. "Thank you."

"Did you get my present?"

She looked down. "Yes, we did. It's very beautiful. Thank you."

"I mean every picture," I said, my eyes refusing to leave her face.

She glanced over at Angus, but he hadn't heard. "Oh, well."

"Where are you going on honeymoon?"

She hesitated. "South Africa." She turned toward Angus again and I realized Angus and the woman he was with had stopped talking and there was almost the feeling of a surge from the line, as if I was holding everyone up.

"You're on table fourteen, I think," V said, her smile back on her face. "The plan is just over there."

I walked over to the seating plan, but my eyes had lost focus and it took me ages to find my name and then my table, which was in a far corner, under the slope of the marquee. I was the last person to my place and had to fit myself in next to a mousy-looking woman and an older man.

The mousy woman turned out to be a cousin of Angus's, although she hadn't seen him for three years, and the older man was a family friend of V's parents. I spoke first to the mousy woman, who was interesting only in that she was able to impart some facts about Angus. She didn't appear to like him much. She called him "the family star" and said she wasn't surprised he'd ended up with someone as fabulous as Verity and didn't I think they'd have beautiful children, a thought so disgusting it made me want to gag. She was keen to tell me how fabulously wealthy he was and what a success he'd made of his company, which he'd started from scratch, although I thought Angus's scratch was probably a lot nicer than mine. She also confirmed he was older than V, thirty-eight to be precise, a bit younger than my estimation, which meant he hadn't weathered well.

I moved on to the man toward the end of the main course. He said he knew who I was, although we'd never met, which seemed strange, but also made me think that I had obviously featured strongly in all their lives over the years. He had been in the army, he told me, and asked if it was a career I had ever considered. Banking is a hiding to nothing, he said, playing around with numbers and pretending things were important that were not. It was, he continued, why the country was in the mess it was in, this inability we had to grasp what was really important.

But my brain felt suffocated by the fact that V was going to South Africa and I was finding it hard to concentrate on what he was saying. South Africa had been where we had always wanted to go and the thought that she would be seeing it for the first time with that repulsive upstart Angus was almost too much. I couldn't help looking over at him throughout the meal. He was sitting at the long table that ran across the top of the room, between V and Suzi. His arm was lying along the back of V's chair, but he was saying something to Suzi that was making her laugh. V was chatting to an older man on her other side who could only have been Angus's father. I wondered what V thought, looking at him, ruining the surprise of what her future would hold in store were her marriage real.

And all at once I was struck by the thought that when we got married I would have two blank spaces where my parents were supposed to be. In fact, I would have blank spaces everywhere. I wouldn't have cousins to sit next to ex-girlfriends. I wouldn't have ex-girlfriends. I wouldn't have friends or even acquaintances. I thought stupidly of Kaitlyn and her washed-out face, perhaps the only person I knew whom I could legitimately invite, apart from Elaine and Barry of course.

I put down my knife and fork as the salmon defeated me and thought I might have to get up and excuse myself, when it came to me. I realized suddenly what V was doing with this marriage, almost like she'd written it on a piece of paper and given it to me. This was not the marriage she wanted. This was the marriage Suzi wanted. V was not this traditional bride, this doting daughter, this white virgin. V in fact was the complete opposite of this. V was dark and musty and throbbing. V craved. V craved me.

I lied when I said the Crave in that nightclub in Piccadilly Circus was our last. Our last Crave actually happened in America, the first summer I was living there. And it wasn't even a proper Crave, although now I realize it was the moment when V knew that the rules could change and how fun that could be.

V came out for two weeks and we flew south, picking up an old Chevy in which we drove routes we'd heard about in songs. We slept in hokey motels that looked like sets of horror films and ate in diners where the waitresses were all too old and sad. We swam naked in rivers and drank beer on the side of the road, sleeping it off in the car.

"I feel like a Crave," V said one evening. We were lying in bed in a cheap motel with the neon lights from the sign leaking in through the window onto our naked bodies. The motel was on the edge of an even cheaper town, where we had seen people dressed in cowboy boots and Stetsons.

"They'd probably shoot us out here," I said, kissing the top of her head.

"No, I was thinking something different," she said, her voice slightly muffled against my chest.

"Different how?"

She sat up and her spine was ridged in her back as she curled her arms around her legs. "I want to sleep with a woman. Just once. And I want you to be there."

I didn't know how to answer at first. I was torn between the desire to do anything to make her happy and repulsion at the thought of anyone else getting that close to V.

She turned around and I could see the need in her face. "It wouldn't mean anything. It would just be sex. I want to know what it's like."

"Okay," I said. And if I am being totally honest the thought was quite pleasant, desirable even. I knew how much V loved sex and what we made each other feel like and if she wanted to try something different then it was better that it was with me.

We dressed quickly, V looking all the more seductive for her sex-tousled hair and hastily applied red lipstick. We both probably stunk of the sex we'd had, but neither of us even applied deodorant.

The bars were like ones you see in films, dark and sordid, with loud rock music and pool tables. People stopped talking and looked at us when we came in and lots of them looked as if the beer had soaked right through their skin. The room smelled of farmyard and sweat and broken dreams. We drank neat whiskey for courage and its warmth spread through our veins.

We found what we were looking for at the third bar, sitting on her own at the edge of the room, on a high stool next to a high table that wrapped around a tall wooden pole. She had frosted hair and smudged eye makeup. Her skin was pale and her teeth were yellow. Her skirt was short and her legs were dimpled and mottled, and she wore what looked like a kid's T-shirt bearing the emblem "Little Miss Trouble." She said she was up for anything if we bought her a bottle of vodka.

She swayed on her walk back to the motel and kept tripping over her feet, which both seemed to point inward. She looked younger in the darkness, out of the lights of the bar, and she smoked with a defiance I had never seen before. V linked arms and whispered something in her ear that made her giggle, and I wondered if I would regret what we were about to do.

She stripped as soon as we got inside, before I'd even had a chance to shut the curtains, standing in front of us in cheap, grubby, once-white bra and panties. I sat in a chair, my head groggy and fuzzed, un-sure of my role in the whole charade. I desperately didn't want to have sex with the girl and my dick felt useless.

V walked toward her, removing her own T-shirt as she moved. The girl spat her chewing gum onto the floor and then they were kissing. They fell on the bed and I found I couldn't stop looking at them, at how they fit together, at how their bodies mirrored each other. Even when V arched her back and screamed, the girl's head buried between her legs, still I looked, still I didn't feel the need to rip them apart and beat my fist into the girl's face. And of course I was so hard by then I stood up and my movement attracted V's attention, so she beckoned for me and I went to her, moving straight for her mouth, kissing her fast. The girl sat backward onto the floor and I heard the click of a lighter and smelled the enveloping smoke. But I didn't care by then and neither did V, who was tearing at my jeans, rushing to get me inside her.

Y

I had forgotten there were speeches at weddings.

Angus stood to loud applause. He wasn't holding any notes and V was looking up at him, as were all the faces in the room.

"Thank you all so much for coming." His voice was clear and confident. "It means so much to Verity and me to have you here to share this special day with us and I know some of you have traveled pretty far to be here. We're very touched." He droned on about how amazing Suzi had been with the organization and how welcome she and Colin had made him feel. He said some sentimental crap about his own parents and his brother and his mother dabbed away a tear. He complimented the bridesmaids who just looked like generic little girls in white dresses to me.

"But now, to the most important person," he said, turning to V. "My beautiful, amazing, clever, talented wife, Verity." He gazed down on her, but she had looked away and I saw her nervous blush begin to extend from her breastbone upward. "I don't need to tell you how ravishing she looks today because you all have eyes. I don't need to tell you how kind and clever she is because you all know her. What I do need to tell you is how much she means to me." His voice broke slightly and he reached for his champagne, taking a sip.

"I really cannot believe that we've only known each other for a year. In fact, we realized just the other day that we first met exactly a year ago last Saturday, which feels rather fitting. Not of course that we got together immediately because it took me a bit of time to build up my courage first to speak to Verity, then to ask her out, then to actually take seriously the fact that she might like me." Laughter rang out and I wanted to stand on my chair and shout at everyone to shut the fuck up,

so I didn't miss a word. "So it has amazingly only been ten months between our first date and this moment. Some might say that's not long
enough to know you want to spend the rest of your life with someone,
but I knew after ten minutes. Verity is quite simply the best thing that
has ever happened to me." He lifted his glass. "I ask you all to raise a
toast to my wife, the most wonderful woman on the planet."

I lifted my glass automatically, downing what was left in it. Ten
months. A year. Ten months. A year. The words were like a steam train
rattling through my brain. Verity and I had broken up at Christmas, it
was now the middle of September. I counted down on my fingers even
though I knew very well what the result would be. Nine months. I looked
at Verity but she had stood and was kissing Angus. My vision thinned to
a small, white pinpoint.

I endured Colin's and the best man's turgid speeches, only because
I would have drawn too much attention to myself by leaving. I had to listen to how much everyone loved Angus and how Verity'd had to overcome some difficulties, which was news to me, but was so happy now. I
even had to hear Angus described as "the most eligible man in London,"
a plainly absurd moniker for someone like him.

They finished in the end, as everything does, and the music began,
so I was able to slip out into the now darkened night. Someone had lit a
million candles and the garden seemed to sway with them. I stood by
the side of the marquee and breathed deeply, letting the air expand my
chest until I couldn't hold any more, concentrating on the movement
alone. The night was clear and the stars were sparkling, dotted across
the sky like a message.

A woman was walking toward me, her steps small and her gait
unsteady. Only when she got closer did I see it was Louise. She had a
cigarette in her mouth, which she took out and waved at me. "You don't
have a light, do you?"

"No," I said. "I don't smoke."

She laughed. "Of course you don't. You couldn't possibly have the strength to grow those muscles if you had a disgusting habit like this." She had stopped but her body was still rocking and her speech was slurred. "They're about to have their first dance. You should go and watch."

"No thanks."

"Do you still love her?"

I looked over but it was dark where we were and I couldn't make out all her features. "Why do you ask that?"

"Because you always loved her too much."

"How can you love someone too much?"

She laughed. "In the same way you can love someone too little. It's like the three bears' beds, it's very rare you get it just right."

I felt lost in the conversation. I didn't know if she was trying to tell me something, maybe even something V had asked her to tell me.

"You shouldn't waste your time," Louise said. "Verity and Angus have got it just right and the rest of us can only marvel in their brilliance."

"You're wrong."

"What is it about Verity? Why do all the boys go potty over her?"

"Because she's perfect." I couldn't believe anyone needed to ask that question.

Louise stepped a little closer to me. "You know, I always fancied the pants off you, Mike. Not that you'd have noticed. You were like a puppy around Verity, only ever had eyes for her." She closed the gap between us and put her hand against my dick, on the outside of my trousers. "I hate James," she said. "He fucks like a rabbit."

"This is Verity's wedding."

"So?" she said, her hand still on my limp dick.

I pulled back, raising my hands as I did so to remove hers from my body, but she was so drunk she lost her balance and toppled backward, her high heels skidding from under her. She fell in an undignified heap, landing by the side of the marquee.

She looked up at me. "What the fuck."

I knew I should help her up and apologize, but something about her crumpled figure on the grass disgusted me. The flickering of the candles was adding to my headache and I found all I could do was turn and walk away across the grass.

"You pushed me, you fucking maniac," she shouted ridiculously after me.

I walked back down to the village but the last train had long gone, so I went into the pub and ordered another pint and asked if they knew of a taxi that would drive me back to London. My headache was so bad by then my vision had become jarred and jagged. I couldn't answer the barman when he asked if it had been a good wedding and he shrugged and moved on to the next customer. I feigned sleep in the back of the cab to avoid talking, but something about the movement must have lulled me because I woke as we were pulling up outside my house. I paid the £250 requested and let myself in, where I went to the kitchen and opened a bottle of red that I didn't even really want.

There was just so much I didn't understand. People said things they didn't mean the whole time. Or maybe they didn't know what they meant? Or most terrifying of all, maybe nothing in the world made sense. What would have happened, for example, if I had fucked Louise behind the marquee? What would she have said to James? Did she really hate him? How do rabbits fuck?

And was it possible that V had known Angus for a year? That they'd had their first date a month before I came home for Christmas? Did they really have it just right like Louise said or was he nothing more than a part in our Crave? If I hadn't been such a massive idiot and fucked everything up by screwing Carly, perhaps V had planned to tell me all about Angus.

I banged my fist against the marble of the countertop, the pain spreading comfortingly up my arm. "V," I shouted into the air, "I just want to understand. I just need to know what you want me to do." But the silence kept its counsel and all I could do was sit at my long kitchen table and drink the bloody wine.

PART
TWO

The week following the wedding wasn't good.

I had terrible trouble sleeping and felt sick and woozy during the day. At work the chairman put me on the new deal; we were taking over a large company called Spectre and it was pretty straightforward. Most of it had to be stripped away and lots of people were going to lose their jobs, but I have never felt the queasiness others talk about surrounding situations like this. The way I see it is if everyone in a company is good at their jobs, then the company survives and if, as a boss, you're too stupid to get rid of the deadwood, then what do you expect?

The chairman laughed when I said this to him as we sat in his sumptuous office. "Between you and me," he said, "that's why women generally never rise to the top in business, they're too damned sentimental." Which is obviously a load of horseshit, but I smiled and nodded my head as I knew I was supposed to. Except the simplicity of the operation didn't seem to help matters. I took all the files and folders back to my desk and logged in to the secure sites that held all the figures and found I couldn't make anything stick. It felt like the numbers were dancing across the screen, disappearing behind algorithms, and vanishing into graphs. I was able to conceive of a route, but then lost it halfway through, allowing predictions to tumble around me as if they had never actually existed.

The problem was that my head felt occupied by V, as if she were a burrowing animal who had taken up residence in my skull. It seemed absurd to be attempting anything normal, when at any given moment she could be experiencing things for the first time that I would never be able to share with her. I kicked myself for not asking her more specifics about their trip, so I could get a clearer handle on what she was doing at any given time. We had talked about going to South Africa ourselves and I felt sure she would be drawn to some of the places we'd discussed.

I googled the country incessantly, refining and extending my searches around the terms *tourism, high class, unusual, exotic.* There was a dazzling array of things to do and most of them looked like the sort of things V would enjoy. And of course Angus had the money to make it spectacular, which he would be doing. I took virtual tours around the top hotels, I booked helicopter flights in his name, arranged tastings in vineyards, looked into the best spas, read the menus of the best restaurants. But nothing ever felt like enough; I wanted to break the computer screen and jump in, I wanted to peel away all the PR, I wanted to install cameras everywhere. I wanted to know exactly what they were doing.

I continued the process at home every evening with a bottle of wine and dinner eaten out of cartons next to my laptop. V would never stand for such sloppiness, but as the week stumbled on I became more and more angry with her. What she was doing began to feel out of all proportion to my crime. I knew I had massively fucked up sleeping with Carly, but I regretted it and I had apologized and prostrated myself. She must have known that it meant nothing, she must have known that she was always and forever the only one for me.

What I don't understand is how some men get away with the things they do, while others, like me, are made to crawl over hot coals for moments of madness that we would take back in a heartbeat.

I can still hear the thwack of connecting flesh that accompanied so much of my childhood. V has never known what it feels like to be lying in your bedroom and to hear your mother's body slump against a piece of furniture. To crawl on your hands and knees into the hall and to watch from the door as a man hauls her up by her hair and slams her face into the wall. To feel the desire to move and yet the overpowering fear that turns your knees to jelly. I always crawled back to my sheet-less mattress and pulled my threadbare duvet over my head, hoping for sleep that never came immediately, instead ambushing me sometime in the night so I would wake in the morning with a shot of dread, convinced I would find my mother dead in a pool of blood.

V has no idea what the body looks like after it has been beaten. How it swells and protrudes, how it colors into sickly shades of crimsons and blacks before fading to yellows and grays. She doesn't know what it feels like to run your hand over that skin when the person's body has gone limp from drink, how it feels hard and unnatural and how you can't imagine it ever looking normal again. She doesn't know how easy it is to leave scars, how sometimes just a tiny brown oval will remain, but whenever you look at it you know why it's there.

On the one-week anniversary of her wedding, I wrote V the following e-mail:

> Verity,
> I don't think this is fair. How many times do you want me to say sorry for what happened in America? It meant nothing. Less than nothing.

If it were possible I would reverse time like Superman and never even speak to Carly. If it made you happy I would fly over there now and exterminate her, rid her from the world so she couldn't infect us anymore. But this is too much now. I shouldn't have let it get this far, I should have stopped the marriage before it actually happened. Because it's going to be so difficult to get out of now and I'm still not sure what you want me to do or how we're going to achieve it. And the time you are having to spend with Angus is ridiculous. Every second you are with him is like a dagger in my heart. I get it, a hundredfold I get it. But you've even gone on our honeymoon with him and that is something we will never get back. It doesn't feel like you are teaching me a lesson anymore, more like you are actively being cruel.

I love you, V. You know as well as I do the connection that exists between us. I would do anything for you. As ever, I crave you.

Your Eagle

The next morning I went on a long run, across the Common and down by the river where I pounded my feet along the towpath next to the scum-filled water. The sky was blue above my head and my breathing was even and regular and I felt as if I could have run forever. If V had asked me to, I probably could have enacted my promise to her. I probably could have beaten such a fast path around the world that I could have turned back time and made everything bad that had happened between us go away.

When I got back home my head felt a bit clearer and I went to the shops to buy the sort of lunch V liked. Fresh vegetables and fish, fruit and cream. I prepared it the way she preferred, simply, and poured us both a glass of cold Sancerre. We ate looking out over the garden and discussing our plans for it for next spring. Seeing it through her eyes made me realize it was too clinical and it would be nice if it resembled Suzi's garden a bit more. You shouldn't ever see soil in flower beds, Suzi told me once, and looking out on my garden I realized there was lots of soil and gravel on show and that all the plants were spikey and architectural. They were in almost direct contrast to the beds at Steeple House, which were heavy with color and flowers and soft, gentle foliage that undulates silver and green. You could stand by Suzi's beds and watch the wind stroke them, you could marvel at the shades and shapes before you. You could wonder at nature that produces the most beautiful, intricate versions of perfection for such short amounts of time. I was glad then that V wasn't actually sitting beside me and that I had some time to make things perfect for when she came home.

On Monday I called a garden designer and the builder whom I had liked the best and arranged meetings for later on in the week. The Spectre deal was still sliding and the chairman asked for a meeting in which he made it clear he was surprised things weren't progressing faster. I made up an ill-judged excuse and he asked me if it was perhaps too large a project and if I needed some help. I was quite shocked because I hadn't realized that anything had seemed amiss at work, although I also realized I didn't care that much. Jobs were easy to come by and paled into insignificance next to making sure everything was perfect for V.

I took a morning off to meet the garden designer, a woman called Anna who had a very posh accent and was as tall and thin as a sapling. She agreed with me that the garden currently was very harsh and outdated, although they were her words, not mine. She asked me to describe what I was after and I told her about Suzi's flower beds at Steeple House. I said my girlfriend was very keen to get that country-garden look and Anna said it was her favorite as well. We agreed that we might as well keep the hot tub and outdoor eating area, and Anna assured me they would be so softened by her planting that they would almost become invisible. She thought maybe some mirrors at the back, perhaps even an old rusty gate in front of a mirror to give the illusion of another secret garden beyond. She told me I was lucky to have the tall brick wall at the end, which made this particular trick of the eye possible. I loved the idea. She said she would go away and do some drawings and send me a quote, although I think we both knew I was going to say yes to whatever.

The builder told me he could start on my plans for a gym and sauna at the beginning of the New Year, but he warned me it would be very disruptive. I was lucky, he said, that I had a bit of a basement so a full excavation wasn't going to be necessary, but it would still take the best part of six months to complete and involve lots of heavy digging and lifting equipment. I balked at the idea of waiting so long, but he pointed out I would need planning permission and agreements with my neighbors, neither of which I had considered. You can't just do what you like, he said, shaking his head and handing me a quote that would have bought two houses on Elaine and Barry's street. For an extra £10,000 he offered to handle the architect and planning permission so I said I would transfer the money later that evening. It felt good to be achieving something and working toward our future. I don't know what I'd been thinking of before, dragging my heels at making the house perfect for V.

Toward the end of the second week I was feeling slightly regretful about the tone of the e-mail I'd sent V. I had after all massively betrayed her trust and the normal rules could not be applied to us. I hadn't actually said the words to V, but when I had written the first e-mail I thought I had been subconsciously comparing her to my mother, which was insane. My mother was a weak and pathetic person who allowed herself to fall into the situations in which she found herself. V was nothing like that and, ergo, what I had done with Carly was as bad to her as if I had smashed her head against a wall. All in all I owed her an apology and so I sent her another e-mail.

Dearest V,

I'm sorry if I sounded angry in my last e-mail. I do understand what you're doing and I know I am responsible for what is happening now. It's just that the wedding threw me off-balance slightly. It was horrible seeing you with Angus, even though I know it is nothing more than I deserve. In a funny way I feel sorry for him and all you are going to put him through, but there does I suppose have to be collateral damage in any situation such as this.

I just want you to know that I'm here. I can swoop in and rescue you at any time, and I am prepared to do anything for you, V. You are, as ever, all that matters to me, my darling.

Please get in contact when you get back. There are lots of things we need to discuss.

I crave you,

Your Eagle

After I sent the e-mail I thought about my childhood, which is not something I have done actively for many years. When I left for university Elaine made me a box that, when she gave it to me, I planned to throw away at the first opportunity. Somehow though this has never happened and it travels with me, always tucked somewhere out of sight, at the back of a drawer.

I got it out and laid its contents on the kitchen table. Elaine had stuck a note to the underside of the box's lid, which I knew by heart but still read: *For all the times you need to remember that you are loved,* she had written in her neat, round hand. Inside there was a photo of me standing outside the front door dressed in my school uniform on the first day I left from their house. Another of a barbecue in their back garden, Barry with his top off tending the meat and Elaine and me in stripy deck chairs, laughing at something he's saying. There's a birthday card for my eighteenth birthday from them and my letter of acceptance to university. There's the ticket stubs from the time Barry and I went to Thorpe Park, and Elaine's handwritten recipe for spaghetti Bolognese, which was always my favorite.

Then there are the other pictures in which I can't really recognize myself. A chubby baby on the lap of a small, pretty woman with her hair in a bowl cut and a nervous smile on her face. We look like we are in a back garden somewhere and there is a tiny round paddling pool in the corner of the shot. A lock of hair in an envelope with my name written across the front, which Elaine told me was found in the drawer next to my mum's bed. I like to run my finger along this word, written in a small spidery hand that almost looks scared of taking up too much space on the paper. It has made slight indentations into the envelope, which makes me think she must have pressed hard.

A dog-eared book called *Learn Your ABC's* whose pages I have turned many times, looking for codes and secret messages I have never found, although there is something familiar about the pictures, like a dream I can only half remember. A tiny, battered red car that I was apparently holding when they took me away, even though I was ten, so it seems unlikely it could have meant anything much to me. And finally a photo of an old black dog that, Elaine told me, was the only decoration in the room that passed as my bedroom in my mother's flat. Elaine liked to think it had been a pet of my mother's and she had given the photo to me because she didn't have anything else to give. But Elaine has always liked to think the best of people and I never wanted to shatter her illusion. Really that photograph was stuck on the wall when I first walked into my room, left by the people before me. I dragged my mattress over to where it was and I would often lie and stare at it, wondering at lives in which dogs not only existed but were photographed. It always gives me a jolt to see it there at the bottom of my box and it always makes a mockery of what Elaine wrote on the lid. But for some reason I never throw it away because sometimes it's the only thing I properly recognize.

My mother might be dead by now. It is a very strange thought: that she could simply not be in the world and I don't know it. But she was certainly heading that way the last time I saw her. She was in hospital, yellow against the white sheets, her mouth a cavernous black and her eyes so sunken they looked like they would never return. After that I told my social workers to stop informing me when she was ill and they didn't question my decision. I was at that point taking my A Levels and I had a bright future ahead of me and Elaine was with me, so it didn't look like I needed to be bothered anymore. All my mother ever did anyway was cry and apologize and try to take my hands, which repulsed me so much I would have to wash them afterward. She made little sense and often I thought the kindest thing would be to hold a pillow over her skeletal face.

I was checking flight arrival times from South Africa on Saturday afternoon when there was a knock at my door. I looked up from the screen and could almost see through the door to where V was standing. Because of course it had to be her. My e-mails had no doubt been all that was needed and she had come straight from the airport to me. I closed the computer and went to the door. But it was Kaitlyn, holding a bottle of wine in her hand.

"Sorry," she said, "there's a few of us next door at Lottie's and we've misplaced the corkscrew. I don't suppose you have one."

I opened the door a bit wider. "Yes."

She followed me into the kitchen. "Wow, I really like what you've done in here."

"Thanks. I've got a gardener coming to soften the back." I got the corkscrew out of the drawer and held it out to her.

"Did you choose the colors?"

"Yes." Seeing Kaitlyn in the house was a bit strange, almost like watching a film even though you know it's really happening.

"Can I have a look at the drawing room?"

"Okay." We traipsed back to the drawing room where Kaitlyn exclaimed at how gorgeous it was. It didn't seem right that she should see the house before Verity did and I desperately wanted her to leave. I could have easily picked her up and deposited her outside the front door, without any fuss.

She walked to the mantelpiece and picked up the photograph of V and me dressed in evening wear, taken at one of Calthorpe's Christmas parties. We're both smiling at the camera, my hand resting on the small of her back, not that you can see that. "So this is Verity?"

"Yes." I had to keep my hands by my side to stop myself from marching over and ripping the photograph from her hands.

"Very pretty."

"Anyway, you wanted the corkscrew."

She laughed. "Sorry, yes." We went back into the kitchen where Kaitlyn picked the corkscrew up off the counter. But she didn't leave. "Verity's not here again then?"

And it all felt too much. The fact that she wasn't Verity and she was standing in her house talking about her. "No."

"Do you want to come back with me? Lottie wouldn't mind. And you have provided the corkscrew."

"No, thanks. I've got a bit of work to catch up on." I motioned to the laptop on the table.

"Oh come on, Mike. All work and no play makes Jack a dull boy."

I tried to smile but it felt like the corners of my mouth were being pulled downward by some internal magnet.

"Are you okay?" Her voice was wonderfully tender. I tried to nod, but it was like the movement dislodged something in my head and I felt my eyes fill terribly with tears. She stepped toward me and put her hand on my arm. "Shit, has something happened, Mike?"

"I don't really know," I said, hearing my voice crack, the allure of actually speaking to another human being about what was in my head too strong to ignore.

"Sit down." She led me toward the table, bringing the wine and two glasses with her. She opened the bottle and poured us both some, sitting down beside me. "Now tell me everything."

I took a gulp of the warm liquid, the very idea of telling Kaitlyn everything too appalling to even consider.

"It's Verity, isn't it? Something's happened. Have you split up?"

"No, but we've had a row. Or more like a disagreement."

"Has she moved out?"

"Not permanently."

Kaitlyn sipped at her wine. "I thought it was odd how she was never around. What was the disagreement about?"

I tried to sift through everything in my brain to find a way to answer Kaitlyn's question. "Sort of how we should live."

"Does she want to get married? Weddings often do that to people."

I looked up at Kaitlyn, trying to work out what she was talking about and realized she must have meant Verity's wedding, which I'd told her was Verity's sister's wedding. My brain was starting to feel like a blender and I reached for the bottle to replenish my glass. "No, no. We both want to get married."

"Oh." Kaitlyn held her eyes on my face. "Well, what then?"

"It's hard to put into words. I did something when I was in America she's finding hard to forgive."

Kaitlyn smiled. "Oh right, I get it."

"No," I said too quickly, "I don't think you do. What I did was irrelevant."

"All men say that," Kaitlyn said, drinking her wine.

"No, really, it was nothing. I love Verity. More than anyone. I'd do anything to make it all right again."

Kaitlyn snorted. "God, I've heard that before." Her tone had hardened and I felt a gap growing between us.

I leaned forward with my elbows on the table. "I don't know what to do. I don't know how to put it right."

I felt Kaitlyn's hand on my back, warming the space it was touching. "Was it your first irrelevance?"

"God, yes. And I would never do anything like that again."

She was quiet for a while and her touch felt so good I didn't want her to stop. "You're not like the other City boys, are you, Mike? I don't know how women stand them. I hear them lie to their wives every day. It's disgusting."

"I don't understand why people bother with people they don't love completely," I said into the table.

"That's sweet, Mike."

"I just have to make it right again."

She sighed. "I guess if you two love each other as much as you say then you'll work it out. You'll just have to give her a bit of time."

Her hand dropped and my back felt so lonely that I leaned against the chair. "But it's been so long already."

"Maybe you need to make a grand gesture or something then. Show her you really mean it." She stood up. "You know, Mike, sometimes what you think you want isn't what you actually want. Sometimes the thing that makes you really happy is the thing you least expect." She paused momentarily. "Why don't you come next door with me? It'll do you some good."

I looked up at her. "No, thanks, really. I just want to be alone." And I did. I wanted to be alone with Kaitlyn's words because they made perfect sense. V loved a grand gesture and I had been a fool not to think of that myself.

She shrugged. "Okay, well the offer's there. Mind if I take the corkscrew?"

"No," I said, standing up as well. She picked it up off the table and walked to the front door, turning to smile at me as she opened it. She looked like she was going to say something else, but the moment passed and she let herself out, closing the door behind her.

There was something very comforting about the sounds leaking through my wall from Lottie's for the rest of the afternoon. Something comforting about knowing Kaitlyn was just there, ready to listen with her wide eyes and pale face. She felt like the sort of person you could really open up to and be yourself with and that was like a release after so long holding myself together and always trying to be one step ahead.

As the day drifted into evening and they turned on some music, I thought about going round, but at the last minute I kept stopping myself. Kaitlyn was right, I did need to make a grand gesture and it was important I readied myself for that.

V replied to my e-mails the next day. I doubted they had gone to South Africa for much less than two weeks, so it must have been the first thing she did on her return.

Dear Mike,

I was very sad to receive your e-mails. You sounded so angry in the first and so desperate in the second, and I can't bear thinking of you in either state. I was worried something like this might happen and I probably shouldn't have invited you to the wedding. But you meant so much to me once and I was hoping we could still be friends, although maybe that was very selfish of me.

The truth is I love Angus very much. I have never loved anyone like I do him, which I am sure is a terrible thing for you to hear, but it's the truth. If you want to know the full truth I did meet him a couple of months before you came back for Christmas last year. I was going to tell you and finish things with you, but then you told me about Carly and I used that as an excuse. I am so sorry I did that, it was cowardly and foolish of me. But I can't pretend I wasn't hurt by what you'd done. Angus and I hadn't slept together by then and I was shocked that you could do something like that, as if we meant nothing to each other.

You need to move on with your life. You are a great person and whomever you end up with is going to be one lucky girl. I do still hope we can be friends sometime in the future, but for now you need to sort out a few things in your head. I know I said it to you so much when we were together, but I do still think you would benefit greatly from some counseling. You've always blamed yourself somehow for how your mother behaved. But you were an innocent victim and you can't worry that you will turn out like she did just because you share some genes. Everything you've done so far is nothing short of amazing and you should be very proud of yourself. Look forward, Mike, it's the only way.

Wishing you much love, Verity

I did a little jig around the kitchen after I read it. Everything I had suspected was true. V had been heartbroken by my sleeping with Carly. She also clearly loved me as much as I did her. She cared about my welfare, she thought about me, she saw herself in my future. What I had perhaps got wrong was the sense that she was punishing me for what I had done. Going over the e-mail it seemed more likely that my infidelity had affected her so deeply she'd had some sort of mini breakdown, attaching herself to the first man to pay her some attention (and V was never going to be short of men wanting to do that). She had transferred all the love she felt for me to Angus and convinced herself that this was how she really felt. The fact that she said they hadn't slept together by Christmas made me dismiss him further. I knew better than anyone how important sex is to V and there was no way she would have abstained that long if she had really fallen for him. No, it was obvious he was nothing more than a stooge and I was going to have to help her see this.

V's mention of counseling was particularly pertinent here. In telling me I needed it she was really talking about herself. I wasn't going to mention it, but she had quite a bit of counseling before we met, even afterward. In fact, she had to take antidepressants for a while after university. Real life, she used to say, was a shock. I never really got to the bottom of why she was unhappy, I'm not even sure she ever did. She told me once that her therapist thought she carried a lot of expectation from her parents. She was a longed-for and only child. Suzi and Colin certainly both idolized and pushed her, something I saw with my own eyes. One minute telling her how clever and talented she was, the next remonstrating that she hadn't done well enough on an exam. She told me that her therapist had told her this constant state of anticipation had heightened her emotions, so that she now associated intimacy with excitement and danger. She needed to learn to relax, he told her, she needed to allow herself to let go.

When she was at her worst, just after graduating, I learned how to meditate so I could teach her. We would sit cross-legged on the floor of our flat and I would talk her through the moments, helping her to regulate her breathing and calm her mind. Sometimes I would open my eyes and she would be sitting there with tears rolling down her cheeks. When I asked her what was wrong, she would say that it was just nice to feel calm, so good not to feel fear in her veins. And then I would hold her and tell her I would always be there to make her feel better and she would cling to me like she was drowning. Once, she called me on the way to work and begged me to come home, saying she couldn't breathe without me by her side. And I did as she asked, calling in sick, to go and tend to her.

The night I received her e-mail, I slept with V in my arms. It sounds like a strange thing to say because I knew she wasn't physically there with me, but in all the important ways she was right by my side. It was as if her very essence was in our bed; I smelled her musky scent, felt her hair tickle underneath my chin, fit my body against hers, held her breasts in my hands.

I woke the next day feeling totally refreshed for the first time in months and when I looked in the mirror after my run my cheeks looked fuller and flushed. Even Kaitlyn commented on how well I looked when I got into work and asked if V and I had made up. Nearly, I told her, with a wink.

Elaine called me during the day and I didn't have a moment to return her call until I was walking home from the Tube that evening. I had decided to give V a day to settle back into work and then pick her up on Tuesday evening. I had googled restaurants near to her work and decided on a good Lebanese one a short walk from her office.

"Oh hello, Mike," Elaine said when she picked up. "Thanks for calling back." I imagined her in the hallway, patting her hair as she spoke.

"How are you?" I asked, my mood so buoyant I wanted to share it with her.

"I'm good. I was ringing to see how you are."

"I'm great. Everything's really good."

"You certainly sound happy," she said, but her voice was tentative. "I haven't spoken to you since Verity's wedding. How did that go?"

I felt slightly irritated that she should bring that up. I was probably only a few weeks away from announcing our engagement and I didn't need this reminder. "It was fine. A bit over-the-top, but you know Suzi."

She hesitated. "Actually, Mike, Verity rang last night."

"What?" It felt like a stone had dropped through my stomach.

"She's worried about you. So am I in fact."

I tried to laugh but it sounded hollow even to myself. "What do you mean?"

"She told me about the e-mails."

I stopped on the road and took a breath into my stomach. A man and woman were having an argument in a lighted window, the woman gesticulating wildly at him. "They were nothing. We've spoken since."

"Have you?" Elaine's voice rose hopefully.

"Yes, it was stupid of me. The whole wedding threw me off-balance, but Verity explained it all to me and I understand now. I was wrong to be angry with her." I started walking again.

"But Verity said you wrote that you still love her."

"It's all a lot of fuss over nothing." I turned up my path and opened my door, balancing the phone between my ear and my shoulder. The house was dark and cool.

"I don't want you to get hurt, Mike."

I leaned against the shut door, feeling suddenly weary.

"Verity would never hurt me."

"Not intentionally, no." Elaine's breathing had quickened. "Have you thought any more about seeing someone?"

"No."

"I think it would do you good. So does Verity."

There was a clear line of sight through to the garden from where I was standing and even in the dusk I could see something was wrong, which made my heart quicken. I walked forward purposefully, but then slackened my pace as I remembered that Anna had started that day.

"I'm fine, really." I unlocked the bifold doors, so they could glide away.

"Yes, but sometimes people don't realize they need help until they get it." Elaine and I had had this conversation a hundred times before when I'd lived with her.

"That's my point about Verity." I walked into the garden, Anna's team had begun to hack away at the stone structure of the garden so it resembled a Greek ruin.

"What do you mean?"

"You know she's pretty highly strung. I think she might be having one of her episodes."

"Really? She sounded fine to me."

I picked up a bit of the chipped stone. "I know her so well, Elaine. I can tell she's in a bit of a state."

"Oh dear. You two have always been so volatile. I just want you both to be happy."

"Well, I'm fine, and I plan to help Verity as much as I can."

"We all care about you, Mike. You know you can come and stay anytime."

"Yes, I know," I said, feeling a sudden surge of love for her. "And you and Barry must come here for supper or something."

"Well, that would be lovely."

"I'd better go now. I'll call again soon."

"Bye, Mike." The hope had vanished from her voice and now it was dripping with melancholy.

Others might have been depressed by that call, but V and I are not like others. V would have known Elaine would call and it was just another move in our Crave, which I felt coming closer and closer to its climax. We had played enough times to know that the end moments often seem cruel; that for us to get what we want others have to get hurt. If we could have done it another way then no doubt we would have, but there was no other way; cruelty was a necessary part of our game.

They say that hate is the closest emotion to love. And passion certainly exists in two forms. The passion of sex and the passion of arguments.

For V and I one would merge into the other all the time. One second shouting, the next fucking. We needed each other in a way that sometimes made me feel like it wouldn't be enough until we'd consumed each other. I read a story once about a Russian man who ate his lovers and I sort of understand why he did it. Imagine your lover actually traveling through your blood, feeding your muscles, informing your brain. Some would see that as the basest level of cruelty, others as an act of love. Ultimately, that is what it means to Crave.

I sat in the bar opposite Calthorpe the next evening, waiting for V to emerge. The day had been bad and I drank whiskey as a way of eradicating it, although it refused to leave my mind. The chairman and I'd had a meeting with the managing director of Spectre in which he had cried and told us about the lives of some of the people who were losing their jobs. The chairman had looked at me and I'd known he wanted me to answer, to spout our well-rehearsed PR spiel. But something about seeing a grown man crying over the curved maple desk in the meeting room had repulsed me.

I heard words come out of my mouth even as I felt the chairman's stare willing me to stop. The man stopped crying, staring at me openmouthed. You're not even an animal, he said, getting up and leaving. We sat in silence for a while after he had gone, my heart thudding in my ears. In the end the chairman stood up and sucked in his breath. I'm going to make an appointment for you with the company doctor, he said before leaving.

I had forgotten that other people do not necessarily live in a world of bad words.

One of Mum's boyfriends, I think his name was Logan, used to put his face very close to mine when he shouted. So close I had to screw my mouth shut against his spittle. You useless fucking cunt, he'd scream at me for knocking over his beer, or You fucking pansy twat, for sneezing when the football was on, or You cheeky fucking gobshite, for when I pretended not to hear him. My mother looked out the window when he spoke, her neat profile blurred by the skyline, as if she couldn't hear. Naturally he spoke to her in the same way and we both tiptoed around him as if we were visitors in his life and not him in ours. He wasn't one of the thwackers though; Logan was cleverer than that, his violence more insidious. Logan knew that the threat of his temper hung like a cloud of poisonous fumes over the flat and that it was enough to exterminate the life we knew.

I don't know why Logan left. I don't know why any of the men left. All I do know is that they left my mum in ever worsening states, which always seemed bizarre to me. Most people would celebrate their passing, but my mother clearly didn't feel like she ever deserved anything more than the lowest form of existence. I would watch her snivel on the sofa after another Logan exited our lives, a full ashtray balanced on her legs, beer cans littered by her feet, her eyes losing focus, and I would want to jump up and down in front of her. I am here, I used to want to shout, but I'm not sure she'd have noticed me even then.

You are not like her, V said to me time and time again, when the fear used to overtake me. But I was never honest with my reply. Because, before V, I was like my mother. I didn't care, I found it easy to shut down, I turned away and found it too easy to be cruel to others. I think the truth is that V made me a better person and without her I could easily slip into the person my mother became.

V taught me not just what it felt like to really care about someone else but also what it felt like to care about myself. She didn't just sculpt my body but my mind as well. When we met I ate crap and got out of breath walking up the stairs. I was skinny as a whippet and my unwashed hair hung long over my ears. I only asked her once why she had spoken to me at the party. I was too scared I'd jolt her into the realization that she had been mad to do so. We were in bed at the time, her head on my chest, which had already started to change shape and fill out.

"Your eyes," she said, her hand resting on my lower belly. "I genuinely did just want a light, but when I looked at you to say thanks, you looked so lost, so vulnerable, I couldn't just walk away."

"But why did you agree to go on a date?" I asked into the blackness surrounding us.

"Because I liked you by then. I could see your potential."

V wasn't my first girlfriend, but she was the first one who meant anything to me. And when I say *anything*, I mean that word literally. Before V, I couldn't understand anything about women and how they worked. I had no idea what they meant when they spoke, no desire to see them after we'd had sex, no comprehension of why they sometimes got angry and cried. It was like my heart hadn't been used before I met V, like I'd never really noticed it or felt it beat. I mean, I know I care for Elaine and Barry, and I must have loved Mum at some point, but when I think about them it doesn't feel like a real connection. When I think about V it is like there is a thread reaching from my heart to hers, tautening and relaxing with both of our breaths.

I could look at V when she came in from wherever she'd been and know instantly how she was feeling. Every time she rang I knew it was her without looking at the screen. When we watched a film or listened to music I knew what her reaction would be without speaking. I knew how to make her scream and moan and thrash, every inch of her body mapped indelibly on my mind. Connections like that cannot be broken, however much we are separated.

I was unsteady on my feet when I finally gave up on seeing V that evening and left the bar. I stumbled on the pavement and had to lean against a wall to right myself. My head felt dislocated and nothing seemed real. People walked past me into the night and I forgot where I was going or where I had been. Nausea rose into my throat, squeezing my heart and constricting my breathing.

The next day at work felt like torture, a steady stream of needles beating into my skull, my body hot and shaky. I hadn't run in the morning and I didn't go to the gym at lunchtime, instead eating a bowl of pasta at a cheap restaurant filled with tourists around the corner. The food landed on the acid of my stomach making me want to retch, but I forced it down and then drank two strong coffees.

During the afternoon the company doctor rang and said he had an appointment for me for the next day at three and I was too befuddled to think of an excuse. I lay my head on my arms on my desk and looked sideways out the window at the birds riding the wind currents. I've always known that if I had to kill myself it would be by jumping from a great height because that way you would at least have a few seconds of knowing what it felt like to fly.

George put his head around my door just after six, when the thought of the Tube was defeating me. I had already decided not to go that evening to meet V as I didn't want her to see me in the state I was in. "A few of the chaps are going to this club," he said, with a wink. "Wondered if you'd like to join."

"A club, at this time?" I said, my brain beating against the side of my head.

"You know what I mean."

"I've got a really bad headache."

He came in, closing the door behind him, and walked toward my desk. He put his hand in his pocket and held out two red pills on the palm of his hand. "These'll perk you up."

The pills were no larger than the head of two pins fused together and the thought of anything making me feel better was too delicious to refuse. I reached for them and swallowed them in a gulp.

"Good lad," he said, laughing. "Come on then."

There were five of us, all walking purposefully through the old streets of the City into the East End, an area at once totally and not at all changed. I have always thought that the history of the East End is still written in the buildings and streets. The air hangs heavy with death and poverty and sex, however many gray coffee shops you plant along its highways.

We turned down a cobbled street with the houses so close together, I could imagine people passing things to each other from high-up windows, or washing lines stretched between rooms, or mothers shouting for dirty children far below. My mind felt loose and my internal organs fluid in my body, as if suspended in liquid.

George knocked on a black door, which was opened by a man who was almost as wide as the door, his nose smashed across his face, his head shaved, his eyes wild. But he smiled incongruously and opened the door wider, ushering us inside. All the other men had clearly been there before and they peeled off up and down dark stairways and into dimly lit rooms. George beckoned for me to follow him, up a narrow flight of stairs toward a thumping beat that seemed to be part of the stone and plaster of the house. We climbed ever higher and the beat turned into music, which rested in my stomach like something primal. At the last door George turned and winked at me again before opening it and releasing the heat and stench of the place into my face. It took me a while to figure out the space, which was surely much larger than the house allowed, but when I did I thought it was fantastical. It was clearly the top floors of most, if not all, of the houses along this street, an endless stretch of cavorting degradation.

The space had been sectioned into hundreds of booths and the walls were all mirrored, so it was impossible to tell what was real and what was simply a reflection. The air hung heavy with smoke and the musty, salty stink of semen. The carpet underneath our feet was sticky and the backs of the chairs looked greasy and grimy. The lights were off, apart from ill-placed spots that stabbed the air, blinding you if you looked too close. Only the music felt natural, as if it had become part of me, lifting and guiding me toward something I could almost remember.

George pulled me forward and I realized as we got closer that we were heading toward a round stage on which twenty women, maybe more, writhed. Their bodies glistened like plastic, their feet distorted by the sort of heels even Kaitlyn would draw the line at. Some were completely naked, but most were wearing a sparkling V over their vaginas, with a corresponding line cutting through their buttocks, like an electric sign announcing their wares. They danced as if they were in a trance, dropping often to the floor and opening their legs, licking their lips and closing their eyes, their hands never far from their breasts.

There were lots of men just like us standing around the stage, some not even looking at the girls but instead at their phones, which illuminated their faces and made them look dead. One or two men were cheering, reaching out to grab at passing legs and breasts, saliva dripping from their mouths. Every so often a man would step forward and motion to a girl, usually by a click of his fingers or a well-directed point and the girl would stop her dance and step unsteadily off the stage, following the man to one of the curved booths.

"Which do you want?" George asked, his voice hot in my ears.

I turned to look at him and could see his face was puce even in the dark. I almost expected his hand to clench his dick as we stood there.

The air was close and heavy and I thought the floor might be tilting. I shook my head. "No. I have a girlfriend."

He laughed, exposing his perfect white teeth. "Don't be a poof. I've got a wife and two kids." The floor was undulating now, as if an earthquake were shaking the building, and I could feel bile rise into my mouth.

He leaned closer to me, so I could hear every word he said. "You don't have to worry about them." He jerked his finger at the stage of women. "They all love it. Sex-mad they are. Not like normal women. They're like some sort of witches or something."

I tried to take a step back, but another man was pressed close behind me. I could imagine George at boarding school, masturbating an older boy, drenched in fear and loathing. I looked back at the women. "I have to go."

But George took my arm. "Don't be an idiot." His voice was harsh. He clicked his fingers at two women standing next to each other. "Mine's the blonde," he said, as they teetered off the stage.

The woman assigned to me took my hand and led me to a booth, where she ducked under the curtain, pulling me with her. There was a fake-leather seat that took up half the booth, and she pushed me onto it. I felt my buttocks slide on the fabric and wondered whether, if a fire broke out, anyone would get out alive.

She stood in front of me, her hand on a hip, so she jutted out at an unnatural angle. Her heels were as high as all the others' and her sparkling V was a bright pink. Her hair was jet black and fell in greasy waves around her face. Her makeup was smudged and she stank of sweat and coconut.

"We get champagne." Her voice was heavily laden with an accent I took to be eastern European.

"Okay."

She ducked under the curtain but was back in a few seconds. Her breasts, I noticed, were small and empty and I saw the flicker of silvery stretch marks across her lower abdomen, the flesh puckered and grainy. She lit a cigarette as she stood over me, smoking it in short, angry bursts.

The curtain parted again and a man came in with a bottle that looked like the sort of sparkling wine Elaine might serve on special occasions and two glasses on which I could see traces of finger marks. He was carrying a card machine that he thrust under my face. "One hundred and twenty-four pounds," he said.

I laughed. I could have laid waste to him with one punch but I guessed if I did it would be the woman's fault, so I paid the absurd amount, my plastic skimming through the machine. The woman opened the bottle when he was gone, pouring out a glass that she handed to me.

"Don't you want one?" I asked.

"No, I don't drink."

I sipped at the liquid and it was as warm and sweet and disgusting as I'd known it would be. I put the glass down.

"What you want?" she asked.

"Nothing," I answered.

She glanced at the curtain. "I can dance, suck, or fuck, or all three."

"No, really." I wasn't sure I was ever going to find my way out of this place. It felt possible that life as I knew it had ended and there was no way back.

"You have to pay whatever," she said.

"That's fine. What do you get most for?"

She looked at me like I was simple. "All three."

"How much?"

"Five hundred pounds."

I knew she was lying, but I didn't care. "I don't have any cash."

She shrugged. "Okay, three hundred."

"How much do you get of that?"

"Fifty. And twenty for every bottle of champagne."

I tried to hold her flickering gaze. "Get him back. Say we want another bottle of champagne and all three."

She smiled at that and I saw her front teeth were chipped. She ducked out again but was back even more quickly. The man returned with another bottle and the machine. I swiped away four hundred and twenty-four pounds and wondered what Elaine could do with that sort of money.

"Sit down," I said, when he'd gone.

She shook her head. "I dance for you." I opened my mouth to tell her no, but she had already started, her body contorting and gyrating. She raised her hands above her head and I could see the shaving rash in her armpits and around her groin. She turned and the tops of her thighs were pitted and uneven, a large yellow bruise winking in the crease of her knee, another midway down her calf. Her hands were on her own body, kneading her nonexistent breasts, her mouth pouted into an O. She came toward me and straddled me, dipping her face against mine, her mouth nipping against my ear. Her body felt slimy and I thought I would have to burn the clothes I was wearing.

And then I thought I was going to be sick, I felt the sensation rushing through my body, contorting my insides. Because I knew if V could see me now she would never forgive me.

"Get off," I said. But the woman kept up her demented thrusting against me. "Get off me," I shouted, the need to stop what was happening now so imperative I wanted to scream.

I stood, perhaps more forcefully than I meant, because the woman shot backward, her body landing against the wall of the booth, her head jerking. She whimpered and for a ghastly moment I thought her arm looked broken.

I went to help her up but she batted away my attempts, struggling to her feet on her own. We looked at each other in the flashing, smoky half-light.

"I'm sorry," I said. "I didn't mean . . . I asked you to stop." I felt a strange desperation for her to understand that I wasn't like the other men she had to deal with night after night.

But her lip curled as she walked past me and held the curtain to one side. "Your time is up," she said.

I felt surprisingly all right when I woke the next morning. I went on my run and my legs moved smoothly beneath me.

I thought of Stacey while I ran, a girl whom I'd been in the home with and who was brought back by the police one night for soliciting, a word she educated us in while the social workers discussed her with the uniformed men downstairs. She was fourteen and told us she'd already turned tricks, which I fully believed at the time but wonder now if it was really bravado. She called it the family business and told us how her mother used to bring men back to the bedsit they shared and how she'd have to wait in the corridor. She'd ended up in care because one of the men had asked her mother how much Stacey cost and her mother had stabbed him. Stacey said she needed the money for the train fare as she wasn't supposed to visit her mother in prison. I hadn't thought of Stacey for years. She must be in her mid-thirties, too old probably to be a woman like I'd seen the night before, although I doubted life had turned out well for her.

When I got to work George put his head around my door. "Didn't see you leave last night. Bloody good time though."

"Yes," I lied, knowing it was the only possible response.

"Got a rollicking off the missus," he said. "How did you fare?"

"My girlfriend's away. Does your wife know where you went then?" The rules of the upper classes are so foreign to me that I am always lost in their world.

But he laughed. "God no. Just that I got in late stinking of booze and fags. She always makes way too much of a fuss about stuff like that. You know what women are like."

"How old are your children?" I asked.

"Six and four."

"Girls or boys?"

"One of each." He shifted his weight and I noticed how pale and clammy his skin looked. I let what we were both thinking hang in the air and looked back at my computer screen and started tapping away until he left. Kaitlyn waved at me on the way past my window at lunchtime and I felt myself blushing, ashamed of what she would think of my behavior the night before.

At two o'clock a note flashed up on my screen: Your appointment with Dr. Lucas Ellin is in one hour at 3 p.m. I groaned loudly, sure that there was a good excuse for me to cancel the appointment. But if there was an excuse it eluded me and I found myself waiting outside Dr. Ellin's office an hour later, my suit feeling a little tight and sweat breaking out across my palms.

It was I suppose a credit to Dr. Ellin that I hadn't known of his existence at Bartleby's until the moment the chairman had mentioned him, but somehow I found this disconcerting. His room was very different from all the other offices in the building: It was a pale blue and his desk was glass, so I could see his whole body stretched out on his chair. He only had one computer and it was pushed into a corner, as if it were a minor irrelevance. And the chair I was supposed to sit on was a plush wingback, with a cushion in its center. There was a large fern in one corner and a bookcase stuffed with books and papers.

He stood as I entered and extended his hand to me across the desk, which I shook as firmly as I could.

"Sit down, Mike," he said. "I'm glad you came."

"I didn't realize it was optional," I said, sitting on the edge of the large chair.

Dr. Ellin laughed as he too sat. I didn't think he could be much older than me. "So do you want to tell me what brought you here?"

"The chairman."

He laughed again, but I wasn't sure why what I'd said was funny. "Yes, but I mean the incident."

"I shouted at one of our clients."

Dr. Ellin pulled his glasses down from the top of his head and consulted some notes in front of him. "I believe you called Daniel Palmer a fucking useless waste of space of a man who needed to get some balls."

I felt my color rising. "Yes, it was very rude of me. I don't know what happened."

"Do you often find it hard to control your anger?" Dr. Ellin leaned forward over his desk. His feet, I noticed, were crossed at the ankles. I had a sudden urge to punch him in the face, an answer if ever there was one. "What do you find amusing about my question?"

I drew down the smile I hadn't realized was there. "Sorry, nothing. And of course I don't."

"Our chairman, Lord Falls, has noticed that you have seemed distracted recently. Your performance at Schwartz's was exceptional, but you haven't got off to such a good start here, would you say?"

I thought it was probably a trick question. "Well, I closed the Hector deal and we're close with Spectre."

Dr. Ellin nodded. "Perhaps you're finding the adjustment of moving countries hard?"

"No," I said, hearing my tone had risen. "London's my home. I wanted to come back. If anything I found New York hard."

"How do you find making friends, Mike?"

I wanted to ask if I had to go on sitting here, but I knew I couldn't. "Fine. In fact I was out with a few of the guys from here last night." I wondered what Dr. Ellin would think if I told him about where we'd been. Probably he would laugh again and think nothing of it. I knew in this world it was me who was considered strange for shouting, but George's behavior at the club would be considered rational. I thought of Kaitlyn suddenly and how she'd told me that we were both outsiders. I longed for V to explain it to me and help me understand.

"It says in your notes that you were brought up in care," Dr. Ellin said, placing the tips of his fingers together in front of his face.

"How do you know that?" A familiar streak of shame ran through me like a piece of glass.

"We like to know who we employ at Bartleby's. I'm not saying it as a judgment. Just trying to get a clearer picture of where you're at, Mike. We want our employees to be as happy as possible."

I felt like I was looking at Dr. Ellin from under water. "I was with my mother until the age of ten, then in a home for about eighteen months, then I went into permanent foster care until I went to university."

"That must have been hard."

I was sure Dr. Ellin had no idea what hard was. He had probably been to the same school as George and the chairman and half the bloody office. "Not really. I was lucky. My foster parents, Elaine and Barry, were great."

"Why were you taken into care?"

I looked over Dr. Ellin's shoulder to the window and told myself I could just turn and walk out. I could have walked out of the whole building. "My mother had a problem with alcohol."

He didn't say anything, waiting for me to give him more, but I stayed quiet. It was none of his business.

"Did she ever get violent?"

It's amazing that people like Lucas Ellin get paid to make such obvious connections. "No."

"And what about your foster parents? How was your relationship with them?"

"It was and is great. I was there for Sunday lunch just a few weeks ago." I shifted in my chair. "Look, I'm not sure what relevance this has to anything. I mean, I lost my temper and I'm sorry, I know I behaved badly."

Dr. Ellin held me with his stare. "Have you ever spoken to anyone about your childhood?"

"Only my girlfriend."

His eyebrows raised slightly. "Oh, you have a girlfriend? Do you live together?"

"Yes. At least, she's not living with me at the moment."

"You've separated?"

"No, not exactly." The chair felt lumpy, like a bad approximation of what it should be.

"Do you know that how you spoke to Mr. Palmer is unacceptable? That you can't always just say what's on your mind?"

It was my turn to laugh then. "Of course I know that. I was having a bad day and he irritated me if you must know. A grown man sitting there blubbering."

Dr. Ellin's fingers were tapping against each other. "A grown man who was losing a company he had created, a grown man who felt responsible for all the people who were about to lose their jobs. It's interesting that you find that show of emotions irritating."

This felt as close to hell as I ever wanted to get: sitting in a fake-friendly doctor's office giving the wrong answers. I knew I needed to find the words that would make him shut up. "If you want to know the truth, it had nothing to do with Mr. Palmer. My girlfriend had moved out the day before and I was in a bit of a mess. But I'm fine now. We're fine."

Dr. Ellin relaxed at that. He would, after all, have something tangible to report back to the chairman. "And of course being left is particularly hard for you, isn't it, Mike? I expect it stirs up feelings you would rather forget." I would have laughed in his stupid face if the need to get out of his office hadn't become imperative. So I made do with looking down and nodding. "I think you might really benefit from us meeting regularly."

"I'm not sure about that."

"There are also some pills I could prescribe, to help you relax. Do you have trouble sleeping?"

"No. And I don't need pills."

But Dr. Ellin was already writing something on a pad. "There's nothing to be ashamed of. Half the people in this building are on one type of pill or another." He waved the prescription at me and so I leaned forward and took it, folding it into the inside pocket of my jacket. "And you know, because I am a private doctor this is a totally private meeting. What I mean is that none of this goes on your record, if that's what you're worried about."

I couldn't really understand what Dr. Ellin was trying to say so I didn't answer.

He looked down at his diary. "Shall we do the same time next week?"

"I'll need to check and let you know." I knew I would have to change jobs if sitting with Dr. Ellin once a week were to become something I was required to do. To have that moron poke about in my brain and jump to the wrong conclusions with psychology lessons any monkey could learn from a textbook. The only person I trusted in my head was V. I stood with the impatience of a child, desperate to be anywhere other than where I was. But Dr. Ellin was slow with his handshakes and goodbyes and by the time I left it felt like my blood was fizzing.

Kaitlyn happened to be leaving at exactly the same time as me that evening, which I was pretty sure wasn't a coincidence. I had planned on picking V up, but I couldn't think of a reason why I wasn't going home, so I fell into line with Kaitlyn. She chatted about nothing on the Tube, about things I couldn't care less about and I stopped listening, watching instead only her mouth as it moved up and down. There were dark, bluey circles around her eyes and she almost looked as if someone had punched her.

"I made way too much shepherd's pie last night," she said as we emerged onto Clapham High Street. "Do you want to come and help finish it off? It is veggie mince though, just to warn you."

I hesitated and in that moment I saw the sadness in Kaitlyn's eyes and the desperation not to be rejected. And what was I going home to anyway? I didn't think I had any food at all in the fridge. "Okay, thanks," I said.

Kaitlyn lived in a flat in a large mansion block that overlooked the Common. I could hear the yapping from inside before she'd even put her key in the lock and I thought her neighbors probably hated her. The dog flew at her as soon as the door opened, leaping into her arms and licking her all over her face, which I found disgusting. She pretended to turn away, but I could see she loved it really, loved even the tiny pink tongue flicking over her lips.

"Sorry it's a bit of a mess," she said incongruously as we went into the drawing room, as the flat was as tidy as it could be. "Sit down, take off your jacket. I'll get you a drink."

Kaitlyn's drawing room was almost as white as she was. It was also very sparse, so you got the impression that everything in it had been chosen with care and consideration. The only bit of color, if you can call black a color, were the calligraphied words stenciled above the couch. I twisted around so I could read them: "Blame it or praise it, there is no denying the wild horse in us."

"Virginia Woolf," Kaitlyn said as she handed me a glass of wine.

V hated any type of slogan and I took to buying them for her as jokes whenever I saw them on cards or embossed on fake metal signs. Her favorite four were:

> *Dream as if you'll live forever. Live as if you'll die tomorrow.*
> *The pessimist sees difficulty in every opportunity. The optimist sees the opportunity in every difficulty.*

No matter how long you have traveled in the wrong direction,
  you can always turn around.
We are punished by our sins, not for them.

Does anyone actually believe this crap, she'd say. I mean do these random words put one in front of another by a moron make anyone feel better?

"Who's your favorite writer?" Kaitlyn asked, sitting next to me. Snowdrop immediately leaped onto her lap and she began to pet him under the chin. I hoped she was planning on washing her hands before serving the food.

"I don't know. Verity likes Virginia Woolf though." I couldn't remember the last time I'd read a book. V used to sometimes jokingly call me a philistine and I felt hot suddenly as I wondered if Angus liked to read. If they read to each other in bed.

"You said you were on the verge of working things out," Kaitlyn said.

I looked over at her expectant face and wondered what it must be like to live in such an unattractive body. "We're talking. I'm confident we can work it out."

"How long have you been together?"

I pretended to consider this. "Nine years."

"So you met at university?"

"Yes." We both sipped at our wine. When you are asked a question you should reciprocate, V had told me. "What about you? Any significant others?"

She laughed. "Well, maybe. Early days, you know."

"I've only ever lived with Verity," I said.

She turned back to me. "Yes, but that's all you need, isn't it, one person?" I smiled because of course I totally agreed. "Sometimes I wonder what it's all for, this making money, I mean. I could have bought a large family house with my bonus last year but I didn't, because I mean what would be the point, rattling around some big old thing, just me."

I thought of my own house and it made me feel itchy. "You could invest it."

"I could," she said, although her tone was harsh.

A faint smell of burning reached us and Kaitlyn jumped up. "Come into the kitchen, we can eat there."

I followed her through to another white room, with white cabinets running along one side of the wall and a round white table encircled by white chairs in the center.

"Open another bottle." She motioned to a laden wine rack in the corner. I went toward it and picked out a fine bottle, easing the cork out with a satisfying sigh.

We sat next to each other with the plates of steaming shepherd's pie, and I filled our glasses. It smelled as good as home.

"I'm thinking about jacking it all in, actually," Kaitlyn said. "Buying a business on the coast somewhere and living a better life."

"Whereabouts?" V had taught me not to blow on my food, so I was waiting for the steam to subside.

She shrugged. "I don't really care. I fancy the sea." It smelled too good to wait so I forked at the food, bringing it to my lips. Kaitlyn did the same, blowing hard on it before putting it in her mouth. "Why are you smiling?" she asked.

"I was always taught not to blow on my food."

"My mum told me that as well. But, you know."

"What business?" She looked better animated I thought.

"I don't know that either." She laughed. "An old-fashioned sweet-shop, maybe, selling candies like white mice and rhubarb and custards, in those big glass jars. And you have to scoop them out and weigh them." The food was as good as I had expected and it landed in my grateful stomach like a kiss. "Don't tell me you've never thought about jacking it all in."

"I plan to retire by forty-five."

"But that's ages away."

"Fifteen years."

"Exactly."

And it did sound like a long time when she put it like that.

"Did you know anyone when you went to New York?"

"No."

"How was that?"

"Awful." There was something about Kaitlyn that made being honest with her very easy.

She laid down her fork even though her plate was still half full. "Why was it awful?"

"Mainly the loneliness. I missed Verity terribly."

Her cheeks colored slightly. "I don't understand why you went in the first place. I mean, if she couldn't go with you."

"I, we . . ." But I stumbled over the words, not entirely sure what the answer to that was. I had momentarily forgotten why V had thought it was such a good idea. "I don't know. It was good for my career."

Kaitlyn kept her eyes on me. "God, don't you think there's more to life than that? It's like, what are we all waiting for?"

"What do you mean?" I poured us both more wine.

She sat back, holding her glass against her chest. "I know this sounds like a terrible cliché, but I saw an interview with Joan Collins once and the interviewer asked her if she looked that good every day and she said of course she did, because life isn't a dress rehearsal." She took another deep sip of her wine and when she looked up at me her eyes were glistening. "I mean, I spend all my life behaving like it's a bloody dress rehearsal, waiting for the real bit to start. And it's such a fucking waste."

We sat in silence for a bit and I could feel my heart through my cotton shirt, pounding along its own godforsaken path. I thought of V in her life, sitting with Angus, no doubt at their kitchen table, while I sat here with Kaitlyn, and it all suddenly seemed appalling. Because what were we doing? Why were we pretending like this?

I felt Kaitlyn lay her hand over mine and I looked down at the paleness of it against my pinker skin. She was so translucent I could see the blue of her veins pumping her blood around her body and I was struck by how fragile she was, how easy she would be to break.

I pulled my hand out from under hers. "I guess I'd better be heading home."

"Sorry. I was just—"

"No, it's not you."

She smiled lightly. "Oh no, Mike. I mean, I really like you, but not, I mean . . ."

"I can't . . ." I started.

"I know you're still in love with Verity." She looked up at me and her eyes were quivering. "But from where I'm standing she doesn't seem to make you that happy."

"She makes me very happy," I said, although something about the words sounded faintly ridiculous.

"Happiness is so odd, don't you think. I mean, sometimes we can mistake feelings for happiness or love, when they're the exact opposite."

It sounded like a terrible thing to say, but I supposed women like Kaitlyn were used to feeling that way. I stood up. "Look, thanks very much for dinner. It was delicious."

Kaitlyn laughed.

"No, really, I'm sorry. Please, can this not ruin our friendship?" I didn't know why I was saying such soppy words, why I cared even. But there was something unbearable about seeing Kaitlyn's tiny figure sitting on the chair, Snowdrop snuffling by her feet. I felt an odd need to put my arms around her shoulders and give her a hug, but obviously I didn't as I didn't want to encourage her in any way.

She stood as well and the movement seemed to compose her. "No, I'm sorry, Mike. I think I've just drunk a bit too much. Of course we'll still be friends, don't be daft."

She walked me to the door and we kissed awkwardly on both cheeks, raising our hands in stupid farewells and tripping over our words.

I breathed deeply when I reached the outside world and looked up at what I could see of the stars behind the hazy pollution. My body felt jangly and so I began to walk, not admitting to myself where I was going at first, but in the end accepting that my feet were taking me toward Kensington. I trampled along the messy, chewing-gum-littered streets, stepping over what looked like people wrapped in filthy sleeping bags, lying on thin strips of cardboard. Never mind the women on the stage, it was much more likely that one of these homeless people was my mother.

Kaitlyn's words slid around my brain like a ball bearing in a slot machine. I knew she had said things that were worth listening to and yet their meaning eluded me. I couldn't work out if she had been giving me advice or, if she had, if it had been worth heeding. I couldn't work out if she was right or wrong. I couldn't work out what I thought. I needed V to tell me, because only she could make sense of the world for me.

V's house was dark, except for the gleaming light on the porch. The shutters and curtains were all drawn, apart from in the kitchen, but this room was dark as well, the moonlight glinting off all the steel and concrete. I knew V was inside, although I stopped my mind from wondering at what she was doing. I checked my watch and it was nearly midnight, which made me feel better. V got tired and she would no doubt be asleep, dreaming maybe of me.

I walked to the opposite side of the street and leaned against the ivy-laden wall I had stopped in front of before. I looked up at the window where I had seen V draw the curtains and felt her presence so strongly it was like I could have flown through the window at that moment. I imagined the shattering glass and the screams of Angus, I could feel her as I took her in my arms and we flew away, back to our nest at the top of the mountains. I thought it had started raining, but then I realized I was crying, hard and fast.

Anna, the garden designer, rang me at work the next morning and asked if I'd had a chance to look at the various planting options she'd sent me. I admitted I hadn't, but said I would get right on it, clicking onto her e-mail as we spoke. I had no idea of the names of any of the plants she suggested and spent an annoying hour googling each one for pictures that yielded little joy. The exercise depressed me anyway, as I should have automatically known what flowers V preferred. In the end I told Anna to go with what she thought. How about colors, she asked, I was thinking pinks and yellows. I thought immediately of Suzi's mother-of-the-bride dress and told Anna absolutely no yellow. We agreed instead on blues and whites.

Kaitlyn blushed when she saw me and kept her eyes down every time she walked past, which was also unduly depressing. Without Kaitlyn, I realized, I had almost no one to speak to.

After lunch I texted her:

Thanks for supper last night. I had a really nice time.

No worries. I probably shouldn't have said so much.

Don't be silly. It's all forgotten. I just don't want it to be awkward.

Of course it won't be.

Thanks.

But maybe, I think you should consider how healthy a relationship is where one person holds all the cards.

????

> I just mean, she has quite a hold on you. You should trust
> yourself more.

I do.

> Sorry, not my place to comment.

It's fine. Friends?

> Friends x.

It was odd because what Kaitlyn was saying should have irritated me, but I found myself strangely elated by her words.

I also sent an e-mail to Daniel Palmer, offering my sincere apologies for everything I had said. I explained that the stress of the job sometimes got to me and that firing people was a terrible consequence of what we did. I said I'd been having some personal issues and that I'd said things to him that I really wanted to say to myself. I hoped very much he could forgive me and that we could move forward and find the best solution for him and his employees.

An hour later the chairman called me and said he was pleased I'd had a good session with Dr. Ellin. He wanted to reassure me that my work was of the highest standard and that they liked to think of themselves as more of a family than a business at Bartleby's. The only reason he had referred me to Dr. Ellin was that they wanted the best for me. Our working relationship was not, he hoped, short term but something we were both in for the long haul. He understood that I was going through some personal issues, and maybe I hadn't had the best start, but he was impressed with how I handled myself. It took a big man to apologize, he said. I mumbled and acquiesced in all the right places and I got the impression that he left the conversation satisfied.

Everything is a game, V used to tell me; only stupid people forget that.

Y

V was wearing her blue dress with the white flowers on it when she left work that evening and it made my heart surge for two reasons. First, I had been with her when she bought it from a little shop in Brooklyn. And second, I had been right to tell Anna to go with blue and white plantings, which meant I clearly knew V's tastes better than I realized. Or maybe we were simply telepathic. Maybe she had spoken to me as I sat at my desk without me even realizing.

"V," I shouted, bounding across the street from my bar.

She turned and her face contracted slightly. "Mike, what on earth are you doing here?"

"I just wondered if you had a moment. If we could perhaps have a chat."

She looked around. "Have you come here to see me?"

"Yes. I really need to talk to you."

She stood with her feet resolutely where she had placed them. "What about?"

I hadn't anticipated it being hard to get her to agree to a simple chat. "The e-mails. And other stuff."

"I . . ." She looked down, then up again. "I'm not sure that's such a good idea, Mike."

"Please, it won't take long. There are just some things I need to say."

She bit the side of her cheek as she always did when she was thinking and twisted her mouth to one side. "Just quickly, then."

"There's a Lebanese restaurant around the corner."

"That bar's fine." She pointed to my bar across the street. The thought of going back in there with her was horrible, mixing my thoughts of her with the reality of her, but I sensed the tenuousness of the situation, so I let her lead me across the road. She asked for a vodka and tonic, so I had the same and carried both our drinks to a table in the corner, far away from my usual one in the window.

As we sat I saw she was wearing the eagle around her neck and my heart did another tiny jig. Her hair was loose and her beauty left me slightly light-headed. It made me want to reach out and touch her, made me want to check that she was made of the same flesh and blood as the rest of us.

"So?" She sounded tired.

"I just wanted to apologize for that e-mail I sent you when you were on honeymoon."

"Which one?"

"The first one, obviously."

"So you don't think you need to apologize for the second one? The one in which you talked about me leaving Angus?"

"I know you think you love him."

She laughed, but the sound was hollow. "I know I love him."

"I don't think you do. I think you still love me."

We looked at each other across the table and I thought that from the outside we must have looked like lovers. We always shared a bubble, me and V, we were always a unit against all those awful people outside our Crave.

"Mike," she said. "I love Angus."

"I know I hurt you very badly and I will go on saying sorry till the end of time, if that's what it takes. But you don't love Angus. You're using him to get over me."

I saw her eyes flicker and her breathing quickened. "Are you okay, Mike? I'm worried about you."

"If you can't admit you love me now, will you admit to loving me once?"

She sipped from her drink, leaving an almost invisible layer of lip balm on the rim. I had to stop myself from reaching over and licking the mark. "Of course I loved you, you don't have to ask that."

"But love doesn't stop. You must love me still."

She kept her eyes down. "But love changes, doesn't it."

"I still crave you," I tried, because I didn't know what she meant. Love never changes.

"Don't," she said, but the word sounded stretched, desperate even. Her chest was moving up and down, up and down.

"We could try the Kitten Club again. Angus won't go with you, but I would."

"For God's sake, Mike," she said, but her breathing had quickened.

"What we had doesn't just vanish. I know you remember what it felt like to be in bed with me."

"Stop." I knew I had gone too far. The eagle swung annoyed around her neck.

"Sorry, I shouldn't have said that."

"You need to stop this, Mike. For both of us."

"Do you ever Crave with Angus?" I asked, a mist rising through me.

"For God's sake. Don't be ridiculous." She stood up but I grabbed at her wrist and she sat down again.

"Sorry, sorry. I just want you to be happy."

"I am happy."

"No, I mean properly happy, with me. Not this pretend happy with Angus."

"Why do you think it's pretend?" she asked, and I saw a real question in her eyes.

"Because you're not the sort of person to fall in love so quickly, or have that big stupid wedding."

She drew a pattern on the table in some of the spilled vodka. "Maybe you don't know the person I am. Maybe I didn't know the person I was until I met Angus. Maybe you don't know yourself yet." I didn't like those words and they shot through me in a way that made me want to look down and see if I was bleeding. "I'm not your mother, Mike. I didn't abandon you. What we shared was amazing and special, but it's over now. You have to move on."

My hand was tight around my glass and I felt my eyes sting with tears. "Don't say that."

She swallowed hard and the eagle bounced. "Look, Angus is going away tomorrow for a few days, but when he gets back you should come over and we could talk to you together. Maybe then you'll understand this isn't some fake marriage."

"No thanks." I couldn't think of anything worse than talking to monkey-man Angus.

She sighed and stood up, but more slowly this time. "I'm going now."

I let her walk away while I sat and looked into the vibrating liquid in my glass. I've always hated vodka and how it can sneak up on you. How it looks like water but is really very potent. I gulped at it and it shot through my system, waking and charging it.

It was clear that V had constructed an impressive fantasy around Angus to shield her from the pain I had caused her with Carly. She seemed to have even herself fooled and that thought scared me because how do you show someone that what they believe to be true is really not the truth?

I had finished my vodka so I took V's and downed it. And she must have left part of herself in the glass because as I drank it was like she was opening my eyes and my ears. I realized that I'd been an idiot. Angus is going away for a few days, V had said. And if that wasn't an invitation to be there when he wasn't I didn't know what was.

The next day was Friday and Elaine rang to say she was coming into London on Saturday and could she take me up on my offer and pop in for a cup of tea. It was slightly annoying because I had been considering visiting V that day, but Sunday was probably better anyway, so I said yes.

She arrived just after lunch, carrying no visible reason for a trip to London. She walked all around the house, exclaiming at every room. I realized that she was the first person, apart from myself and the builders and decorators, who had ever been upstairs since I'd moved in. It made me wish that I'd made an excuse and pretended to be busy, because surely V should be the first person to see her new home, not her sort-of, soon-to-be mother-in-law. But Elaine lingered in every room, running her hands over the furniture and opening cupboard doors, turning on light switches, and even once bizarrely running the taps. If she could have waited just a few more weeks, I thought, V and I could have shown her around together, which would have been a far more pleasant experience.

Predictably she wasn't so keen on the garden, which was still a mess. I could see how much better it was going to look, but Elaine is one of those people who can't bear to change things for the sake of it. There were always cellophane-wrapped plates in the fridge at her house, unfranked stamps steamed off envelopes in drawers, and so-called scrap paper that had to be written or drawn on both sides before she'd buy more. The motto "Waste Not, Want Not" was pinned by the clock in Elaine's kitchen, which was, I realized, nothing more than an early version of Kaitlyn's wild horses, a thought both pleasing and disconcerting at the same time.

We sat at the kitchen table to drink our tea, Elaine saying she didn't want to risk spilling anything in the drawing room. I had bought some fancy cupcakes from the deli and she picked at one but didn't seem to enjoy it.

"So, you've really set yourself up here," Elaine said, looking around the kitchen.

The house felt vulgar seen through Elaine's eyes, as I had known it would. You could have probably fit her kitchen into mine four times over. "Yes."

"It's a very large house," she said, and the words hung in the air. "You must be making an awful lot of money."

"You know I am." I knew my face was red and it felt no different from being a child and having her tell me off for sneaking another biscuit.

"I don't think I've ever asked you, Mike. Do you enjoy the work?"

Remnants from my conversation with Kaitlyn floated back to me. What she'd said about selling up and moving to the coast had stuck to me like flotsam, and I realized as I sat with Elaine that I didn't particularly enjoy what I did. "I don't know really. I suppose it's okay." But even as I said that I thought of the way I jumbled figures and numbers to make them behave as I wanted them to. How I never actually saw anything I had created, how nothing real ever changed hands, how my whole working life was intangible.

Elaine sipped her tea, her hands encircling the mug. "I suppose there must be a point where you've made enough."

I thought of all the zeros in my bank balance. "I suppose."

She looked me straight in the eye. "What would you really like to do, Mike, I mean if you could choose anything?"

I hate questions like that, they go nowhere apart from deep inside. "I haven't really thought about it."

"But there must be something?"

I tried to search my brain, but it seemed stopped by mud or grease. If I thought about what I wanted it was only V and it felt like it had only ever been her. Although, that couldn't be entirely true because I hadn't known her all my life. I couldn't at that moment remember why I'd gone to university or what I'd hoped to achieve. Everything just seemed blank.

Elaine sighed. "You could do a lot of good with all this money."

I nodded, my throat feeling inexplicably full. I needed to make money to make V happy, but it didn't feel like something I could say to Elaine. "I'm hoping to have a family in this house one day," I said, and as I did something tugged at my chest. I had never thought about having children before but of course that's what married couples did, and V and I would have perfect children.

Elaine smiled. "Well, that would be lovely. But you've got to meet a nice girl first."

I smiled back, but my mouth felt taut. Because if you followed that thought through, and if V really believed she loved Angus, then what would stop them having children? I stood up. "Sorry, I just need the toilet," I said, walking to the downstairs bathroom, where I locked myself in. I leaned over the basin, breathing deeply into my stomach, my hands clenched on the white porcelain. Just the thought of Angus's baby invading V's body sent convulsions of fear through me, which fizzed from my head to my feet, popping through my blood and making me weak. It was an abomination, too repulsive to consider. I knew then that I had to get her away from him as soon as possible.

Elaine was putting on her coat when I came out. "It's been so lovely to see you, Mike," she said. "And to put you in some sort of context. Barry won't believe it when I tell him about the house."

"You must bring him next time."

"I'll do that."

I walked her to the door. I think she'd worn the same coat when I lived with her. It was her autumn coat, not as thick as her winter one, but good in a rain shower. She rubbed my arm at the door and her eyes were twinkling. "You take care of yourself, Mike. And call me anytime. You know our door is always open to you."

"I know." She looked so tiny standing in my giant hall, the top of her head only reaching my shoulder, and I longed for her suddenly. Longed for my room now occupied by Jayden. She would be going home to cook tea and then she and Barry and maybe Jayden would watch *Strictly*

Come Dancing and they'd share a can of Guinness and at some point someone would say something that made everyone laugh. I bent down and kissed her cheek. "Thanks for coming, Elaine."

"You're a good lad, Mike," she said. "Don't you forget it."

I opened the door and the wind had picked up, so you could feel the first chill of a dying summer in the air. At the gate she turned and waved at me and I had to swallow down my tears as I shut the door.

I had an irrational and stupid desire to call Kaitlyn. I knew if I did I could go and sit in her white flat with her wild horses running across the wall. I could imagine her making me a cup of tea and letting me lie on the sofa. I didn't think she'd even mind if I cried, although she would ask me what I was crying for and I wouldn't know what to tell her. And anyway it would be a mean thing to do, leading her on unforgivably.

Instead I went back to the kitchen and opened my laptop, googling again 24 Elizabeth Road, trying once more to see past the sterile image. After that I googled V, but there was still nothing online beyond the very basics. But then I had an idea and I typed Angus Metcalf into Facebook. Sure enough his profile popped up, which of course it would, considering what a self-centered, show-off type of person he was. His last post had been from the day before when he'd checked in at Virgin Atlantic's upper-class lounge. A stupid graphic showed a dotted line between London Heathrow and LAX. He was very far away.

I spent the rest of the day and night trawling his Facebook page, reading every comment and post. The past year was dominated by Verity, with shots of them in various locations, with people I didn't know, in places I couldn't decipher. He had been tagged in endless shots of their wedding, so I was treated to the first dance I missed in actuality, the cutting of the cake, the throwing of the bouquet. It was easy to tell how happy he was, but I thought V's smile seemed a little bit forced, her eyes not quite as sparkling as they should have been, as if she were holding back in a way only I would recognize. And the more I looked and the more I read, the more I realized what a prize idiot Angus Metcalf was. How everything he did was clichéd and contrived and designed to be noticed. His life appeared to be nothing more than one big boast, one big lampooning monstrosity. He enraged me, so that my blood danced in my veins and my head throbbed with a deep, sickening beat. I felt violated by him, as if I had somehow let him inside me, as if his existence on the computer alone was an outrage.

I snapped the lid shut but it wasn't enough, I knew he was still there, still existing within the virtual wires. I picked the laptop off the table and felt its lightness in my wrist, so light I could lift it up and over my head easily, my muscles tensing and readying. I hurled it through the air, watching it arc and fall, watching it connect with the wall, splintering and shattering, all its innards tumbling to the ground. The floor was strewn with a mess of plastic and wires and pieces I didn't even recognize. Circuits, letters, numbers, signals—it was all there but would never go back together again.

I arrived outside V's house early on Sunday morning, but the curtains and shutters were still drawn so I went to the park, where I walked along the deserted paths. Kensington Palace was right there, overlooking everything in its grandeur, and it struck me as outrageous that it just existed among us normal people. How it didn't fence itself in or cower behind walls. How it assumed its right to be there, and so it was. And I was aware as I walked around ponds and up and down giant alleyways that we were all trespassers in this private garden, and that the residents of the palace had had to make compromises as well.

The curtains and shutters at number 24 were still drawn when I got back, but I couldn't wait any longer, so I knocked on the door. I could hear the sound echoing inside and I knew suddenly that V wasn't there. My heart sped at the thought that she might not be where I had placed her in my mind.

I bent down and lifted the letter box, but all I could see was the black insides of a metal box. I straightened up and leaned over the stone balustrade, cupping my hand against the glass. One of the wooden slats of the shutters hadn't quite met its partner and I could see a sliver of the drawing room beyond, some pale sofas, a streak of a fireplace, nothing more. I ran down the stairs and into the basement area, but this time there was a blind across the window, its billowy fabric concealing everything. Finally I went and stood on the opposite side of the road again, against the ivy wall, looking up at the tall house. But it was still and silent, giving nothing away. I wondered if she had gone to Steeple House for the weekend and considered for a moment getting on a train and joining her there. But I knew that would be all wrong and that Suzi was the last person I would want witnessing our reconciliation.

I walked instead toward Islington and our old flat, the thought of not seeing V so disappointing that I had to find some way to be close to her. I hadn't seen the flat for more than a year now, hadn't even been there when V had packed it up and left. From the road it looked no different, dark windows reflecting the sky, and yet I was filled with a strange longing just by looking up at it. I crossed the road and pressed our old buzzer, still nameless. A woman answered and I nearly walked away, but by then it seemed imperative that I stand once more inside the place where V and I had been our happiest. I told her a stupid story about how I'd used to live there and my girlfriend had lost a very precious ring and how I'd suddenly had a brainwave that it might have fallen between the loose floorboards in the kitchen. She sounded dubious but I guess knowing about the floorboards must have done the trick because she buzzed me in.

A man opened the door to the flat. He extended a skinny arm toward me and tried to hide his nervousness behind his beard. But I was as friendly and calm as possible, as we all know I could have snapped them both in half in a minute. We went to the kitchen and looked under the floorboard and there was nothing there and I said it had been worth a shot and they agreed. I told them I liked what they'd done with it and she said she was an artist, so she loved experimenting with color and I had to hide my smile because of how much V would have hated the bright tones. I shook their hands and thanked them as I left and I really meant it, because it was like the flat still retained our energy and I had sucked it all up, storing it deep in my stomach.

I bought a new laptop on the way home since it was stupid not to make use of the gift of Angus's Facebook page. But he still hadn't posted anything new, which I found surprising, expecting a barrage of photographs of him in Los Angeles. But then again what would be the point in pictures without V in them?

There was one Crave that V and I never did. She said she'd always had this fantasy about fucking a really disgusting man. Her idea was to go to some shithole of a bar and pick up an ugly freak whom she would take back to our flat. I obviously would follow close behind and let myself in with my key. She didn't actually want to go as far as having sex with him; she wanted me to pull him off her just moments before. It was never a serious suggestion and never something we were actually going to do. We'd talk about it sometimes, lying in bed, but we both knew it was never going to happen. It was just one of those fantasies we liked to bat about between our brains.

I spent most of the next day checking Angus's feed, which stayed stubbornly silent until five, when it informed me that he had checked in at Virgin Atlantic's upper-class lounge to fly from LAX to London Heathrow. He would be home the next morning, which meant I absolutely had to see V that night. I remembered how she'd casually said that he was going away for a few days and how I'd been too embroiled with everything else to listen to her properly. What if she'd gone away on Sunday because I hadn't shown up on Friday or Saturday? What if she had been waiting for me and I'd been too stupid to realize it?

Y

I went straight from work to Elizabeth Road. The shutters and curtains were open, but there were no lights on. I knocked on the door anyway, but no one answered. Still, she had clearly been home since the day before and was probably on her way home from work.

I went to sit in a pub around the corner and ordered a double whiskey and soda. It was only six thirty and I knew she didn't usually leave work until around six, so I made myself give it an hour before I went back. And I had been right to do that because there were now lights on in the hall and the kitchen. I paused on the curb, feeling the second double whiskey melt into my blood. This was the moment I had been waiting a very long time for and it was important that I get it absolutely right.

I climbed the stone stairs and stood under the porch light, which hadn't yet been turned on. I took a breath and knocked. It was amazing how much more alive the house felt this time, as if it loved V's presence as much as I did. I heard footsteps on the stairs and then she opened the door. She looked like she had recently changed as she was dressed in baggy sweatpants and a white T-shirt, which strained across her bust. The eagle was around her neck.

Her eyes widened at the sight of me. "What are you doing here, Mike?"

"Can I come in?" I said, giving her my best smile.

But she stayed standing in the doorway. "I don't think that's a good idea."

"Please. I just want to have a chat."

"We've tried that." She started to close the door but I put out my hand and she was no match for my strength. It was easy to push the door slightly more open and step inside. "What are you doing?" she said as we stood facing each other in the hall.

I shut the door behind me. "I didn't say what I really meant the other evening."

She glanced behind me at the door. "I've got a friend coming in a minute." It was an obvious lie.

"V, this is ridiculous. I love you, you love me. We know each other like we're the same person. This has all got to stop now. You need to tell Angus it's over and come and live with me."

She didn't answer at first, but then she said, "You need to leave."

And that's the thing about V. She makes you work hard. She's not easy like women like Kaitlyn or Carly because she's worth it. She's like that TV ad, she's what every woman wants to be and what every man wants to possess. I smiled at her.

"I crave you, V."

"Mike," she said, but then she stopped and her hand went to her throat, clutching at the eagle. It was all I had been waiting for. The moment we had both always known was coming. The signal only we understood.

I stepped toward her and took her in my arms, pressing her against my chest. She was very still, but we fitted together in the way we always had. I knew she would be able to feel my body through my clothes, the way it worked only for her, the way it throbbed between us.

"My darling girl," I whispered into her hair. "I've missed you so much."

I let her go a bit then, holding her by the shoulders so we were standing opposite each other. We were both crying, overcome with the emotion of the moment. "It's okay," I said, "I'm here to save you. I'd never abandon you."

"Mike, please," she said, but her voice was very weak, drowned out by the force of the desire that existed between us.

I leaned down and kissed her on the mouth. At first it felt hard against my own and I worried for a mad second that she wasn't going to let me in. But then I felt something give in her body, some recognition of all we had ever meant to each other, a realization of desire. I encircled her waist with my arm, pulling her toward me.

I could feel her breath on my face, her body shaking and quivering. I lifted her and laid her down on the rug on the floor, which made her exclaim slightly. I was so hard I thought I was going to burst. V was crying, releasing all the lies and tension of the past few months, and I felt such a surge of love for her that I brought my face so close to hers that our breath was conjoined. She looked beautiful lying there, her hair splayed out around her head, her eyes wide, her skin pale. The eagle lying quietly on her neck. I pulled at her sweatpants and eased her legs apart with my knees.

"Oh God, Mike, no," she said. But the moan and her words were ones of pleasure. It is hard sometimes to get what you want, to succumb to what you need. I kissed her and felt her lips part to reveal the sumptuousness of her tongue, traced the outline of her teeth.

There can never have been two people who have ever or will ever exist who fit together more perfectly than we do. We are like superheroes together. If sex could save the world, then we would rule the planet.

I reached for my zip, but I felt her hand on mine. "Hey, Eagle. This isn't the way it should be."

Her words cut through my thoughts and I raised myself onto my arms. "V, please."

But she smiled so sweetly through her tears. "Come on, you know this isn't right, Mikey."

"Of course it's right," I nearly shouted.

"No, no, we're not the ones who skulk around."

I hovered over her, unsure what she meant.

"Mike," she said, more firmly now. "I don't want it to be like this. Do you understand what I'm saying?"

I rolled off her and we lay next to each other on the floor for a while, neither of us speaking or moving. In the end I rolled onto my side and traced my finger down the side of her face. Her eyes were open and she was staring at the ceiling. I leaned over and kissed her cheek. "Do you want to come home with me now?"

She sat up slowly, her back turned toward me, and I saw she was shivering. It wasn't cold, so it made me worried that she was ill. "Do you want me to get you a jumper or something?" She shook her head. "You should pack a bag at least."

"You can't expect me to just leave Angus like that."

I sat up as well and turned her around, so we were facing each other on the floor. "For fuck's sake, V. Enough about bloody Angus."

She reached forward and took my hand. "Come on, Mike, we're not mean people, are we? I can't very well just walk out on him. I've treated him pretty shabbily, you must agree?"

Personally I would have let Angus stew, but V is nicer than me. "We've never cared about the other people before."

"But this is different. We've gone much further this time. I think you should go home and I'll tell Angus everything tomorrow. I have to do it in person. He's going to be devastated."

"I hate the thought of you spending one more second with him." The hall light was very bright and it made it hard to think straight.

"Come on," she said, soothingly. "I want to do this properly. Or it's going to color our life together."

"I wish Angus just didn't bloody exist."

I stared at her dipped head concealing her whirling brain, wishing with every fiber of my being that she would repeat the words I had just said. Yes, that's what I wish as well, was all I wanted to hear. She breathed deeply into her chest, so it rose and fell, then looked up at me and it was like looking straight into the old Verity, as if the artifice and pretense of the last year had evaporated and we were all that was left.

She held my gaze as she reached over and put her hand on my chest, her eyes welling with tears. "Oh God, Mike, I hate this. Sometimes, I wish things were different." Her gaze flickered as she drew in a breath and her eyes clouded slightly. "But life can be cruel," she said, her voice quivering on the words.

"How about if I come and tell him for you? I can't bear you doing it alone."

But she stood up and with it I felt the moment dissolving into tiny fragments of dust that I wanted to scrabble about for on the floor. "I'll be fine," she said firmly, even though her voice was shaking. "It's getting late, Mike. Why don't you head home and I'll be in touch tomorrow."

I looked at the stairs leading up and down. I had imagined taking her home with me and how she would feel in our bed, curled into my body. The thought of leaving her here was almost more than I could bear. "You know I'd do anything for you, don't you, V?"

"Yes, of course I do." She walked toward the door. "And you must know that for now it's best we do this."

And naturally she was right. There would have been something underhanded about slipping away into the night, as if we were ashamed of what we'd done, which would have been absurd as nothing was more right than V and me.

She opened the door and I stood half in, half out. "Let me know as soon as you've done it," I said. I leaned back down and kissed her again on the lips. "This was our best ever Crave."

I e-mailed her as soon as I got home:

> Darling V,
> I love you, my sweet, my everything. I am so glad we've sorted it all out and you will be back with me where you belong. You're going to love the house, but of course you can change it any way you like. We can even move if you want to. I've been thinking recently about making a change. Maybe even going to live by the coast. But we've got acres of time to discuss all that and of course I'd never make you do anything you don't want to.
> E-mail me as soon as you've spoken to Angus. Or if you need to contact me quickly my phone number is 0770090073.
> As ever, I crave you,
> Your Eagle, Mike

I slept better than I had since Christmas, waking to the blissful realization that by that evening V would be in the house. I called in sick to work and spent the day preparing for her arrival. I told Anna that I would pay her triple if she could get the planting finished by the end of the day and she made a phone call and five Polish men arrived. I went to the shops and bought flowers, champagne, halibut, salad, the water in the blue bottle V likes, and a bottle of her favorite perfume for the bathroom. I cleaned and tidied all day, straightening straight sheets, plumping plump cushions, shining shiny taps. I carried all my weights to the basement and emptied the bins.

I checked my e-mail throughout the day, but I didn't start to wonder at V's silence until about three-ish. There was an e-mail from Kaitlyn asking if I was okay and whether or not I needed anything, but I didn't bother to reply. Anna came in at four to say they'd pretty much finished. She'd be back to completely finish up in the next couple of days, but it was as good as done. I walked around the space with her and I don't think I exclaimed as much as she expected, but I'd paid her a small fortune, so I didn't really care. Although I probably should have been more effusive because she'd done exactly what I'd asked and the garden was very beautiful, swaying and sashaying in the breeze. The Polish men traipsed back through the house and I hoovered and washed the kitchen and hall floors.

There was still no e-mail from V, so I sent her a quick one:

Darling,
Is everything okay? I'm eager to hear from you. I can be there in a shot.
    X

My in-box pinged almost immediately and I dived for my phone. It was a message from the postmaster: message undeliverable, address not recognized. My breath was suddenly hard to catch and my vision dimmed, so I had to lean over the table. There had to be some mistake. And then it struck me that I'd been a fool to leave V alone in this task, whatever she'd said. It was no different than if I had left her alone in one of the bars with a man pawing at her and expecting her to walk through the door of our flat half an hour later. What if Angus had become angry and was right now holding her prisoner at home? Or worse? I grabbed my coat and my phone and rushed out of the house.

I ran the length of my road, arriving into the mass of people and traffic on Clapham High Street. The path to V seemed unbearably long and I wanted to explode a bomb and remove everything and everyone between us. I jigged on the pavement, unsure whether a taxi or the Tube would be quicker. I heard my name being called and turned to see Kaitlyn walking toward me.

"Feeling better, then?" she said accusatorily.

But I was too preoccupied to think of a good excuse. "Yes, I'm fine."

"You look a bit feverish."

My eyes were still on the road. "I'm fine."

"I don't know what you're doing, Mike, but you should be careful."

I turned to look at her and her eyes were as watery and disconcerting as ever. "What do you mean?"

"The chairman called me in today and has asked me to have a look through all the Spectre stuff. He said he was worried it had all gotten to be a bit too much for you."

I tried to feel irritation at the news but couldn't muster any. "I don't care. Take it if you want."

"I don't want to do anything that might harm you. Have you been offered another job or something?"

"No, nothing like that. I just don't really care." And it was a relief to say it, a bit like when you exhale after a deep breath. "Look, I have to run. V needs me."

Kaitlyn took a small step toward me. "Mike, are you sure she needs you? There's something I've been meaning to say to you—"

"Shut up, Kaitlyn," I said because I couldn't bear her commenting on my life or V one moment longer, especially when she had no idea what she was talking about. "Just leave me alone."

I turned and ran toward the Tube as I'd decided it would be quicker.

Every second of that journey dragged against my skin, so it felt like time was moving backward and I was in a bad dream where I would never reach my destination. I ran all the way from the Kensington High Street Tube to Elizabeth Road, but I am very fit and I wasn't even out of breath when I knocked on the heavy black door I had come to know so well.

Angus answered, dressed in jeans and a gray shirt, nothing on his feet. His hair was messier than usual and his face looked almost crumpled. There were black circles underneath his eyes and I thought he held the air of a discarded man. We looked at each other for a few heartbeats, neither wanting to be the first to break ground.

"I need to speak to Verity," I said eventually.

"Sorry, who are you?" he asked, his face screwed up as he leaned against the door.

"Mike," I said, but the fact I had to introduce myself deflated my momentum.

"God, so you are." He stood straighter, his face hardening. I couldn't work out if he was knocking me off-balance on purpose. "I'm afraid Verity's in bed. She's ill."

"I still need to come in."

His face contorted slightly, but I knew he was from that class of people for whom rudeness is very hard. He was not the type of person to slam a door in anyone's face, even if that person was about to make off with his wife.

"You and I should talk," I added.

He opened the door wider and I stepped over the threshold exactly as I'd done the day before. He motioned for me to go into the drawing room and I was able to see the pale sofas I had glimpsed through the shutters, as well as the marble fireplace, the huge Venetian mirror, the pale gray walls, the beautiful works of art.

"You've got a nerve turning up here," he said. "What the fuck's wrong with you? I think Verity's made it pretty clear where you stand."

"Verity hasn't told you, has she?" Her sickness suddenly made the silence of the day understandable.

"Told me what?" He folded his arms across his chest.

"We're in love. She's leaving you and coming to live with me."

He laughed, a schoolboy splutter. "Don't be ridiculous."

I composed myself and tightened my jaw. "I'm really sorry to tell you, but you're part of this game we play, that's got a bit out of hand. Verity is really sorry about how much she's hurt you, but it's impossible us not being together."

"What the fuck are you talking about?" I saw a flash of fear in his face, which hadn't been there before, and it renewed my courage.

I spoke slowly. "I am very sorry. Verity and I are in love and she's going to divorce you and come and live with me."

He stared at me for a moment. "Have you lost your mind? You don't think I'd know if my own wife was in love with another man?"

I was taller than him by a couple of inches and definitely stronger. "You know we were together for nine years before she met you?"

He snorted. "Of course I know that. You know she started seeing me before she'd finished with you?" He shifted his weight and kept his eyes locked on mine.

My mind jolted slightly, but recalibrated itself quickly. "Yes, I know. I had a stupid one-night stand in America, which she was furious about and this has all been to pay me back. But it's finished now, we've reached the end of our Crave."

"Your what?" He spat the words at me.

"The game we play."

"Stop, Mike." We both turned to see V standing in the doorway. She looked as terrible as it is possible for V to look. She was as pale as paper, but with livid red spots high on her cheeks. Her hair was matted and stuck to her head and her tiny body was shivering inside her cotton pajamas.

Angus took the blanket from the back of the sofa and wrapped her in it, which irritated me as I was the one who should be doing things like that. "What are you doing up?"

"I heard you both," she said. She stayed standing close to him.

"I've told him, V," I said. "It's okay, we can leave now."

But she started to cry. "Oh God, Mike, please don't."

Angus put his arm around her. "You need to fuck off, mate, before I call the police."

I hate posh boys calling me mate, as if they have any idea how to use the word. I directed my speech only to V. "I know you wanted to tell him, but it doesn't matter. All that matters is that we can be together now." I took a step toward them but she jarred back.

Angus stepped in front of her, his arm stretched out to me. "If you don't leave in the next thirty seconds I'm calling the police."

I turned to him then, the pathetic monkey man, thinking he had something that was clearly not his. "If V doesn't love me then why were we lying together on that rug last night, pulling ourselves back from making love, planning our future?" I swung my hand toward the hall and Angus followed my movement.

He looked between me and the rug a few times, his face dropping and falling. "Verity," he said, turning to her. "What's going on?"

V was still crying, her whole body dropping downward as she sank slowly to her knees. "Make him leave, Gus."

"I'm not going anywhere," I said.

But V looked up at me, her eyes hard and straight and I knew I'd angered her. "Leave, Mike." She'd told me she wanted to be the one to tell Angus, she'd even explained why that was the right thing to do, but my impatience had got the better of me.

"I'll be back first thing in the morning," I said. "And this time we really will be going home."

Angus stayed mute during our exchange, no doubt seeing the superior connection that existed between us. He knew he was defeated and there was no point in saying anything more to him. I simply turned and let myself out.

I walked home to dissipate some of the energy rushing through me. I was satisfied that V wasn't in any danger from Angus. He was simply an irritant who needed to be pushed to one side. It was highly frustrating that we would have to wait one more night, but then again, we had the rest of our lives to look forward to, so what was twelve or so hours.

I didn't feel like eating when I got home, so instead opened a bottle of wine to cool my blood and smooth my nerves, both of which were still jumping inside my body. When I was a boy and things were bad, I used to think I had an army of ants living inside me, patrolling my borders. I could never decide if they were on the same side as me or not and sometimes I would wake screaming from nightmares where they had crawled out of my nose, mouth, and ears.

Maybe Mum had the same ants inside her, because when you drink they go to sleep. Then they lie down in your blood and flow through you like Moses bobbing down the river in his basket. Fetch my medicine, Mikey, Mum would say when I got big enough to open the fridge and reach for the cans on my own. I wished suddenly and violently that she could see me right now, that she could witness all I was and all I had achieved. You're not a bad lad just because bad things have happened to you, Elaine used to say. Maybe your mum had a rough time herself when she was a girl, Elaine also used to say, maybe she just couldn't do it right, however much she wanted to. I reached for the bottle and was surprised to find it empty. The night was dark outside and I was suddenly very tired. I went into the drawing room and lay on the couch. I wanted to cry but I couldn't work out why.

I had no idea where I was when I woke up. I lay in the darkness with something vibrating underneath me and thought I was back in the flat with Mum getting pulverized in the next room. But where I was lying felt too soft and the air didn't contain either bitter cold or the heavy stench of fags. And then the pieces of my mind fell into place and connected and I knew where I was. I scrambled for the phone in my pocket, seeing an unknown number on the screen, although I knew immediately who it was.

"Mike," V said. "Is Angus there?"

"What? No." I looked at the clock on the media system, it was 2:12 a.m. "Why would he be here?"

"Because he's not here." Her voice was stretched and rushed. "I told him everything and he's so angry. And our wedding file is open on the computer with all the names and addresses of everyone we invited, so he must have been looking you up."

I stood at this. I hadn't drawn the curtains and the moonlight had cast the room silver.

V was crying. "I'm calling a taxi now, Mike. I'll be there in fifteen minutes. Promise me you won't open the door to him."

"Why shouldn't I? We might as well have the discussion now."

"No," she shouted. "He's drunk and I know how strong you are. Mike, please promise me. I don't want either of you getting hurt."

"No one's getting hurt. We can discuss it like adults and sort it out."

"Oh God, Mike." Her tone had risen even higher. "You don't understand. Don't open the fucking door."

"Okay," I said, "okay."

I stood still for a minute. V was coming home. It was actually happening. Within the hour she and I would be enclosed in our warm, safe space and Angus Metcalf would be making his sorry, solo way back to his house. It had almost been too easy, too perfect. I quickly straightened the cushions on the sofa and took the empty bottle of wine to the recycling in the kitchen, rinsing and then drying my wineglass before replacing it on the rack. Even in the moonlight the garden swayed in the breeze and I was so pleased with myself for making every detail perfect for V.

There was a loud knock on the front door, a fist pounding heavily on the wood. I stayed standing in the kitchen, looking out at the plants whose names I couldn't quite remember.

I heard the metallic twang of my letter box flip open and made a mental note to buy one of those letter-catching boxes I'd seen at Angus's house.

"Open the fucking door," Angus shouted, and V was right, he was drunk, his words slurring into each other.

I leaned against the sink, my arms tensing so I could feel my muscles curling around my bones.

"You fucking coward," Angus shouted. "You don't get to come to my house, then not let me into yours."

My fingers were turning white against the porcelain of the sink as the blood stopped flowing to them, and I wondered how long you would have to stand like this before they died.

The banging increased, as did the shouting. Angus's entitled voice telling me what to do, demanding my attention. "What are you scared of?"

"Nothing," I said to the sink. "Nothing that you could ever do."

I walked down my hall toward the banging. It was not enough to simply walk away with her this time.

I opened the door and Angus barreled into me, his arms flailing and his eyes wide and wild. He had spittle at the corner of his mouth and he kicked at my shins. I teetered backward, taking a minute to recover my strength and meet his punches. I didn't want to hit him back, but I wanted to stop him and I held my arm over my face.

"You fucking animal," he was shouting, "you fucking waste of a human being. You disgusting, repulsive excuse of a man." I could smell whiskey on his breath and could feel the weakness in his punches.

"Stop it, Angus," I shouted. "There's no point in this."

"There's every fucking point," he screamed. "You cowardly fuck. You useless cunt."

I let him go on hitting me, while the insults poured over me. I thought of V and how she would stop me with a kiss at the end of a Crave. I tried to feel her hand on my arm as it twitched to lay waste to the loser who'd just tried to kiss her. But V wasn't there and Angus had done more than that; he'd kissed her and his hands had covered her body. And I'd heard his words before: They'd been screamed in my face by other people, other people who were with us now, looking through the window, laughing at my passivity.

How many times can you be told you are a Useless. Fucking. Cunt.

Excuse. Of. A. Person? How many times can you be punched and stay quiet? How many times can you sneak back to your mattress and hide under your threadbare duvet? How many times can you go on believing life is a rehearsal and not the real thing?

I threw open my arms, which made Angus's hands spin away from him, knocking him off-balance so he stumbled backward. He had blood on his hands and down his shirt, which I knew was mine. I hate men like Angus. But then again I hate men in general. Angus might as well have been George or even Logan or any of the other fuckers who've waded through my life. Angus had broken the rules of the Crave, he had gone on where others had been made to stop.

I walked toward him, clenching my hand and drawing back my arm so it was level with my chin. He flinched as I threw my fist through the air and into his face. It connected with a force that sent him spinning backward, his legs flying from under him. I felt the crack of his bone, the tear of his muscles, the dislodging of his teeth. I saw the final terror in his eyes as he fell through the air. But it wasn't enough. I followed his fall with my body, my fist pumping into his face, pushing him ever farther back into himself, rubbing out the fact that he had ever been here at all.

I don't know how long I went on hitting him, but I became aware of noise and someone pulling on my arm and I looked up to see V. I stopped immediately because it was all right now that she was home. I sat back, my legs inexplicably skidding on the wet floor. V folded her body over Angus, a strange moaning sound coming from her.

I needed to calm myself, so I did my meditation exercises, breathing into my toes and working up through my body. Angus twitched once, his hand grasping for nothing. And then I couldn't bear the thought of what V was doing, how Angus's blood was drenching her, contaminating her. I stood and pulled at her shoulder, so she looked up at me, her eyes huge and miserable. I held out my hand, but she hesitated.

"Come on, V," I said, "it's going to be okay."

She looked back down at Angus, who now had blood bubbling at his mouth. "I don't know what to do," she whimpered. "I don't . . . I don't know what to do."

I leaned down and took her hand, pulling her upward and over Angus's body, so we could back farther into the house. I pulled her into me, feeling her tiny body succumb to my arms, so that I was the only thing holding her up. It was all going to be all right; she was home.

I was holding her very tightly but I wanted her to look up just once, to look down the hallway and see what I had created for her. I wanted to take her by the hand and walk her up the stairs and into her new bedroom. But it wasn't the right time and it was enough that she was there at all. That we had finally arrived where we were meant to be.

I became aware of people and noise and for some bizarre reason Kaitlyn was standing on my doorstep, her hand over her mouth. The blue flashing lights arrived in minutes and I stood as the police and paramedics came into my hall. I held out my hands to them, with V still slumped against my chest, almost as though she had fallen asleep on me.

We didn't need to continue with this torturous cruelty we had been inflicting on each other. We could enter a new realm, one in which we could show each other how much we loved each other.

And as I stood there holding my beloved in my arms, I realized that when it comes to grand gestures there is nothing grander than killing for love.

PART
THREE

y barrister, Xander Jackson, returned this document ten days ago. It might sound stupid but I've missed it, even felt worried about it. I've missed the act of writing it, almost like it is in control of the end of the story. And I'm desperate to know what happens next, where we go from here.

"This is dynamite," Xander said when he handed it back to me. "In both a good and bad way. There's loads we can use here, but also I think you should destroy it."

"No way," I said.

"I thought you might say that," he said. "But if you don't destroy it you have to absolutely promise me you'll never show it to anyone. Our case is fucked if you do."

"Why?"

"Because it makes you sound a bit unhinged."

"What are you talking about?"

He laughed. "Sorry, unhinged is probably too strong a word, I didn't mean that. It's just, well, some people might not entirely understand what you feel about Verity. They might misinterpret some of the things you did, like waiting outside her office and walking past her house. You know."

"Not really."

Xander composed his face and leaned forward, his hands clasped in front of him. "In all seriousness though, Mike, we're going to plead not guilty."

"But I did it," I said. "I'm not denying I threw the punches. I mean, there were witnesses apart from anything else."

"Yes," Xander said. "But you've been charged with murder and I'm pretty sure we can get it reduced to manslaughter. If we plead not guilty, then the charge of manslaughter is still on the sheet and the judge can direct the jury to convict you of that rather than murder. It makes a massive difference to sentencing."

Xander is an idiot like all the others, but an idiot my lawyer assures me we need. He is a dick-slapping show-off who might not go to the clubs George frequents, or beat up women like the men my mother chose, but he's still an arse. I'm sure he's married with a couple of kids but still looks at pretty girls on the street, still allows himself the odd fumble at Christmas parties. His cheeks are ruddy and I expect he gets excited by bonfires and how to cook lamb and chopping wood, a type of person I didn't even know existed until I went to university, but they do, I promise. He thinks he got into being a barrister to help people and do good, and doesn't like to admit that sometimes it gives him a hard-on defending impossible cases. And also he likes the money. But right now he is the best chance I have of getting out of here and starting my real life with V.

Initially I didn't want to implicate V at all. But Xander had some powerful arguments. "Do you really think she'll be outside the prison gates waiting for you if you're in here for ten or more years and she gets off scot-free?" he asked, after we'd sweated out the argument in a strip-lit cell for hours and hours. I could feel the sweat pooling under my prison-issue clothes and the ants in my bloodstream were running riot.

"A girl like that? Especially after all the media coverage? She could write a book, be the toast of the town. There'll be loads of men queuing up to take her on dates. Besides. I think it's damned unfair for you to take all the blame. I hadn't thought of it before I read your document, but you were clearly coerced and you have to ask yourself why she did that."

"It was part of the Crave," I said. "I thought I explained that. And she didn't coerce me. I enjoyed it."

Xander waved this away. "Do you know she was the sole beneficiary in Angus Metcalf's will? That girl is a multimillionaire now."

I shook my head. "V would never do any of the things you're suggesting for money."

He smiled. "Just an added bonus then, shall we say."

I didn't like his tone, but there was no point in losing my temper. "I don't want to shift the blame to her."

"Look, there's no doubting you threw the fatal punch. But there are so many unanswered questions, so many ways we can get the jury to question her and then start to see you in a different light. I mean, for a start, why hadn't she told Angus that you were in contact? Why didn't she report the assault straight after it happened? Why didn't she tell Angus as soon as he got home? Why the fuck did she ring to warn you he was coming around that night?"

"It wasn't an assault," I said, thinking back to the glorious kiss V and I had shared, which still rested like velvet in my soul.

"Exactly. So, you have to ask yourself why she's saying that now, all of a sudden. Doesn't it make you doubt her intentions all along?" Xander leaned forward as he spoke, his Adam's apple bobbing and his cheeks flushed.

"I don't expect you to understand. It's part of our game. I don't want people to doubt her."

He looked straight at me. "Mike, they either have to doubt you or her. We can't go after Angus because he's dead and juries tend to feel sorry for the victim. If they believe you did it out of jealousy it plays very badly. Murder carries a mandatory life sentence and even if we got manslaughter you'd be looking at ten to fifteen years. We can say you didn't mean to kill him until we're blue in the face, but they won't believe you. You beat him up pretty badly, apart from anything else, which doesn't look good. But if you were so distressed you lost control then maybe we can turn them toward a more lenient version of manslaughter. What if your mind was turned by Verity? If her hold over you was so strong that you thought you were doing what she wanted? Then, then we've got a chance."

My mind felt fuzzy. "But I'll still have to go to prison."

"I think that's going to be unavoidable. But what I'm suggesting is the difference between ten and five years, maybe less. You won't even be forty when you get out."

"What will happen to Verity?" I was thinking about how I would visit the prison gym in the evening and press weights.

Xander sucked in some air, as if he really was human. "That's what we need to discuss, Mike. And I need you to listen carefully and think about what's best for both of you. It's not going to be pretty for her either way. We'll have to tear her apart in court a bit and all your secrets will come out. But I think we need to go further. Maybe"— he tried to look uncomfortable, but it didn't sit well on his smooth features—"maybe she'll have to pay for what she's done. Literally, I mean."

I decided on heavier weights. "I don't want her upset."

Xander sighed. "Come on, Mike, this is serious. This is your life we're talking about." He stood and leaned over the desk. "Bottom line, you're going down for this and I don't think it's fair for you to take this all on your own. Verity might not have thrown the punch, she might not even have actually asked you to do it, but she's as guilty as you are in some ways. Come on, she was clearly in love with you and wanted out of her marriage."

"I don't understand what you're saying."

"Mike," Xander said, his voice lowered like I would imagine him speaking to his children when they were naughty and he was being reasonable. "I'm duty bound to go to the police with what you've told me."

"But I haven't told you anything."

He tapped my document. "It's all in here. You know they've had Verity in for questioning a few times already?" I shook my head. "They're obviously suspicious about her involvement. If I tell them what you've told me I think there's a chance she could be charged with accessory to murder."

"No. Absolutely not."

"You'll be tried together," Xander said. "You might even get similar sentences. And think about it. When you get out you'll have this shared experience. She won't have been out in the world getting on with her life while you've been rotting away in here. You can start a new life together, put all this behind you."

I looked at Xander and his blue eyes, which reminded me sometimes of Kaitlyn's. He smiled slowly as his words sunk in. There was something intoxicating about them. Something that demanded surrender. That felt like stepping onto warm sand or into a proper hug. It was a part of the Crave neither of us had anticipated, but maybe that wasn't such a bad thing. There was an undeniable beauty in the idea of V safely packed away in a cell just like mine, waiting to be taken out like a precious jewel in a few years' time. It almost sounded romantic, like something we might tell our grandchildren.

Xander told me to expect certain aspects of our story to be leaked. He was sorry, he said, but there was nothing he could do about it. Office juniors like to gossip, he said, sighing as he stopped his hands from rubbing together. But I didn't expect these ridiculous, bald headlines that leave out so much. I have started cutting them out and sticking them in here so that I never again forget what the world is really like.

MAN KILLS RIVAL IN TRAGIC SEX GAME

DESIRE, DEATH & DESTRUCTION

THE LOOK OF GUILT

THE COLD-EYED WIFE

WAS ANGUS METCALF MURDERED BY JEALOUSY OR DESIGN?

THE CARE-HOME BOY WHO NEVER FIT IN

THE CARE-HOME KILLER

IS VERITY REALLY TELLING THE TRUTH?

THE TRUTH BEHIND VERITY'S EYES

VERY CLEVER VERITY

THE BRILLIANT EXECUTIVE SUCKED INTO A DANGEROUS GAME

CONSTANT CRAVING

THE KILLER CRAVE

THE BOY WHO CRAVED LOVE

I also cut out this article on Saturday. It's an opinion piece, written by someone called Helen Bell, whose name I will remember, published in the bestselling national newspaper in Britain.

IS VERITY METCALF A MODERN-DAY
LADY MACBETH?

What an odd name for a woman at the heart of a seedy and deadly love triangle: Verity, supposedly the teller of truth. Except I've always thought it was asking for trouble to give your children any of those Faith, Hope and Charity names. What a task to set a child, almost as if you're goading them to rebel before they're even out of the pram.

Verity Metcalf, 29, was, however, not someone you would look at and consider a rebel. On the surface she has in fact lived an exemplary life. She excelled at her £12,000 a year private girls' school, Haverfield in Sussex, near to the £3 million house where she was brought up. She was a straight A student at school and from there went to Bristol University, where she received a First in applied sciences. She then moved to London and secured a six-figure salary at the world-renowned Calthorpe Centre, taking part in pioneering work in artificial intelligence.

To top it all, she had recently married the so-called most eligible man in London, Angus Metcalf, a high-flying advertising executive at the top of his game. They lived in a house estimated to be worth more than £8 million on one of London's smartest streets, with pop stars and Russian oligarchs as their neighbors. They attended charity balls and dined with the rich and famous. They had works of art on their walls that wouldn't have looked out of place in the finest galleries, and holidayed in some of the most exclusive resorts in the world. Their honeymoon to South Africa, taken only in September of this year, reportedly cost more than £20,000.

So what went wrong? How has Verity Metcalf found herself at the center of a tawdry ménage à trois, as her brilliant husband lies dead and her ex-boyfriend, Michael Hayes, 30, languishes in prison awaiting trial for the murder?

The truth, as it always is, is much more complicated than the perfect face Verity presents to the world.

An undeniably beautiful woman, Verity has shown almost no emotion since the death of Angus Metcalf. She has been photographed countless times—near her house, at the police station, running in the park, at her parents' country mansion—and yet her expression is always the same. The steely eyes, the pursed lips, the upturned chin. There is often jewelry at her ears and neck, sometimes she even appears to be wearing a bit of makeup. Certainly her eyes are never puffy or bloodshot, as one would expect from a devastated new widow. She walks almost with her head held high, her gait strutting, as if daring us to cross her.

I look at Verity and I see not a shocked woman in mourning but instead a calculating temptress. She telephoned Mr. Hayes to warn him that her husband was on his way over on the night of the killing. And she was apparently found embracing Mr. Hayes by police called to the house by a neighbor, as her husband lay dead at their feet.

By all accounts, Verity liked sex and she liked to experiment. An ex-boyfriend has been quoted as saying that she sometimes "scared him with her passion." We will never know if this was the hold she exerted over Michael Hayes, but many testify to how enchanted he always seemed by her.

Hayes is an interesting character. Brought up by a violent, alcoholic mother until the age of ten and then placed into the care system, with all its failings, he was an unruly and difficult child. Expelled from three schools, he only found stability from the age of twelve, when he was placed in the permanent foster care of Elaine and Barry White. His behavior certainly appeared to settle with them and his obvious intelligence blossomed enough for him to do well in his exams and secure a place at Bristol University to read economics.

Verity and Hayes met toward the end of their second year, and looking at photographs of them from that time it is hard to put the beautiful, confident girl with the shy, awkward boy. Friends say he was infatuated by her from the start and would follow her around like a puppy.

After graduating, Hayes went into banking, where he excelled. Not as rich as Metcalf, he still earned a substantial sum of money, with bonuses that regularly topped a million.

Verity and Hayes split up at Christmas last year, but she had already met Metcalf by then and begun an affair. Friends describe them as seeming blissfully happy and they were engaged within months and married this September at a lavish ceremony on the grounds of her parents' home. Bizarrely, Hayes attended the wedding, but guests have said he seemed agitated and out of place.

No one knows when Verity and Hayes reconnected or what happened. All we know for certain is that they were seeing enough of each other for her to now accuse him of assaulting her in her own home

24 hours before the murder took place, while Angus was on a business trip in Los Angeles.

Perhaps they never stopped loving each other? Or perhaps Verity never loved Hayes or Metcalf? Perhaps she saw an opportunity in both men and played one off against the other? Because Verity Metcalf is now a very rich woman, being the sole beneficiary of her husband's substantial fortune.

We've all known a Verity Metcalf; I certainly have. She's the prettiest girl in school, the one who gets all the boys. She's clever and bright and funny and always invited to all the parties. She looks good in clothes but never seems to work out. She gets the dream jobs and the sunniest holidays; she eats in the best restaurants and drives the fastest car. She knows the power of her sexuality and isn't afraid to use it.

Except, when you try to have a proper girlie chat with her, you realize there is something missing. She doesn't want to curl up in her pj's with a bottle of pinot grigio and compare dating disasters. She keeps herself aloof, with one eye trained over your shoulder in case a good-looking man should walk in.

The last time I trusted a woman like Verity Metcalf, she walked away with my husband, and since then, I've been able to see past the glitz and the glamour and look into these women's eyes. They're dangerous, the Verity Metcalfs of this world, and they know it. It's just a shame it takes the rest of us too long to learn the lesson.

One thing's for sure: Whether or not Verity is responsible for her husband's death, I doubt she's really innocent or truthful underneath all her perfection.

Xander looks more and more pleased with himself every time he comes to visit, bringing bundles of news clippings, which I've now stopped reading. I can't look at one more picture of Verity with her eyes meeting the camera as the flashes pop in her overexposed face. I know what it is costing her to hold herself together like that, how inside she will be crumbling and weakening, how all that might be left of her is a ruin.

I think of my garden sometimes. Anna said that we had to tear it all down to rebuild it and make it better, and I have to believe that is right. Verity and I might appear as nothing more than rubble at this moment, but I am doing this for the best reasons. Out of this mess I am going to create something truly spectacular, something so much better than what we had.

The police have been to see me a few times about Verity. They go over and over the same questions, asking me to repeat stories about our lives so that it almost feels salacious. They ask me about the things we've done together, the promises we made, the connection we shared. They can't understand why V's tone was so friendly in the e-mails she sent, and they go through them line by line, asking me to show them where she is talking in our secret code. Why do you think she didn't tell any-one about your contact, they ask again and again, and I tell them it is because we are in love.

Mainly though they want to know why she rang me on the night of the murder and why, when the police arrived, she was in my arms while Angus lay dying on the floor at our feet. Don't protect her, Mike, they say, sounding like Xander, she's not worth it.

Sometimes, after these interviews, I feel guilty, not because she didn't do all those things but because I could never have imagined a moment in which I wasn't laying down my life to protect V's. But I'm starting to see that is a very simplistic way of thinking. My life belongs to V as hers does to me. We do not exist without each other and as such we can't be parted, we can't go off on different paths. We have to stay together, whatever that means and whatever it takes to get us there.

It's odd to think I'm only down the road from home. Clapham to Wandsworth prison is only a couple of Tube stops, a brisk half-hour walk. I can't see anything other than sky from my small, high window, black birds circling like vultures in the gray clouds. But still I can trace the route between here and home, walking the streets so thoroughly in my mind, I can almost feel that wonderful ache in my legs when I stop. There is nowhere near enough exercise given to us in here. No wonder the men all scream and shout and spit and swear. Our bodies are useless, leaving only our minds to puff and pant along. I spend hours each day exercising in my cell, even though Fat Terry says he'll deck me if I don't shut the fuck up. But we both know he won't, or more accurately he can't. That tub-of-lard wouldn't stand a chance against my taut muscles and he knows it. I don't even bother to answer him as I dip toward the floor on my hundredth push-up or exhale my breath against the pain of razor-fast sit-ups. I cannot let my body wilt and falter. I have to look good in court for V and I have to be strong enough to save us both.

V said we had a bright future and because of that I always imagine us bathed in golden sunshine. She wanted us to work hard and earn lots of money so we could kick back and relax later on. What is the point, she used to say, of working three-quarters hard all your life and dying of a heart attack the day after you retire, when you can push yourself when you're young and fit and have fun, then retire early and have even more. I wonder how what is happening now fits into her plans and I wonder if we will still have enough money to live the life she dreamed of when I get out. I don't want to have to ever use a penny of Angus's money and I doubt she would either. Thoughts like this can keep me awake at night as I spin through scenarios that see me searching for a job as I approach forty, a blackened criminal record hanging over my head.

Xander says I'm not allowed to write to her or try to contact her in any way. He says it would be very bad for my case if I so much as ask to do so and he's made me promise not to. Instead I talk to V all the time in my head. I know she's still angry with me for telling Angus in the way I did and she's right to be. If I'd just waited a bit longer and let her handle it she would have known how to let him down gently and he wouldn't have gotten so angry. He wouldn't have drunk too much or attacked me and he wouldn't have made it necessary for me to punch him so hard.

Xander calls this self-defense and he says I must not forget the facts: I was woken from sleeping, Angus was threatening and intimidating, he threw the first punch, I tried to reason with him, I never wanted to hurt him. Say it to yourself every night before you go to sleep, Xander says, remind yourself that you acted in self-defense.

I go over and over the conversation V and I had in Angus's house the night before the incident. How I said I wished Angus didn't exist and how she told me she wished things had worked out between us. But how she also told me to go home and wait, how she needed to be the one to tell Angus. How she was not just giving me what I wanted but also protecting me. She knows me so well she knew I would get angry. I see now that she was trying to save me from myself and I didn't listen to her. If only I had just understood and left when Angus said she was ill, then by now they would be on the way to a divorce and V and I would be living together at home.

That thought affects me physically. It climbs inside me and burrows into my gut like a parasite, so I have to roll onto my side and clutch my stomach. Because we were so close, we were within touching distance of all we had ever wanted, and I had to ruin it.

But I am well practiced in ruining things. If I am feeling weak my mind sometimes pounces, dragging me backward through the detritus of my life. I scramble and scrap, clawing my way back up the hill, but on the way down it treats me to some fine views. Carly of course is near the top, but if I slither farther I can watch myself opening the door to those social workers a thousand times, the film scratched and grainy against the pitted inside of my skull. I see myself standing back; I feel the will to protect my mother drain out of me.

She used to come and see me for the first few years I was in care. Controlled visits they were called and they all took place in a room in the home, which was shut off from the rest of the house. It was painted a sickly yellow and had peeling stencils of rabbits and bears on the wall. There was a sad plastic tub of toys in one corner and a worn purple sofa running along one wall, under a shelf of books. None of the books ever changed places, their spines sagging under the weight of neglect.

She was usually sober, although she pretty much always stank of booze and fags, mixed with a lavender scent that she bought from the market and thought masked the poison that constantly oozed out of her pores. She cried quite a bit and her makeup would clump and run and make me feel sick. Her clothes were dirty in that way where you can see it is layered and ingrained and she smelled disgusting, a mixture of mud and fish and decay, which caught you in the back of the throat. She apologized a lot, her eyes darting over my face, as if I was meant to know how to respond. She told me about where she was staying and said soon I'd be able to come back and live with her, even though we both knew it wasn't going to happen. Or at least I knew, maybe she deluded herself right up till the end. She asked what I'd been up to and I shrugged and told her nothing.

She came a few times to Elaine and Barry's, sitting nervously in their front room while Elaine bustled with tea and biscuits. Her hand shook when she raised the mug to her lips and there was lipstick on her teeth, which didn't wash away when she drank. I could hardly believe it when I saw that. My mother, I realized, was the type of woman who wasn't even lucky enough to count on tea washing away her embarrassingly applied lipstick. It felt, as I sat on Elaine's green couch, like almost the worst of all her sins against me. It felt unforgivable. It felt cruel and vindictive. It felt like a summation of everything that was wrong about her.

I have decided to grant Elaine's application to visit me because sometimes I surprise myself with my need to see her. Maybe it's nothing more than sentiment for me to look back fondly on those evenings with them as Fat Terry's TV drones in the corner, rehashing Christmas songs in a desperate attempt to make us buy trash, in between terrible shows where inarticulate people shout at each other about who has fathered their baby. Elaine and Barry love Christmas and I spent nine very happy ones in their home. I wonder if this Christmas will be better or worse than the last one and then I can't believe it's only been a year since all that. How sometimes life can drag and turn and other times it speeds and shunts, propelling you forward however hard you want to stay back. About this time last year I was fucking Carly and my life.

Xander told me today that V has been formally charged with accessory to murder, although she's been granted bail. She will have to wear an electronic tag around her delicate ankle and report to a police station once a day.

"The things you've both said just don't add up," he told me. "The tone of the e-mails she sent you were too affectionate for you to have been threatening her and she never reported any of your so-called harassment to the police. She didn't tell anyone she knew, including Angus, about the times you met each other. She's now saying you assaulted her the night before the murder, but she didn't call the police or mention it until recently. And then of course there's that phone call she made to you on the night of the murder and the fact that she was in your arms when the police found you. And you keep going on about how in love with each other you are, which just makes the police think you're protecting her. None of it looks great for her, which is no bad thing for us."

I presume V will spend Christmas at Steeple House, but I wonder if Suzi will have gone all out as she usually does. I wonder if they've decked the tree and if there are lavish presents beneath it. I wonder if the turkey is ordered from the butcher, the cake made, the mince pies browning. I wonder if they're lighting candles and opening the door to carolers. I wonder if they'll turn up for the Christmas Eve service at the chapel.

Xander said that he's been told to expect a trial date for early January. In all likelihood it's going to take place at the Old Bailey because of the nature of the case and the public interest. And as he assured me, we will be tried together, sitting for the duration within touching distance of each other at the back of the courtroom.

He knows V's barrister, Petra Gardner, and says she's formidable. I asked if we're on the same side, V and I, and he laughed and said no, not really. It made me feel odd, him saying that. It was nearly enough to make me tell him to stop, but I have to keep remembering how this really will be a new beginning for us. I have to hold on to the fact that we are not fighting each other and ultimately both want the same thing. We both need to look to the future.

Elaine and my mother arrived on the same day. Elaine in person and my mother courtesy of the *Daily Mirror*. I folded my mother in half and laid her on my bunk, but she stayed in my head as I walked down the steps toward the visiting room and Elaine. My mother was alive and the thought gave me an unexpected rush of joy that pricked at my heart and lifted me along.

Elaine had lost weight and her winter coat hung off her frame as she walked between the tables toward me.

"Oh Mikey," she said, reaching over for my hands. "My poor boy, what have you done?"

The shock of her kindness made me start. "I'm sorry, Elaine."

"I just don't understand. What happened?" Her kindly face fell and swayed beneath the weight of it all.

"It was an accident. He came to the house in the middle of the night and attacked me and I punched him in self-defense." Xander had schooled me so well I couldn't remember anymore what was really true and what was necessary truth, as Xander called it.

"And now Verity's been arrested too. It doesn't make any sense." Elaine's eyes were begging me to tell her something palatable, something she could take home to Barry like a present.

"Verity was going to leave him to be with me."

"Oh, Mike. But she says you assaulted her, that you'd been hassling her."

"It's very complicated."

"But were you two having an affair?"

"Not an affair exactly. It was more like it never stopped between us. We'd met a few times and talked about her leaving Angus. She felt very guilty about it all."

Elaine's eyes were small like a mouse's, but she kept them on me. "If that's true then why is she saying all that stuff about you forcing your way into her house and turning up outside her work?"

I was arrested for the assault last week, a technicality really considering I am already in prison. When Xander told me what was going to happen I think I got a bit angry and shouted, although it's hazy in my mind. He said it wasn't ideal and asked if I could be sure I hadn't assaulted V, which was a preposterous question. Then he asked why I thought she might be saying I had. I couldn't answer him at the time, but I can now. I've worked it out. It's another part of the Crave. My information got her arrested and so she's throwing it back at me. She's angry because she doesn't yet understand what I'm doing, but really we're just playing, we don't mean any of this, it will all pass as everything does.

"Mike," Elaine said. "Did she ask you to hurt Angus?"

"It's hard to explain."

Elaine lowered her voice. "Do you think it's possible you have a different perception than Verity of what happened?"

"No," I said, remembering how our lips had met, her gasp of desire, "no, absolutely not."

"I just can't make sense of it," Elaine said again. "Verity was always such a lovely girl. I was so fond of her." Elaine squinted at me. "Your barrister asked me lots of questions about your relationship. I don't believe you planned this together."

I looked down and felt my heat rise. I couldn't think of a way of explaining it to Elaine. "It wasn't like that. It's not a simple case."

They say visiting time lasts for two hours but I often hear inmates shouting from their cells about how they only get an hour and a half and their (insert a female name here) has had to travel seven hours to visit them. Elaine was my first visitor so I have no idea if the hour and a half we spent together was normal or not, but I could have done with the time being halved. She gave up in the end trying to ask me about the case and began one of her polite conversations I'd heard her have too many times with neighbors and shopkeepers. I couldn't bear that and almost wished we could go back to talking about what I'd done. It felt like I was falling away from her eyes, as if the more she looked at me the less she could see me, so all she could think to say was how awful the fog was and what did they serve for Christmas dinner in here.

As soon as Elaine left I wished I'd been brave enough to tell her what I really thought: V had married Angus because she believed herself to be in love with him because of the pain I'd caused her with Carly. She thought I didn't love her anymore and made herself believe she was in love with Angus. It is even possible that she still doubts my love, which would explain why she is accusing me of assault: because she can't believe I meant it when I kissed her. She didn't want Angus dead, but she didn't want to remain married to him and she needed my help to achieve this, help she asked for in a way only I would be able to interpret.

If only I could write to V or speak to her just once on the phone. I want to soothe her mind and lay my reassurances all over her fears. I know V inside out and I know how she works and what she thinks. She isn't as strong as she likes to imply and she isn't particularly sure of herself. I can't bear to think of her out in the world by herself without me, and if that means enclosing her in a concrete box for a few years, then that is the kindest thing to do. We will both be in our protective cells, and that is a comforting thought. Once the trial is over Xander says we will be allowed to write to each other and I plan to do so every day, throwing my love at her until she realizes I absolutely do mean it. I will remind her how she once told Suzi she found the idea of writing letters romantic. We will have years of letters, letters we can tie together with a ribbon and keep forever.

After I got back from seeing Elaine I read the article about my mother and my first thought was to set it on fire, but in the end I just threw it away. My mother, Michelle Hayes, forty-eight, now lives in Bermondsey with Darren Hatton, forty-one, and their nine-year-old daughter, Kimberley. She has "been saved." She regrets my upbringing, but I was a very difficult child. She thinks Verity looks like a nasty piece of work. I'm not a murderer, not her son, no. I must have been persuaded to do it somehow, there's no way she'll ever believe otherwise.

A photograph accompanied the article but I didn't see any point in keeping it either because I don't know anybody in it. I stared at it for a long time before I threw it away, but I can't even be sure if the woman in the picture was really my mother. She was sitting on a beige leather sofa in front of a window with a view of a garden, in a room with large purple flowers on the wall bedecked with photographs in frames that spelled the word *love* or *family*. The floor was carpeted and you could see the corner of a television and a painting on the wall. She had her arm around a podgy little girl with long brown hair, wearing a Justin Bieber T-shirt. Darren was sitting on the other side of the girl with his arm against my mother's shoulders. Darren might have always been on the large side, but my mother had definitely put on weight. You could see a roll of flab that had been exposed by her jeans, highlighted by the pink of her T-shirt. Her hair was now dyed a soft blond and her makeup looked professional, probably done for the paper. I looked at her hands cupped around Kimberley and I saw her nails were neatly filed and painted a pink that matched her T-shirt. She had a few rings on her fingers and a bracelet around her wrist. I wondered if they were all naturally mournful people or if the photographer had told them to look sad; the latter I suspect.

Even though she is now in the bin I find myself hoping that in reality she smiles more. That she has found the happiness she proclaims. Wouldn't it be good for us both to have finally found love, to have finally found what we were unable to give to each other.

Christmas is a dismal affair in prison. There is something about seeing a line of men wearing colored paper hats, queuing with their plastic trays for a meal you know will taste of sawdust, that makes you want to jump out of a window. And I know I wasn't the only one to feel that way. The day had a febrile atmosphere to it, as if the tension existed in electronic waves that zoomed through the air. Men threw punches and shouted, the guards drew their weapons, a small man jumped on the metal netting between the floors and rolled around, someone got a snooker pole wrapped around his head and the blood wasn't cleaned up properly. Terry spent the day with his hand down his trousers watching telly and I lay on my bunk and thought of V.

"You never meet birds like that, do you," Terry said toward the end of the night when our cell was fogged with twisted desire.

I leaned over my bunk and looked at the woman he was pointing at on the telly. She was shouting at someone, her Barbie body encased in a shimmering, sparkling suit that loved her like a second skin. Impossible, Kaitlyn-like heels were on her feet and her breasts were as round and large as two watermelons. Her hair was platinum blond and her face looked painted on, like a modern-day geisha, her ballooning lips a bright, shocking red, her eyes ringed in thick, smoky black. Her skin was the color of yogurt and I wasn't sure she was human.

"Bet she's fucking filthy an' all," Terry said, slapping his hands together and rubbing them with ever increasing motion. "God, I tell you, if I got my hands on her, she wouldn't know what'd hit her. I'd give her a right good seeing to, I would, and she'd fucking love it. Be begging for more." He laughed and it lapsed into his deep smoker's cough.

"Bet you had birds like that flocking 'round you with your fucking loads'a money," he said, but I had rolled onto my back. "Go on, give us a Chrissie present and tell us about them." I lay still. If it came to it I'd be happy to beat Terry to a sorry version of himself, but I didn't want to. "Fucking killjoy," he said beneath me.

I read somewhere that the reason humans are so tragic is because we are only one half of a whole and most of us spend all our lives desperately searching for that missing person to make us complete. But because the universe finds it amusing to watch us suffer, most of us never meet this elusive other half because they have been born on the other side of the world. But you keep searching, not even knowing what you're looking for, or even that you're searching, because that is your biological imperative. And then you start to panic, because you feel this massive gaping hole inside and you know you either have to fill it or die. Some turn to drink or drugs or gambling or TV, anything really to make them forget they are hurtling through life on a lonely, never-ending path to death. Others take a more conventional route and convince themselves that the person they always dismissed as being too boring/fat/ugly/inadequate/bad in bed/smelly/violent/psychotic is actually "the one." The one person in this world who will stop them slitting their wrists next New Year's Eve. But of course they're not, so they're left with a life of recriminations and regrets, which ends up in the same place as if they'd missed out the middle section and gone straight to the drugs, drink, or TV. There is no perfect "one" out there, you hear people say, because for the large majority that is the truth. Your perfection is living on the edge of a mountain in Outer Mongolia and your paths are never going to cross.

Except that isn't true of V and me. We found each other. And not just that, it wasn't even hard. We met in the way all those other not quite right people meet, except we didn't have to ignore the nagging doubt in the dusty basement of our minds. We just were, are, right. We fit together in every way and there is nothing anyone can do to change that. You could send us to America and fry us in the electric chair and still this would be our truth. Still nothing could change this fact.

Today was the first day of the trial. I was taken by police van to the back of the Old Bailey, where I was escorted inside with my hands locked in front of me and a blanket over my head. I felt the crowd around us and saw the flashbulbs bounce off the rain-slicked pavement. A woman shouted, "Repent or die," and I presume it was meant for me. Once inside, the blanket and handcuffs were removed and I was led through what felt like miles of labyrinthine corridors that seemed like they were underground. We stopped at the bottom of a flight of stairs, at the top of which was a shut door. The guard went in front of me and I followed. It took me a minute to realize we had made it into the courtroom as we walked up and through the door. The light was bright and there was a cacophony of noise from all the people who were there. But I soon saw that I was in the dock, as Xander had told me I would be, a long box that ran across the back of the courtroom. He had also told me time and time again that because V and I were being tried together she would sit in the dock with me, which meant we would be sharing not just the emotion of the room but even the physicality of it. It was a delicious thought that had kept me awake at night, as if the whole of the British legal system had been designed for this moment alone.

The guard indicated for me to sit, so I did and he sat down next to me. Xander turned from his table at the front and nodded at me, his absurd wig bobbing into his eyes. I knew that V was somewhere in the building, probably not even that far away. I was about to see her and at that moment I would have given my freedom for just one glimpse.

She arrived a few minutes later via a different door, which meant she had to walk through the body of the courtroom to reach our box. I felt a surge from the people in the room, as if everyone was as drawn to her as I was. A female guard ushered her into our space, but at the other end of the dock, sitting next to her as my guard had done, as if they knew it would be impossible for us to be alone and not touch in such a confined space. V was carrying a cardboard cup that brought with it the scent of coffee; I knew it would contain a skinny latte, we'd drunk enough of those together over the years and, for some reason, this memory was almost worse than all the others. It seemed so carefree and innocent compared to where we were now and I couldn't understand why it was proving so difficult to return to. I looked over at V, desperate for her to even glance over for a second, but she refused to return my stare, her pursed lips sipping from the white plastic lid.

She was dressed in a black skirt and jacket, with a white shirt underneath. Her hair was tied into a low ponytail and she didn't look like she was wearing makeup. But the eagle was around her neck, which made me relax slightly. She kept her eyes focused in front of her and her expression neutral, but I could see the twitch at the corner of her mouth and the drag in her cheeks. I was worried by how pale she was, almost Kaitlyn-color, and she had lost a substantial amount of weight so she was verging on being too thin.

"Don't do anything stupid" had been Xander's last words to me. "You have to seem like the sane, stable one. You can be upset, you can fight your corner, but do not do anything to arouse interest. It is imperative we direct the attention toward Verity."

I looked at the jury as they filed in, but they were no different from a group of people you might see in a train carriage or walking down the street. They ranged in age, gender, ethnicity, weight, height. They all looked at me and then around me to get a glimpse of V, then away again quickly. For all I knew one of them could have enjoyed drowning kittens in their spare time, or going to church, or swimming. None of them looked as intelligent as V and me, and it seemed absurd that they should be deciding our futures. Although I had to check that thought. We were deciding our futures. We had engineered this. We were playing the game and they were just coming along for the ride.

There would be people I knew in the rows in front of us but they felt like a bogeyman, as if by not looking at them I could somehow make them go away. When I lived with my mother there were monsters only I could see in the corner of my room, hidden by the cobwebs and filth that clung to our walls. I came to an agreement with those monsters. If I agreed never to look straight at them, they agreed not to eat me. It lessened the terror a bit.

I looked anyway. Elaine and Barry were seated in the rows in front of me and they both smiled in a low, depressing way. Colin and Suzi were in front of V, both shrunken and thinned, like pruned trees. Suzi was leaning across Colin to talk to Angus's brother and, next to him, were Angus's parents, all of whom I remembered from the wedding.

It struck me then that this was in fact like a wedding, bride's family on one side, groom's on the other. And that made me feel better. I looked again at V but she was still staring straight ahead. I wished I could tell her that this was our conjoining, our true beginning, the end of our ultimate Crave but the start of something more wonderful. A normal, bog-standard wedding was never going to be right for us. This was a much better way of cementing our union.

"All rise for Justice Smithson," said a loud voice, and the room moved as an elderly man in a flowing red robe with a graying powdered wig on his head climbed the steps to the bench. Xander had been very pleased by Justice Smithson, "old school," he'd called him, which was apparently a good thing. When Justice Smithson sat we all copied him and he looked down on us like he enjoyed his job. His eyes rested on me and then I followed them to V.

Y

There is so much empty time in court, so many hours pass in which nothing is really said or established. I find myself looking at the dust that collects between the glass and the wood of the enclosure they have put V and me into. I try not to look over at her too much and she never looks at me. But there are moments when something is said and I feel the pull between us like a wire, feel us reaching and straining for each other.

People stand, people sit, the judge nods and the three barristers speak to the jury. Xander has warned me that while it seems like V and I are on the same side, facing off against the prosecution, that isn't really true. V's barrister, Petra, will want to lay all the blame at my door, as it's the only way to get V off completely, while Xander needs to apportion the blame between us equally to reduce my sentence. The prosecution is going to try to slay us both, as the best result would be if we are both guilty of murder.

All the different scenarios make me feel dizzy and I find it hard to concentrate when the prosecutor speaks because everything she says is so absurd. Everything points to a plot V and I supposedly concocted to kill Angus so V could inherit his money and we could live happily ever after. Xander says she has made a strategic mistake as her story is too far-fetched. He's told me not to worry about her and so I don't; I allow my mind to wander when she speaks and shut down my thoughts so that I can keep them sharp for the important moments.

The jury frequently looks over to V and me; I can feel their eyes on us and I know they have no idea what to think because they are such ordinary people, puffed out by life. The charges seem so large: murder for me and accessory to murder for V. And I know the jury is so far from being able to make these sorts of decisions about us. They seem like nothing more than children being told bedtime stories when Xander and Petra speak to them, and I am not sure they even listen to the details. I see them yawn and rub their eyes sometimes; one of the young men looked hungover a few days ago.

And sometimes I hardly blame them because so many stories have been told in here that it is hard to grab hold of what they mean. Sometimes even the witnesses change their mind halfway through as the questions switch between Xander and Petra. Angus's brother, Frederick, told us that they had all liked Verity and had never seen Angus so happy. But he also said that sometimes it had seemed too much, that maybe you could say he was almost under her spell, that it was a lot of money to leave to someone you had known for such a short time.

I hate the thought of V having Angus's money. I think we should burn it. I think we should fill his stupid show-off house with banknotes and set fire to it, watch it dissolve into the air like the nothing it is.

We had to listen to the man all the papers have been quoting; he was called Gordon Sage and he was paraded in front of us to speak about the things he and V had done together when they were eighteen.

"I must confess I found her scarily sexual," he said, his piggy eyes staring out of his fat, rugged face like they could still see her naked body. "She had this thing for doing it outside." He licked his lips and I felt something rise through me, so I was worried I was going to be sick on my shoes and fill the courtroom with the acrid stench of bile.

I looked over at V but she had shut her eyes and was leaning her forehead against her hand. I turned my attention back to Gordon Sage and saw his fat fingers curving around the wood of the witness box. I imagined them inside V. "But then one day she got a friend to ring and say it was over, no explanation or anything. In fact we never spoke again."

I imagined V screaming underneath his corpulent body and I knew then why she needed me to always save her from men like that. All the Gordon Sages I had peeled off of her in nightclubs, all the times I had stopped them from pawing her body and breathing on her neck, little droplets of spittle landing on her skin, so she would be tainted by their DNA. I would pry his fat fingers off one by one, bending them so far back each one would break and he would end up sniveling on the floor, snot dribbling from his nose.

Xander liked Gordon, or at least what he brought, as he put it. "They tried to call some American woman you worked with over there," he said when we met beneath the courtroom after that day. "I'm presuming it was that girl you slept with. But she's refused to come and the judge said he didn't think it was relevant anyway. He actually said that he wasn't interested in your sexual adventures." He laughed. "I thought Petra was going to burst when he said that. Good old Smithson, never disappoints." I couldn't really understand what he meant, but I didn't care, because the thought of V having to sit in the same room as Carly made my skin itch.

On other days my brain has felt overused, as if words are turning in my head and banging against the side of my brain, chipping my skull so that fragments of bone are imbedding themselves in places they shouldn't be. I wonder now if the woman who called herself Mrs. Lasscles really was my old headmistress, because nothing about her felt familiar. She could have gleaned a lot of what she told the court from any newspaper, like how my clothes were often dirty and I was small and thin for my age. But she also spoke about things I find hard to place, like my "violent temper," as she put it. She said I was always starting fights and that lots of the parents complained about me. She said the other children were frightened of me, even some of the staff. Sometimes I had to be restrained, one teacher carrying my legs and one my arms, to remove me from classrooms.

Her words scratch at my head and at times I have thought I am going to remember something, but it always remains tantalizingly just beyond my reach. She didn't blame me, she said, trying to catch my eye as she spoke. They knew there was trouble at home, but however many times they questioned me I never admitted to anything, always saying everything was fine, even when it so obviously wasn't. They were in contact with social services, but they hadn't known how bad it was. Naughty children are never anything more than bad parents, she said, her understanding radiating off her like a bloody halo.

But then there are others, like Sarah Cross, who felt like being reunited with an old friend. She smiled at me when she stepped onto the stand and I remembered how warm she had always been, how she'd give you a hug even when she wasn't meant to or sneak you an extra biscuit. She was rounder than she'd been when I'd known her and she had heavy bags under her eyes and a nasty cough that attacked her sometimes as she spoke.

"You would be hard put to find a worse case of neglect," she said, "although undoubtedly worse things do happen to lots of children. He wasn't sexually abused, which is always a blessing, but he hadn't been provided with basic care, which certainly left physical and mental damage." On the day I let them into the flat I was ten years old and weighed seventy pounds. I was wearing clothes for a six-year-old. Lots of my teeth were decayed and I was infested with lice.

I could feel V reaching out to me as Sarah spoke, as if she wanted to lean over and take my hand. But I kept my head down because I don't want V to think of me like that. I have told her everything, but I don't want her to hear it from someone else, I don't want the knowledge to be out in the open. It taints me somehow, taints me with the infection of that time.

The court was shown photos of the flat, which I could only bear to look at peripherally. Everyone in the room was able to see the piled-up plates and overflowing ashtrays, the black mold on the walls, the encrusted toilet, the black sink, and the bath so filled with rubbish it was unusable. The pictures weren't lying, but what they didn't show was how the whole flat smelled of rot and decay, how it caught in the back of your throat and made your eyes water. I coughed because it was as if the pictures had released the stench, as if it had found its way back to me so that sitting in court I could taste the yeasty, sour smell of my childhood home that, toward the end, made me think about new life-forms. Sometimes I wonder if the real reason I opened the door to social services that day was not because I wanted to save myself but because I thought something was actually going to materialize out of the atmosphere, something worse than was already there.

As I looked I had to tuck my hands under my armpits, a trick I learned when I lived with my mother, as if they had once again become raw and chapped from how cold the water was when I tried to wash a plate so I could eat off it, using a blackened sponge and no dish liquid. I felt again the rush of sweat break on my forehead as I heaved over the rotten toilet, never learning the lesson not to eat food that had grown white fur. My mouth dried at the memory of days-old pizza stuck to the top of the box, or at least the remnants of toppings.

I noticed an older woman in the jury dabbing at her eyes when they were shown pictures of my bedroom, which made me want to stand up and roar and cover V's eyes with my hands. I wanted to spare her the sight of the curtainless window, like a large bruised eye, the mattress as thin as paper, and the filthy duvet. A shiver started deep in my body, an involuntary memory of all those nights when a freezing wind passed over my head and the cold seeped into my marrow so it felt like I would never be warm again.

But those photos missed something else, something rare but nevertheless true: The times it was just Mum and me on the sofa, snuggled under a blanket with the telly on. When she'd used her money for food rather than vodka so my belly had stopped hurting. Before the fourth can, when she was still the right side of lucid.

"It's going to be okay, Mikey," she'd say, drawing me into her. "I just need to get through this and then we'll start again." I would nestle into her sweaty, threadbare bathrobe and wish she was telling the truth. Wish that I hadn't reached an age when I knew that people could lie to themselves as much as to others.

When Louise gave her evidence I realized that she is a different sort of liar than my mother, a worse sort. There are people out there who see nothing wrong in lying at all. There are people out there who inhabit lies, who let them soak in and devour them. I will never be one of those people, but at the same time I am not sure the jury would understand the bald truth of what happened between V and me. I look over at them and their flat, bland faces and I know they are so disappointingly ordinary. There is no way they could ever understand the space that V and I occupy, no way they could understand our truth.

"None of our friends ever liked Mike," Louise said. "We all tried for Verity's sake, but there was no getting through to him. It was almost impossible to engage him in conversation. He would come out with us, but he always stuck by Verity's side, staring at her and whispering in her ear. And he didn't have any friends of his own, so he was always there and he didn't like it if she went out without him. We found him creepy, the sort of person you didn't want to be left alone with."

"Yes, Verity did confide in me toward the end of her relationship, probably a year or so after Mike went to New York. The things she told me were quite frankly worrying. We all told her it was unhealthy, but she seemed enthralled by him, if that's the right word."

"I think it is fair to say she was scared of him, yes. But also, some of us worried she was a bit obsessed with him."

"Angus was so much better suited to Verity. We all breathed a massive sigh of relief when she met him. It was like getting the old Verity back, fun and carefree, not always looking over her shoulder."

"Mike seemed very agitated at the wedding, almost at times as if he wasn't sure where he was. I bumped into him outside the marquee after the speeches and he was in quite a state—he was bent over, as if he couldn't catch his breath. I asked him if he was all right, but he didn't answer. I tried to rub his back a bit, like you do when someone's sick, but he didn't move, so I asked him if he was still in love with Verity. He stood up at that and pushed me so hard I fell over. Then he stood over me and he looked so furious that I really thought he was going to hit me or kick me or something, but he just walked away."

When Xander stood I could almost believe he was holding a gun as he walked to the witness box. He didn't preamble, he just came straight out with it. "You propositioned Mr. Hayes for sex on the night of the wedding, didn't you?"

Louise's eyes widened. "No," she said, "absolutely not."

"You followed him outside when he went to get some fresh air and told him you'd always fancied him and that your husband, James"—Xander looked at his papers, although I knew it was only for effect—"fucks like a rabbit." There were titters from the jury and Louise turned the color of freshly fallen snow. I wondered if James was sitting somewhere in front of me.

But she recovered her composure and looked straight at me. "Michael Hayes is a fantasist," she said. "I would never do anything like that. And, for the record, I have never fancied him."

"But what reason would Mr. Hayes have for pushing you? He says he removed your hands from his groin and, because you were so drunk, you fell over."

Louise opened her mouth and she looked momentarily like a fish. "That is not true." But her tone had weakened.

"He says you were very angry," Xander continued. "You shouted expletives after him when he walked away. Angry enough to come here and lie about him in court?"

"No," Louise said. "That's not how it happened at all."

"No further questions, My Lord." Xander returned to his table with a spring in his step. I think he would have winked at me if he thought he could get away with it.

Recently a confusion has settled over me, which is blanketing my thoughts. Sitting in the courtroom day after day has made me understand that I must sculpt my story in the best way for the right outcome. I have an idea, but the idea also feels wrong. Is lying sometimes the best policy? Is it possible to want the best for someone and yet act in a way that seems the opposite?

Elaine once told me that writing things down helps to simplify problems. List the pros on one side and the cons on the other, she advised, although at the time we were only talking about exams. And it does undeniably help; when I read our story, mine and V's, over and over it calms me. I have always thought that numbers were my friend, but maybe words are as well?

Before I go to sleep each night I hear Xander saying how I don't want V out in the world having fun while I rot away in here. He is of course wrong, as he is about most things, but the things he is wrong about usually also contain an element of truth. What he is right about is that V and I must continue along the same path, our journeys must be conjoined. I think he imagines I want her incarcerated out of some sick feeling of vengeance or even to keep her away from the world, neither of which is true. I don't doubt V's loyalty to me and I don't think she would be capable of being out in the world having fun without me. I think in fact she would barely be able to function. Which is the reason that I am coming to believe properly in Xander's strategy. V would be lost without me, she wouldn't know what to do with herself, she would be stranded and alone. It has always been my job to keep her safe, and if I am in here, then she must be in the safest place for her.

Every day in court she looks thinner and weaker, which worries me terribly but also makes me feel like she can't be left alone for years without me. I know she must be pining for me and worrying about me, her mind spinning a future she can't imagine. I've noticed she never arrives with a coffee anymore and her skin has taken on a yellowish pallor; even her hair looks slightly unwashed and she picks at the skin at the side of her nails. She looks like she is falling apart and I know some people would think that is because of the strain of the trial, but I know it is the strain of being without me and worrying about my future. If we accept our fate together and continue along the same path then she will get better; she will put some weight on her bones and a bloom back in her cheeks, her hair will shine again, and her mouth will turn upward into a smile. I know she just needs certainty, my lovely girl, and that the certainty will bring with it understanding and peace of mind.

Elaine and Suzi shared a day in court, which seemed strangely right. Suzi went first, dressed in a pale gray suit that was almost the same color as her skin. She could barely keep still and her hands worried in her lap for the whole time she was there, her eyes filling with tears every time she looked over at V.

"We welcomed Mike into our lives," she was saying to Petra by the time I tuned in. "He was a sweet boy, but it was easy to see he was very troubled. There was always something about him that Colin and I never entirely trusted."

"Can you elaborate?"

Suzi has lost so much weight her skin now hangs off her face, making her look like an old lizard. I don't think we will be able to see her when all this is over.

"There was nothing specific. It was more just a feeling that he was too in love with Verity. We excused it because of his upbringing, but it often made us uneasy."

"Can you give an example of something that made you uneasy?"

"I know it sounds silly, but even the way he looked at her concerned us, as if he were looking into her rather than at her, if that makes sense. And he never took his eyes off her. You know how you're aware if you're staring at someone, you look away because you feel embarrassed. But Mike never looked away. He never even seemed to realize how uncomfortable it made Colin and I. And he was always in contact with her, always had to know where she was and what she was doing. And he didn't really have any friends, so everything they did was because of her. She felt very responsible for him and his happiness, and it worried Colin and me that she should take something like that on at such a young age."

"Did you talk to Verity about this?"

"Oh yes, toward the end of their relationship especially, as it made her extremely upset. She was terrified of hurting him. She said it wasn't like ending things with a normal person because his rejection by his mother had made him vulnerable."

I had to turn my head to V at that point, but she only gave me her taut profile. She was sitting very still with her eyes on her lap, but I saw the tension in her cheek, which I knew was how she kept herself from crying. And suddenly this whole thing seemed even more absurd than it already did. Here we are, two people who love each other, being separated by a stupid mistake that could have happened to anyone.

I turned back and Suzi was talking again, so I realized I must have missed Petra's question. "Yes, we knew she had started seeing Angus. She had planned to tell Mike when he came back from New York at Christmas and the stress made her quite ill."

202

It was possible that Suzi had always hated me, I thought then. It was possible that it had all been a sham, all those shared times, all the dinners and conversations. It was possible that nothing she said was real.

"Verity shouldn't have used Mike's infidelity as an excuse for ending the relationship," Suzi was saying and I had missed another question, which made me feel slightly light-headed. "She knows that. But I would have probably done the same."

"And how did Mr. Hayes take the split?"

"Very badly. Verity had to lock herself in her room the night she told him because of his persistent attempts to speak to her. He slept outside her door on the floor and the next morning refused to move. In the end, Colin and I had to basically tell him to leave."

"Where did he go?" Petra asked.

"Back to their flat in London. Although he called all day every day. It was ghastly. Verity didn't answer her phone at all and so he rang the landline, day and night. She got in such a state that in the end Angus drove down and took her away to a hotel for New Year's so she could get a bit of peace."

I thought I might fall forward off my chair, but I recovered myself. Suzi was just lying. Everyone was lying apart from me and V.

"One day Mike sent so many flowers they filled a van. When the woman unloaded them she said she'd never seen anything like it. I had to donate them to the church and hospital." Suzi swallowed. "That was typical Mike, always going overboard."

"Were you ever worried for your daughter's safety?" Petra asked, removing her glasses as she spoke.

As I sat there waiting for her answer, I realized Suzi has never been in love. You just have to listen to Liam Gallagher to realize that people like V and I are going to live forever and Suzi and the rest of them are wrong simply because they don't know what it's like to really, truly love someone.

"Toward the end a bit, maybe," she said, and she couldn't help glancing over at me. I held her gaze without flinching, and she looked away almost immediately. I remembered what she'd looked like at the wedding, how puffed out and proud she had been. She had been so stupid to ever think that was it.

"When he first went back to New York after Christmas the contact was so incessant Verity had to change her phone number and she moved in with Angus, but her e-mail was harder to change because of work and he bombarded her daily with ridiculous e-mails. But then he stopped in February and we thought maybe things had calmed down. When Verity told him about the wedding, he even seemed happy for her. Of course, I never thought anything like this would happen." Suzi's voice caught on her last words.

"And how has Verity handled it all?" Petra asked.

Suzi's head dipped momentarily. "She's been amazing when you take into consideration what's happened to her. Her new husband, whom she loved very much, has been killed, then she's been hounded by the press and had to put up with all the terrible lies that have been written about her. And now this ridiculous trial. It's been awful to watch what she's gone through in these last few months, which should have been the happiest of her life."

"So, in your estimation, your daughter and Mr. Metcalf were happy and in love and Mr. Hayes has a delusional fixation that turned violent?"

"Objection," Xander said. "Ms. Gardner is not a psychiatrist and cannot diagnose my client."

"Overruled," said Justice Smithson. He looked at Xander over the top of his glasses as he spoke, almost apologetically. "Mrs. Walton's observations of her daughter are pertinent here, although obviously the jury must take into account her relationship with the defendants."

Suzi looked over to the jury and I saw two pink spots had appeared high up on her cheeks. "Absolutely. You don't see my daughter when she is behind closed doors. We're not the sort of people to weep and wail in public, but I can assure you that she is as devastated as it's possible to be. I know Angus and Verity were happy and I know Michael is delusional." Suzi swallowed again, her eyes brimming with tears.

"In your mind she wouldn't have wanted anything bad to happen to Mr. Metcalf. Is it possible she could have asked for Mr. Hayes's help to remove him?"

"God no." Suzi's voice rose with each word. "She loved Angus so much. And Mike is the last person she would ask to help her with anything."

"Perhaps you could tell us your impressions of Mr. Metcalf," Petra continued. "What sort of man did he appear to you? Were you ever concerned about his treatment of your daughter?"

Suzi would have laughed if she was capable of such a sound at that moment. "No, the exact opposite. Angus was the most charming, happy, generous, funny man you could hope to meet. He was very in love with Verity and always treated her with nothing but respect and adoration. As a mother it was a pleasure to watch them together."

"So you don't think he would have gone to Mr. Hayes's house that night meaning to harm him?"

"No, but I'm not surprised they got into a fight. I've been on the receiving end of some of Michael's rants and they're not pleasant."

"Could you elaborate, please?" Petra said, and I knew they'd rehearsed this part.

Suzi clasped her hands together on the wooden ledge in front of the witness box. "As I said he rang the whole time after Verity finished the relationship and I ended up speaking to him quite a lot. He was very rude to me on a number of occasions. He called me a scheming whore once, when I told him that Verity had gone away for New Year's."

I heard an intake of breath from the jury, but I kept my eyes on my hands, my face burning.

Petra approached Suzi and put her hand on her arm. "Thank you very much, Mrs. Walton. We can all see how hard this has been for you. No further questions, My Lord."

Xander stood up slowly. He wasn't carrying any notes and he almost ambled over. "Mrs. Walton, let me second that thanks. This must be unbearably hard for you. I'm a father myself and I can't imagine what it must be like to see a child of yours go through all of this."

Suzi looked slightly startled. "No, it's horrible."

"Almost unbelievable."

"Well, yes."

He turned to the jury. "Verity is your only child I believe?"

"Yes." I could see the terror in Suzi's eyes.

"A longed-for only child. A child you have always idolized and adored."

"Of course we adore her," Suzi said.

"A child you've always wanted the best for. The best schools, the best clothes, the best opportunities." He looked at Suzi as he spoke.

"What parent doesn't?"

Xander looked over at me and I felt the jury's eyes follow him. "Oh, there are plenty of parents who don't want the best for their children. Plenty of children out there who don't get riding lessons and extra tuition and expensive holidays and fantastical Christmases." He paused. "I'm just wondering how far the best of everything extends?"

Petra stood up. "Objection, My Lord. What is the relevance?"

"Yes, get to the point," said Justice Smithson.

"Did you have an idea of the sort of person you'd have liked Verity to marry?" Xander asked.

"No."

"But you wanted the best of everything for her, so surely that must have extended to her friends, her lovers, her partners."

"Of course we always wanted her to be happy."

"You were very pleased about her marriage to Angus Metcalf, I take it?"

"Yes. He was a lovely man."

Xander smiled. "But he was more than a lovely man, wasn't he. He was rich and successful and could give Verity an amazing life."

I followed Suzi's eyes to V and saw she was sitting forward on her chair, her face white. "Yes, but that wasn't why—"

"Whereas Mr. Hayes is a more troubling prospect, with his background."

"No. And if you're going down that line, Mike is perfectly rich himself. And besides, Verity earns her own money, she's very well paid."

"Yes, but neither of them is in the league of Mr. Metcalf. Did you perhaps encourage Verity to leave Mr. Hayes for Mr. Metcalf?"

"Objection, My Lord," Petra shouted.

"I'm struggling to see the relevance, Mr. Jackson," Justice Smithson said.

Xander drew in a deep breath, making his chest puff out. "I'm not suggesting Mrs. Walton is lying," he said, pausing. "Just maybe that her adoration of her daughter and her obvious obsession with wanting the best for her might have colored her judgment of not just Mr. Hayes but also of Mrs. Metcalf's involvement in this case."

"Objection, My Lord," Petra shouted again. "There is no obsession in Mrs. Walton wanting the best for her daughter."

"Sustained," Justice Smithson said, although there was a slight smile on his lips.

"Sorry, My Lord," Xander said, bobbing at the bench. He turned back to Suzi. "What did you think about Verity asking Mr. Hayes to her wedding?"

Suzi looked over at V again, her eyes darting. "I didn't think it was a good idea."

"Did you argue about it?"

"Not exactly, no."

"But you told her your views."

"Yes."

"And she did it anyway."

"Yes." Suzi almost raised her hand. "But she did it for good reasons. Like I said before, she was always overly concerned that Mike was all right. She felt responsible for him because of his upbringing, which is ridiculous because it had nothing to do with her."

"But we do feel responsibility for those we love, don't we?" Xander said conversationally, turning to the jury as if he was making a good point at a party.

"I suppose so."

Xander left a beat of space before his next question. "Do you think your daughter was still in love with Mr. Hayes at the time of her marriage?" The line between V and I tightened again. I remembered our meeting on the street just before her wedding, her body ready to run, her eyes searching for me.

Suzi looked like she'd been slapped. "Absolutely not, no."

"But she cared about him enough to feel responsibility for his happiness."

"That's totally different. Verity is a kind, caring person."

Xander walked toward the jury. "Did you know about this game, the Crave, your daughter and Mr. Hayes played together?"

"No, of course not."

"What do you think about it?"

"I think it's strange, but they were young."

"Did it surprise you that Verity should play such a game?"

"I'm not in the habit of speculating about my daughter's sexuality." Suzi looked down and I thought she might cry.

"But, with that in mind, is it fair to say that you don't know your daughter as well as you think you do?"

Suzi looked back up, her eyes angry and hard. "No, of course it's not fair to say that. What you're talking about is different. It's not what matters."

Xander nodded. "If you say so, Mrs. Walton. Did Verity tell you that

Mike was back in touch with her? Did she talk to you about the e-mails or going for a drink with him?"

"No, but that's because she didn't want to worry us."

"Would you like to have known?"

"I'd like to have been able to help her."

"So when Verity came to spend the weekend with you, when Angus was away and after Mr. Hayes had been to meet her after work, she didn't mention anything about this to you or your husband?"

"No."

"And on the Monday after that weekend, when Mr. Hayes came to Verity's house and she claims he assaulted her. Did she contact you that night?"

"No," Suzi said, and her voice sounded shrunken.

Xander nodded. "Thank you, Mrs. Walton. No further questions."

We countered Suzi with Elaine after lunch, as Xander put it. He said the comparison would be brilliant. Naturally we all want to support the underdog, he said, but also our society is still riven along class lines. No one would support a posh, snobby woman with a cut-glass accent over a salt-of-the-earth, foster parent dressed in a secondhand coat. I didn't tell him that Elaine's coat was not secondhand, simply well worn, as I wasn't sure he would understand the concept.

Elaine almost stumbled into the witness box, her eyes blinking and her face creased in worry. She smiled over at me and nodded and every-one could see she would have blown me a kiss if she could have. She spoke in a quiet yet determined tone and, she turned and looked at the jury and Justice Smithson, as if wanting to include them and be polite.

"He was quite a handful when we got him," she said. "But I could see the sparkle in his eye and I knew it was just a question of chipping away a bit at the hard surface he'd had to build up to find the real Mike."

"And who would you say the real Mike is?" Xander asked.

Elaine looked over at me and I smiled at her because I wanted her to feel comfortable saying anything. "He's a lovely lad," she said. "He's always been a bit of a loner, but he's very clever and part of his anger when we got him, I think, was that all his intelligence was frustrated. You know, it took him a bit of time to learn to trust Barry and me, but when he did he was a pleasure to have around."

"I believe you had him for longer than any other foster child?"

Elaine nodded. "Yes and he stayed on with us after he turned sixteen."

"Which is unusual why?"

Elaine turned to the jury. "Sorry, the state stops paying foster carers when a child reaches sixteen. They're supposed to get a place of their own, but there was no way we were going to send Mike out into the world to fend for himself then. Poor lad had spent his childhood looking after himself, it didn't seem right to make him do it again so soon. Plus he'd have had to start working and it would have been criminal for him to miss out on A Levels and university." One of the women in the back row of the jury nodded vigorously.

"But you must have seen something pretty special in him to make you take that on?" Xander asked.

"We did," Elaine said. "He's not really tough like some of the boys are. Sometimes when you've had an upbringing like Mike's you become Mr. Hardman, which Mike did for a while at school. But I think his real response was to look for love, to work hard, and to make sure he was never in the place of his childhood again. Barry and I had to help him achieve that."

"So by the time Mr. Hayes went to university would you say he seemed like a perfectly normal young man?"

"Yes, quiet and studious, but well balanced, I'd say." It was easy to see that the jury loved Elaine. They'd talk about her afterward and marvel at her kindness in taking on someone as fucked-up as me. I balled my hands into fists and held them in my lap.

"And he met Verity in the second year. When did you meet her?"

Elaine looked over at V and her face was open, but when I looked at V she had her head tilted down toward her lap. "We probably met her about six or so months after they started going out. We always loved Verity, she was a gorgeous girl and she made Mike very happy, which is all you ever want, isn't it."

"And did Mike seem to love her too much, like Mrs. Walton suggested, would you say?"

Elaine cocked her head to one side. "I don't know how you love someone too much. He was certainly very keen on her if that's what you mean. There were never any other girls or anything like that."

"So you must have been surprised when they split up?"

"In a way. But they were young. It didn't seem that surprising." And that is the problem with life. No one else ever really sees what you do. Even Elaine, even she hadn't seen what V and I are to each other. Only V and I knew and that was the way it would always be.

"How did Mike seem, after the split?"

Elaine shifted her weight. "He didn't tell us when it happened. I rang him to say happy New Year in early January and he started crying and blurted it all out. About the other woman and everything. He sounded terribly unhappy."

Xander glanced at the jury. "Yes, to be clear. Mr. Hayes had a one-night stand in New York, which he told Verity about and that was the reason she gave him for ending their relationship."

"Yes."

"Even though she had started seeing Mr. Metcalf by then?"

"I don't know anything about that."

"It was a very honorable thing of Mike to do though, wouldn't you say? I mean, he easily could have never told Verity about the one-night stand and she would have been unlikely to find out."

Elaine nodded. "That's typical Mike though. He always did the right thing. He's very moral."

Xander let the comment rest in the air for a bit before asking his next question. "I take it you kept in contact with Mike after that?"

"Oh yes."

"And how did he seem?"

"He remained very upset for a couple of months, but then he started to recover himself and after a while I felt like he was back to normal."

"So, in your estimation, when he came back to London in May, he was happy and over Verity?"

"I would say so."

"When he got back did you talk about Verity at all?" Xander tapped his hand against the wood of his table.

"Only in relation to her wedding. I knew Mike was going, so I asked him about it and he seemed fine."

"No more questions, My Lord," Xander said, beaming at Elaine and then the jury as he sat back down.

Petra stood and walked to where Xander had been standing. "I'm interested by your assertion that Mr. Hayes seemed fine about the wedding, when Mrs. Metcalf rang you to say she was worried about him."

Elaine looked over at me. "That was after the wedding, when they got back from the honeymoon. I rang Mike after Verity called me and he admitted he'd sent her some e-mails he regretted, but he said he'd sorted it out and everything was all right."

"Why did Mrs. Metcalf contact you do you think?"

Elaine looked at Justice Smithson and Xander, almost as if she expected them to stop the question. "Because we'd talked about Mike over the years. She wanted to see if I knew what was going on."

It made me feel strange to think of them discussing me without my knowing; how my name could be pushed into the air and not touch me, how I never, ever wanted anyone to decide anything about me again.

Petra looked at the jury. "Item 15 in your notes." There was the sound of a shuffle of papers. "But perhaps I can read one of the e-mails Mr. Hayes sent to Mrs. Metcalf while she was on her honeymoon."

Petra put on her glasses and looked at the paper in her hand. "'Verity, I don't think this is fair. How many times do you want me to say sorry for what happened in America? It meant nothing. Less than nothing. If it were possible I would reverse time like Superman and never even speak to Carly. If it made you happy I would fly over there now and exterminate her, rid her from the world so she couldn't infect us anymore. But this is too much now. I shouldn't have let it get this far, I should have stopped the marriage before it actually happened. Because it's going to be so difficult to get out of now and I'm still not sure what you want me to do or how we're going to achieve it. And all the time you are having to spend with Angus is ridiculous. Every second you are with him is like a dagger to my heart. I get it, a hundredfold I get it. But you've even gone on our honeymoon with him and that is something we will never get back. It doesn't feel like you are teaching me a lesson anymore, more like you are actively being cruel. I love you, V. You know as well as I do the connection that exists between us. I would do anything for you. As ever, I crave you. Your Eagle.'"

There was a palpable silence in the courtroom when she had finished and I was aware of Xander shifting in his seat.

"I haven't heard that before," Elaine said, and I could feel her look over at me, even though I kept my eyes lowered. I felt frightened for the first time as this would be hard to explain to those who don't know us.

"Perhaps then you also haven't read the e-mail he sent Mrs. Metcalf in January last year in which he details the ways he could exterminate Carly, the woman with whom he'd had a one-night stand. He mentions suffocation, poisoning, hitting her over the head. He says he's sure no one would miss her."

Elaine blanched. "No. But I'm sure he didn't mean it that way."

"Would you say these are the e-mails of a rational person?"

Elaine looked up, down, her eyes darting. "I don't know, I haven't seen the e-mail."

"What did Mrs. Metcalf say when she rang you?"

"She said she'd had a couple of e-mails from Mike while she was on honeymoon and she was worried about his state of mind." Elaine hesitated. "When they were together we'd had a few conversations about how therapy would be good for him. He was deeply affected by his upbringing, as you'd expect. She wanted to talk to me about trying to persuade him to see someone."

Petra nodded. "How would you say Mr. Hayes's upbringing affected him?"

"It made him suspicious of people. He has a hard time trusting them, which is why he doesn't have many friends. But then on the other hand, if he does invest in you he gives everything to that relationship. You know, it really matters to him." She paused for a moment. "But the worst part is how unlovable it used to make him feel, like he wasn't really worthy of attention. It took him a long time to realize that Barry and I wanted the best for him and he never really got the hang of making friends. When he was younger I used to tell him to invite friends round for tea and stuff, but he never did. It used to break my heart thinking about him in that playground day after day all alone. I once asked him what he did at lunchtimes and he said he liked building things out of stones. Sometimes I'd look at the clock at oneish and have a bit of a cry thinking about him."

Something dropped through me when she said that, a bit like one of the stones had found its way back to me, its smooth shiny surface passing through my bones and blood, resting in the end in my internal organs.

Petra removed her glasses and tapped them against her leg. A muscle in her cheek was twitching. "But would you not say his upbringing also made violence seem commonplace? Would you not say his easy chat about exterminating Carly is very worrying and his thoughts about Mrs. Metcalf's marriage extend into a realm of fantasy?"

"Objection, My Lord," said Xander. "This is pure conjecture."

"Overruled," said Justice Smithson. "Although the jury would do well to note that Mrs. White is not an expert, just someone who knows the defendant well."

"I think Mike loved Verity as much as he said," Elaine said.

"Perhaps," Petra said. "But wouldn't you say there are parts of his correspondence with her that contain worrying things for him to have thought. The fact, for example, that he was convinced the marriage was a mistake. And that he was ready to rescue her at any time."

"He would have rescued her at any time, if she had needed it," Elaine said, and I loved her at that moment.

"Yes, but she didn't need rescuing," Petra said. "She was happy."

"I know," Elaine conceded.

"Did Mrs. Metcalf ever give you any reason to believe she wasn't happy in her marriage or that she regretted splitting from Mr. Hayes?"

"No."

"Did she leave you with the impression that she wanted to meet with Mr. Hayes or was thinking of restarting their relationship?"

"No."

I saw movement out of the corner of my eye and turned to see that V had dropped something that she was leaning down to retrieve from the floor. When she straightened I saw it was only a tissue, which she used to wipe at her nose.

I wasn't annoyed with Elaine, because why should she understand the nature of our Crave. That was what made it so special, the fact that only V and I could decipher its intricacies. It was worth being misunderstood for, even worth going to prison for.

"Would you say Mr. Hayes is a fantasist?" Petra asked.

Elaine looked over at me and this time I met her eyes. She smiled ever so slightly at me. "No, just confused." I smiled back.

Petra looked at the jury. "Very confused, some might say." I looked back again at V as surely it was impossible that Petra had just said some Oasis lyrics in the middle of the trial without being instructed to do so.

I kept my eyes fixed on the side of V's head, where her hairline was pulled into a tight ponytail, but she didn't turn toward me. I willed her to, just once, so I could let her know I got it, I too understood that we are the only people ever to have felt the way we do. But her eyes stayed trained on her lap.

"I believe, Mrs. White, that Mr. Hayes bought your house for you from the council eighteen months ago."

Elaine blinked. "Yes, he did."

"That was very generous of him."

"Yes."

"Did you ask him to buy it?"

"No. In fact, he didn't tell Barry and I until he'd almost done it."

"If someone had done that for me I would feel very, very grateful to them."

Elaine looked at me. "We are. We'd have lost the house if Mike hadn't bought it when the council decided to sell."

I smiled at her. I would have bought Elaine's house for her a hundred times.

"I would find it hard to say anything bad about someone who had done that for me," Petra said, ruining the moment.

But Elaine looked straight at her. "I know what you're implying, but that's not right. Mike is as lovely as I said. He bought the house because he's a good lad."

"I understand that you care very much for Mr. Hayes and, in his own way, he probably cares for you. But that shouldn't stop you from telling this court what you really think him capable of."

"I don't know what you mean," Elaine said, and it was as if her hair stood on end.

"I mean," Petra said, "I think Michael Hayes is a dangerous fantasist and I think you feel the same way."

"I do not."

"But can you sit there and say that you have no concerns about him at all? Can you honestly say you find the fact that he killed Mr. Metcalf totally shocking, totally out of character?"

Elaine hesitated, looking over at me. "Mike wouldn't have meant to kill Mr. Metcalf. He would never intentionally hurt anyone."

"Yes, but with his violent past and his stalking of Verity, are you surprised?"

Xander leaped up. "Objection. Mr. Hayes is not on trial for stalking."

"Sustained," said Justice Smithson.

"Apologies," Petra said, "wrong word. Perhaps I should say his devotion to Mrs. Metcalf. Are you surprised this all ended in violence?"

Elaine scrunched up her face and for a moment I thought she was going to shout. "Not much surprises me when you've seen the things I have. When you've listened to the stories I've heard about children that make you wish you didn't have ears."

"I understand that, Mrs. White. I understand the nature of what you do. But you've already said you saw something different in Mr. Hayes. Is part of that difference his instability, his violence?"

"No." Elaine shook her head. "No, it's not."

"Would you like to tell the court about the time you and Verity had to call an ambulance because Mr. Hayes had become so out of control?"

Elaine looked first at Petra, then me. "That was years ago."

"Four years to be precise. And I think we would still like to hear about it."

I wanted to put my hands over my ears, but I knew how that would look.

Elaine drew in a deep breath. "It was his birthday and we were having supper at home, just Mike, Verity, Barry, and me. His mum had sent him a card and I should have handled it better. I should have waited for a quiet time to give it to him, but I just handed it over, across the dinner table. He read it to himself and Verity asked if she could see it, but he didn't reply. He went very red and I wanted to reach out and snatch the card back because I realized what I'd done. He hadn't spoken to his mother or heard from her for years and I just hand the card across the dinner table like a great big idiot. He stayed silent for ages and none of us could make him even look up, but then he threw the card on the table and went into the garden. Then he started screaming and we all went outside and tried to get him to stop, but we couldn't. We couldn't get him to move at all. We called an ambulance because we didn't know what else to do."

It's ridiculous for Elaine to blame herself and I must remember to tell her that when this is over. She wasn't to know how seeing those bald words "To Mike, Love Mum" written around the printed Happy Birthday was going to be too much. If you'd asked me before it happened, I wouldn't have known it was going to be too much. And even though I was sitting at a table with V, Elaine, and Barry, those words seemed like the bleakest, hardest thing I'd ever seen. It was like nothing else existed, as if they had picked me up and thrown me back into my bare room in my miserable flat. I don't remember leaving the table, I don't remember going into the garden, but I can still hear the sound of the scream, or more accurately I can still feel it, because it wasn't a scream of pain; it was more like a release, like an air bubble popping, like an acknowledgment of all the times I never made a sound.

"Were you worried for your safety?"

"No—I was worried about his."

I sneaked another look at V but she still had her head down, although she was shredding the tissue she had been holding, its white fibers falling to the floor at her feet.

Petra put her glasses back on and flicked through her notes. "I have the medical report here. Michael was seen by a Dr. Hahn that evening. He was injected with a high dose of Valium and spent the night on the ward. Is that correct?"

"Yes."

"Dr. Hahn's diagnosis reads as follows, and I quote: 'Severe case of nervous exhaustion, semi-psychotic episode brought on by shock or maybe PTS'—that's posttraumatic stress. 'Am satisfied no need for sectioning, but have advised patient and family to seek help from GP. Patient would benefit greatly from a course of therapy and possibly medication. Have advised they seek this help at the earliest opportunity.'" Petra looked back up at Elaine. "Did Michael visit the GP?"

"No."

"Did you want him to? Did Verity want him to?"

"Yes."

"Did you argue about it?"

"A bit."

"What were Mr. Hayes's reasons for not going?"

"He said he was fine."

"But in your and Verity's opinion he wasn't fine?"

"We thought he could do with some help."

Petra sighed and turned her back on Elaine, placing her papers back on her desk.

"He's a good lad," Elaine said, her voice rising over the court. "Mike is a good lad."

It appears I still haven't learned that people can always surprise you. I told Xander not to worry about Kaitlyn, I said I was pretty sure she was in love with me and either way we were good friends, so she would be on my side. We like to do that, don't we? Pretend to ourselves that we know someone, that we've worked them out, that their motives are clear, that we have insight. But really it's all an illusion. None of us knows anything about what goes on in the heart of another. You have to reach the level

V and I have to achieve that and it takes so many years and so many experiences that there is only ever one person with whom you can hope to have that connection in life.

I even felt sorry for Kaitlyn as she took the stand because she looked so translucent, as if the wood she was surrounded by was reflected in her skin. She was dressed in much the same way as V and I saw Kaitlyn cast surreptitious glances over at V as the courtroom settled. I knew without looking that V wasn't returning the looks and I knew also that the luminosity of V's presence would be intimidating to Kaitlyn. In the end she turned her bright eyes to me and her mouth flicked up into a small smile, which I reciprocated.

"I believe you and Mr. Hayes have spent quite a bit of time together since he started working at Bartleby's?" Petra said.

"Yes," Kaitlyn replied. "We got on well from the beginning."

"And what were your initial impressions of him?"

"I was surprised by how modest he was, if that's the right word. I mean, with his reputation, I was expecting one of those brash City boys, but Mike was never like that."

"What reputation?"

"Mainly how well he'd done at Schwartz's. When his appointment was announced, Lord Falls, our chairman, made a really big deal out of it and we all expected this loud, cocky trader to walk in. But he was the opposite of that." Kaitlyn smiled over at me again, which I was starting to find a bit irritating. I hoped V didn't think there was actually anything between us.

"Although I believe things never quite came together for Mr. Hayes work-wise?" Petra said, which seemed like an odd question.

"No. He was quite"—Kaitlyn looked like she was searching for the word—"quite volatile."

"In what way?" Petra asked, and I too wanted to know the answer.

"I have friends on his team and they would often talk about him shouting at them. He once made my friend Lottie cry. He told her she was useless and incompetent in front of their whole team." I felt a click in my brain, like a wheel I was unaware of turning.

"Is that behavior unusual?"

"Not as unusual as it should be. But also, Lottie lives next door to Mike and he never really acknowledged her. She said they could pass each other in the street and he wouldn't even smile. I stay at her house quite a bit and it often sounded like there was a party going on next door, when we knew he was home alone."

"A party?"

"Yes, lots of loud music and banging."

"Maybe Mr. Hayes was in fact having a party?"

"No, Mike didn't know enough people to have a party." Kaitlyn glanced up at me apologetically, but I didn't mind her saying that because who is there worth knowing? "I know this sounds terrible, but once Lottie and I were so intrigued we stood on a bench to look over the garden wall. All the lights were on in Mike's kitchen and he was sort of running around, banging into the walls and the table, like he didn't even register they were there. He was playing music at top volume, Oasis I think it was, and he was crying. It was really sad. Both Lottie and I were quite upset by it." I tried to breathe deeply but my body felt as blocked as my brain.

"Did you talk to him about what you'd seen?"

"No, I was too embarrassed. I just tried to be as friendly as I could and make it clear that he could talk to me if he needed to."

"Would you say Mr. Hayes is a heavy drinker?"

"Yes," Kaitlyn said, and I felt the room tip. I saw my mother passed out on the sofa and tried to work out if it made it better that my sofa came from Heal's and hers was full of cigarette burns. There is no law that says we become our parents, Elaine once said to me.

"He often came to work looking the worse for wear and he often smelled of stale alcohol. At the time I thought that was maybe what was affecting his performance."

"But you still spent time together outside of work?"

"Yes, a bit. We went for drinks and he came to my house for dinner one night." A faint blush rose up Kaitlyn's cheeks, which in anyone else would have gone unnoticed but in her radiated like a beacon.

"And what did you talk about?"

"All sorts," Kaitlyn said. "He told me about his upbringing and how he always felt like an outsider, which I sympathized with, working in the environment I'm in. We talked about work, a bit. And of course Verity." She nodded over at V when she said this and I couldn't help following her. V was looking straight at her, her face set like a mask. I repeated the word "sorry" in my head over and over as I stared at the side of V's head, willing her to hear. Eventually she rubbed the side of her face and I relaxed slightly, knowing she'd received the message.

"And what did he say about Mrs. Metcalf?" Petra asked, looking over at V herself.

Kaitlyn bit her bottom lip. "He was very protective over her. I could tell something was up between them but he didn't admit it for ages."

"What do you mean by something was up?"

"Well, she was never around for a start and he was always making excuses about where she was and stuff." Kaitlyn looked at me again and I could tell she was sorry for what she was saying.

"So you were under the impression that Mr. Hayes and Verity were a couple?" Petra asked, but I could tell in her tone this was rehearsed and I dreaded the answer.

"Oh yes. He referred to her as his girlfriend the first time we went out after work. I bumped into him once in a deli near to where we live and he said he was buying supper for them both."

"He specifically said that?"

"Yes. He bought steaks because he said they were Verity's favorite. I felt sorry for him because he seemed so agonized by the decision, it felt painful."

"But Verity wasn't there?"

"Not in the shop, no."

"Nor at home?"

"I presume not."

"But he gave you the impression that they lived together at Windsor Terrace?"

"Yes."

"Did Mr. Hayes ever confide in you about his relationship with Mrs. Metcalf?"

"Yes." I felt a wash of shame run through me when Kaitlyn answered, my whole body cringed at V knowing I had ever discussed her with anyone else. "After I'd known him for a few months he told me that she'd moved out, but he gave the impression it was just so they could sort out their differences."

"Which were?"

"I think he said they disagreed about how they should live."

Petra raised her eyebrows and let out a stream of air. "So I take it you had no idea about Verity's marriage?"

Kaitlyn shook her head. "None at all. In fact I bumped into Mike on what I now know was the morning of the wedding and he told me it was Verity's sister who was getting married."

"And you never had cause to doubt him?"

"None at all. I felt sorry for him. If I'm honest I thought it sounded like Verity was playing him a bit, but he was too in love with her to do anything about it."

"But I believe this wedding was how you began to uncover the extent of Mr. Hayes's lies just before the murder."

"Yes," Kaitlyn said, and I sat up straighter, as if called to attention. "I knew Mike was hiding something and I had tried googling him and Verity, but he is virtually nonexistent online and I didn't know Verity's surname, so I didn't really come up with anything. But one night, about a week before the murder, I was scrolling through Facebook, you know the way you do when you're bored, looking at photos of friends of friends without really knowing why you're doing it. Anyway, I came across an album of photos of an acquaintance who'd been to Angus Metcalf's wedding. I'd read about it in the *Standard* so I started looking. I'd seen a photo of Verity at Mike's house and suddenly I'm looking at her in all the pictures and I realized she was the bride." I could feel my breath high in my throat, like a trapped bird.

"What did you do with the information?" Petra asked.

"I confided in Lottie, but we didn't really know what to do." Kaitlyn paused for a second. "It made me realize that he'd built this whole fantasy around Verity and I was worried about what he might do." Kaitlyn glanced up at me and her translucent skin colored slightly. "I know it sounds ridiculous after everything that's happened but I still think Mike is a genuinely nice guy and I think he believes the lies he tells. I don't think he's trying to deceive anyone more than himself. And he's very convincing. Like I said, when I first met him I really thought Verity was playing him, I wanted to help him get out of what I thought was a damaging relationship." She shook her head.

My seat felt too small for me. I couldn't remember if what Kaitlyn was saying was true or not. It felt like there were only versions of the truth and nothing was absolute. Something was opening beneath me, a hole that threatened to swallow me and a feeling of inescapable terror washed through me. "It's okay," I said under my breath, "V and I are in love and that's the only truth worth knowing."

Petra nodded sagely. "I believe you were staying at Lottie's house, next door to Mr. Hayes, on the night of the murder."

"That's correct."

"Perhaps you could tell us what you saw."

Kaitlyn shifted her weight. "I'd been worried about Mike that evening anyway because I bumped into him on the way home from work and he said he was on his way to see Verity. He was incredibly agitated and wasn't really making sense. He said something about her needing him, but it didn't ring true, especially considering what I knew by then about the wedding. He'd called in sick to work that day and he looked feverish. I tried to stop him, but he wasn't paying any attention and was a bit rude, if I'm honest. Lottie and I discussed it all evening and decided I would talk to Mike the next day and, if that didn't work, we'd maybe try to talk to the company doctor or someone about him." She paused for a moment. "We went to bed around midnight, but were woken at about two twenty by shouting outside. We got up and looked out of the bedroom window and saw a man I now know to be Angus Metcalf banging on Mike's door. We talked about going down but he seemed drunk and angry and we didn't know what to do. After about ten minutes Mike opened the door and the shouting intensified. We couldn't see anything because they'd gone just inside the house, but it was pretty obvious they were fighting, so I called the police."

"Did you go downstairs?"

"Not at first, no. We were scared. But then Verity arrived in a taxi and went running up the path and we could hear her screaming so I went outside. Lottie tried to stop me, but I had to help."

"And what did you find?"

Kaitlyn touched her finger to her lip. "It was horrible. Mr. Metcalf was lying just inside the door, covered in blood, not moving at all. But the strangest thing was that Mike and Verity were standing just behind him, embracing."

"I know Mr. Jackson made a lot of this when he questioned you, Miss Porter, but to be clear, when you say embracing what do you mean? Were they kissing?"

"They weren't kissing, no. I could only see Verity's back. She was leaning against Mike and he had his arms wrapped tightly around her."

"Where were her arms?"

Kaitlyn thought for a moment. "By her side I think. But I'm not sure."

"So she wasn't returning his embrace, as you put it."

"I don't know. But whatever, it was really strange. I mean, her husband is on the floor dying or dead and she's allowing the man who killed him to hug her." And of course Kaitlyn couldn't understand this. No one will ever understand V and me, which is what makes us so wonderful.

"Is it possible that she was in a state of shock?"

"I don't know. I can't imagine how it could be seen as normal behavior however you want to say it."

Petra looked down at her notes and I saw her neck had blotches of red on it. "I put it to you, Miss Porter, that you are in love with Mr. Hayes and therefore jealous of Mrs. Metcalf. That you know you saw a woman in a state of shock, being taken advantage of by a delusional man, but your personal feelings have colored your testimony."

Kaitlyn laughed. She shook her head. "No, you're completely wrong. When I said I stay with Lottie a lot, that's because we're partners. She's my girlfriend. I can assure you I have no feelings of those types for Mike. And I have no feelings whatsoever for Mrs. Metcalf." I felt myself blushing as she said the words, a strange shame seeping through me at my arrogance. At my inability to see the signs. Maybe there will never be pictures in clouds for me.

Petra coughed, but Kaitlyn stood firm, her eyes level.

I felt a strange sensation rise through my body as I flicked through all the times Kaitlyn and I had spent together, all the things she'd said, all the fleeting touches, all the half sentences. Knowing this truth about her and Lottie altered it entirely. What I had interpreted as love on her part had really been friendship, concern. The sensation flipped in my stomach and passed out through my head, leaving me feeling dizzy. I had gotten so much wrong, I had misunderstood Kaitlyn in almost every way, and the thought was terrifying.

It was V's turn to take the stand today, which means we are here at the moment I have been turning over in my head. I must testify tomorrow and I only have tonight to make my final decision. To separate wrong from right, truth from lies, fact from fantasy. I must separate and then rearrange and do what is right for only V and me.

She was wearing the same black suit, this time with a pale blue shirt. She had on flat ballet pumps, her hair tied in a low ponytail, and no makeup on her face. There were simple pearls on her earlobes and naturally the eagle hung around her neck, its silver brilliance resting peacefully in the hollow at the bottom of her throat, between her delicate collarbones. She was very pale and because she has lost so much weight her bones jutted out of her face, making her look harsher than usual. My heart sped at the sight of her, so small and delicate, as she stood inside the giant witness box. Fear struck at me with the thought that this strategy is perhaps too much and maybe V is too delicate to handle the scrutiny.

I remembered her suddenly in all those bars, when I'd felt like she was a butterfly surrounded by flies. And fast on the heels of that thought came the next: If we do both end up in prison she will be surrounded by flies for years, except I won't be physically able to save her. I won't even be able to see her. The thought lodged in my throat and I couldn't pull my breath into my lungs so I started to feel light-headed. I shut my eyes and counted to ten. I have to banish the bad thoughts and instead focus on the thought of her packed away like a precious jewel, ready and waiting to be taken out again when the time is right.

"Mrs. Metcalf," Petra began. "Perhaps you could start by telling the court about the history of your relationship with Mr. Hayes."

It looked like it was painful for V to take a breath. I knew where Suzi and Colin were sitting and I saw her glance up at them briefly before she began. "We met at Bristol University, toward the end of our second year. We started dating and after we graduated we moved to London and rented a flat together. He went to America five years later and I stayed on in London. We carried on a long-distance relationship, but we didn't see much of each other because of work and it became a bit strained between us. I ended the relationship about thirteen months ago."

"Was it a happy relationship, before the end?" Petra was keeping her movements relaxed today.

"Yes," V said. "We were very happy for the first eight or so years. It only turned toward the end, I'd say the last six months."

"And why would you say that was?"

"I don't know. Maybe the distance? Or maybe we grew apart a bit?"

"Can you elaborate?"

"I began to find his, his"—V looked up at Petra, but then down again—"his, I suppose, need of me, too much."

"In what way?" Petra asked, and I hated her at that moment, purely and simply, for everything she was making V say.

"He'd always been very connected to me, but when he went to New York it got worse. He had to know what I was doing at all times, and if I changed my plans or did anything spontaneously we had to discuss it for hours." V swallowed. "It felt like nothing was ever enough. I had to send him weekly e-mails with my movements for the week listed in them."

"If I may I am going to read the jury one of these exchanges, although they are all in your files, item 21," Petra said, turning toward the jury as she spoke. She looked back down at her papers. "'Monday gym after work, Tuesday meetings all day so won't be able to speak to you but will go straight home, Wednesday dinner with Louise, meeting her straight from work, Thursday leaving drinks in the office for Sam, Friday will catch a train straight to Steeple.' Mr. Hayes replied the same day: 'Didn't you have dinner with Louise last week? Why do you need to see her again so soon? And which Sam? Why do you feel like you have to go to everyone's leaving drinks? I would prefer if you went straight home and we can have a proper chat.'" She looked up and back to V. "There are lots of similar exchanges between you two. Did you not find them a bit odd?"

"Yes," V said. "But I also didn't want to fight when he was so far away."

"I believe Mr. Hayes also liked you to sleep with Skype on?"

"Yes, he liked the laptop to be on the pillow next to me."

"And you did that?"

"A couple of times, yes. It was easier than saying no."

"Would you say Mr. Hayes is controlling?"

V lifted her hand but then dropped it again. "In some ways, yes."

"Were you scared of him?"

"No, I wouldn't say scared."

Petra moved forward marginally. "So, to be clear, you hadn't minded this attention before he left for New York?"

"When we were at university and after, when we lived in London, I think I was flattered by it. But we were much younger and I think when you're young you want to be adored more, don't you think?" She looked up as she spoke, but really she had asked the question to no one. "Mike and I were in a bit of a bubble and I think when he went away I realized that things couldn't go on the way they had been. I guess I just wanted a more normal life."

Petra looked over at the jury. "I'm asking you this next question because so much has been made of it in the press. But I would like it noted that I don't think your sexuality has any bearing on this case or any other. Unfortunately, though, it is not something that can be ignored." I looked at the jury as well and saw how uncomfortable they were. She turned back to V. "When you say you were in a bubble, are you talking about this game you and Mr. Hayes played, this Crave that the press has made so much of?"

V hesitated and rubbed at a point above her eyebrow where I knew her headaches started. "I think that had a lot to do with it. It felt like something private and special between us and I suppose it bound us together in the way things like that do."

"How often did you Crave?"

"Not a lot. Maybe once a month."

"Would you describe what you did as sexually deviant?"

V almost laughed. "God no, it was just stupid adolescent fun. We went to a bar, I got chatted up, and Mike broke it up. It turned us on, the thought that another man found me attractive. That's it. No one ever got hurt, it was just a bit of fun."

"And who started it?"

V's head flicked toward me involuntarily, but she stopped herself from actually looking at me. "We were at a party once, just after our finals, and someone started chatting me up and Mike got a bit heated. We left the party and laughed about it, but it became obvious that we'd both been turned on by it. A few days later we went clubbing, just the two of us, and Mike suggested I go and stand by the bar on my own. He said he wanted to see how long it took for me to be chatted up. We were both drunk and I did it and pretty soon this man approached me and Mike came steaming over. It sort of went from there."

"So it was Mr. Hayes's idea?"

"I suppose it was, yes."

Petra nodded. "Perhaps you can talk us through the end of your relationship with Mr. Hayes. You said things had been going wrong for about six months."

V nodded. "Yes. I started to feel very stifled by him and his constant need to know everything about me stopped seeming sweet and started to become irritating. My work was very busy and it became exhausting juggling the two things." She paused, her eyes wide like she was scared. "Then I met Angus. He came in to do a pitch and I had to run him through something I was working on afterward and then he rang me the next day and . . ." She trailed off and I thought she was going to cry. "He was just very different from Mike. He was calm and self-assured and he seemed in control of himself and his emotions. We went on a few dates and I realized I was falling for him."

"And this happened when?"

"Well, I met Angus around September the year before last, but we didn't start seeing each other until about November and even then we took it very slowly because of Mike. I knew I was going to have to finish things with Mike, but I felt very confused and I also knew how badly he'd take it. My plan was to tell him face-to-face when he came home at Christmas."

"Would you say you had fallen in love with Mr. Metcalf by then?"

"Yes," V said, very simply. "I've never loved anyone like I loved Angus."

It was possible, I thought, that I had died and gone to hell. The room had become very hot and I could feel sweat dripping down my back. My mind slithered, not able to keep up with what V was saying, not able to process it into the meaning I knew was there, into what I knew she would be wanting me to hear. Stop listening to the words, I kept telling myself, except they were all I could hear.

"But you were still concerned for Mr. Hayes at that point?" Petra asked stupidly.

"Yes, very much so," V answered. "Naturally we'd talked lots about his childhood over the years and I knew he was much more affected by it than he admitted, even to himself. I know the reason he doesn't get close to many people is because he finds it hard to believe anyone will love him. He was always going on about how he wasn't good enough for me. And I understand that. My God, it's amazing he's done as well as he has with a start like he had." Her voice caught and my brain stopped slithering. "But I couldn't let that mean that I sacrificed my life to make his happy. I knew telling him was going to be awful and I knew he was going to take it badly, but I had to do it."

"Of course you did," Petra said. "Your mother said it made you ill."

"Yes, I felt very agitated for weeks before he came home. I barely slept at all. I had to take time off work and go and stay with my parents."

"But it turned out Mr. Hayes had been unfaithful to you in New York, which he admitted to you?"

"Yes. I can't tell you how relieved I felt when he told me that," V said. "Looking back now, I can see how cowardly I was to use that as an excuse and I wish I hadn't done it, but at the time it just felt like a massive release."

"Perhaps you thought Mr. Hayes didn't care as much about you as you'd thought?"

"There was that as well. I mean, I was surprised that he'd done it, but his excuses were very irritating. He tried to blame me for it, going on and on about how lonely he'd been, as if I was the one who'd made him go to New York."

"Which you hadn't?"

"No, of course not. In fact, when he applied for the job I remember being very upset. But Mike had this obsession with retiring by the time we were forty-five. I don't know why, but I always presumed it had something to do with his upbringing and how out of control he'd always felt. I think it's very important for him to feel in control now and I suppose money helps with that."

I reached out and put my hand against the solid wood of the box in which I sat, contained and safe. I felt the warden look at me and I would have punched him if he'd touched me. Because at that moment I still hadn't entirely worked out what V was doing, why she was swapping and spinning our story.

"How did Mr. Hayes take the ending of your relationship?"

"Very badly. It was dreadful. He started screaming and crying and begging me not to end it. He grabbed me around the legs and I had to slap him to get him to let go of me because I was so scared. My parents had to ask him to leave our house the next day because he wouldn't leave me alone and then he bombarded me with phone calls and texts and e-mails. He sent so many flowers my mother had to donate them to the church. Angus came and took me away in the end and I think if he hadn't done that I might have gone mad."

I concentrated on the feel of the wood beneath my fingers, old and ridged, and ultimately unconcerned.

"But Mr. Hayes went back to New York in the end?"

"Eventually, yes. He'd bought me a ticket to come and spend New Year's with him there even though I'd told him a hundred times I wasn't going to, way before our conversation about splitting up. When I didn't turn up for that flight I think he began to get the message and then I changed my phone number and told him I wasn't going back to our flat. In the end he went back to New York, but the e-mails continued for about six weeks. It got to the stage where Angus would go into my account every morning and evening and delete them so I wouldn't even have to know how many he'd sent."

An image of monkey-man Angus reading my private words to V flashed into my brain and I almost wished he wasn't dead so that I could feel my hand smash into his face again.

Petra walked toward the jury. "Item 13 in your folders. And then they just stopped?"

"Yes. One day they stopped and that was it. At first I didn't believe it but as time went on I really thought things were okay. Then Angus and I got engaged and I was so happy I let the thought of Mike drift to the back of my mind. I always knew I was going to have to tell him about the wedding, but I kept putting it off and then one day, out of the blue, I got this e-mail from him saying he was coming back to live in London and so I replied and told him about the marriage."

"And how did he react to that?"

"It took him a few days to reply, but when he did he sounded fine. He congratulated me and I really thought we'd moved on and could be friends."

Petra was still over by the jury and she put her hand on their box, so she could have almost reached out and touched the fat man nearest to her if she'd wanted. "Now this is where I think some people might question you. Why did you still want to be friends with Mr. Hayes?"

V looked over to Petra so I knew the jury would be getting the full shock of her beauty. "We'd meant so much to each other," she said, and I saw her throat move with the words. It was as if I was able to watch them form in her before she said them. "And I knew how vulnerable he was and how few people he had in his life. I didn't want him to be unhappy. I wanted nothing more than to see him settled with someone nice. It was stupid of me."

"Or kindhearted," Petra said, removing her hand. "So he came to your wedding and you didn't see him before then?"

"We bumped into each other once. He was shopping on Kensington High Street and I lived just off it."

I waited for more because V must have known, but she held her counsel.

"How did Mr. Hayes seem?"

"Fine. We chatted about his new house and the wedding. It was a five-minute meeting, nothing more."

"And how did he seem at the wedding?"

"Again, I only saw him briefly when we said hello in the line, but I've heard what everyone else has said. Perhaps he did seem a bit anxious. I don't really remember."

"Then you went on honeymoon."

"Yes and that's when I received the next two e-mails."

"Item 16 in your folders," Petra said to the jury. I heard the rustle of paper and I knew what they were reading.

"They were a terrible shock," V said. "I got in quite a state about them. They ruined a couple of days of the honeymoon. Angus was furious, he wanted to call the police, but I stopped him. We agreed that the best thing to do was leave it till we got home and then compose an e-mail that made Mike feel valued and listened to but that spelled out the fact that I loved Angus and didn't want to be with Mike."

"Why did you stop Angus calling the police?"

V opened her mouth but then she swallowed and her shoulders clenched, so I knew she was trying not to cry. "I think I still felt guilty. I wish I had now. It was a massive mistake."

"Why do you say that?"

"Because after we got back Mike turned up at my work and made it clear that he thought the marriage was a sham and I really wanted to be with him. It became clear that he thought it was all part of some sort of Crave."

"And he told you this when you went for a drink with him in the bar opposite your office?"

"Yes."

"But you didn't go straight home and tell Angus?" Petra said, which was the first reasonable question she had asked.

V looked down and swallowed again. "No. He was going away on a business trip and I knew he'd have freaked out and called the police and worried the whole time he was away. I thought if I waited till he got back then we could deal with it together. I really didn't think Mike would do anything more than he'd already done. I thought I could handle it."

"Except that didn't turn out to be the case, did it?" Petra walked toward V who looked like she was shivering. "I'm really sorry to ask you to tell us about the next part, Verity, but I'm afraid you need to tell the jury what happened."

"I know." A tear rolled down V's cheek and off the bottom of her face. "I went to my parents' for the weekend and got back on Sunday night. Angus was due back very early on Tuesday morning and I hadn't heard from Mike, so I thought maybe he'd got the message. But then he turned up at the house on Monday evening, stinking of alcohol. He forced his way in and it became apparent that he thought we had some sort of agreement. That I was planning to leave Angus and move in with him."

"I believe Mr. Hayes kissed you. That you ended up on the floor together."

V nodded, more tears falling. "Yes. I think he would have raped me if I hadn't stopped him."

"Objection," Xander said, standing. "Mr. Hayes denies assaulting Mrs. Metcalf. He says this encounter was entirely consensual."

Justice Smithson looked at the jury. "The jury will take into account that this case has not been heard yet and a verdict has not been reached, so Mrs. Metcalf and Mr. Hayes have differing versions of this event."

V gasped suddenly, as if she was drowning, pulling her head upward and forward. "That was the worst part," she said in a strangled voice. "Mike seemed to think I wanted it all to happen. I had to play along to get him to leave. I had to pretend that I wanted to leave Angus and be with him." She put her hand over her mouth, as if containing the words, and her eyes looked desperate. She looked in fact momentarily mad, like she had when she'd been ill before, when she said life felt like it was happening behind a wall she couldn't climb. And that is when what she was doing started to make sense to me. When she'd been ill she used to say she couldn't understand anything that was said to her and it was as though words churned in her head. And of course she is feeling that way now, of course all of this is more than she can bear. I forget sometimes how much I hurt her with Carly and how delicate this new life of hers is. The reality must collide with her construction of events in her mind and cause her to misthink. She must be terrified at the moment and I am the only one who can make her feel safe again.

"Can you describe to us what happened when Mr. Hayes kissed you?" Petra asked ghoulishly.

"Mike is very strong," V said, and I felt the jury turn to look at me. "He had me around the waist and I could, I mean, I could feel he was excited. I tried not to kiss him at first but I thought if I did then he might go away."

"How did you end up on the floor?"

"Mike had me in a really tight grip, pressed against his chest, and I could feel that he was trying to maneuver me to lie down, but I wasn't giving in. So he sort of picked me up and put me on the ground. Then, before I could get up again, he laid right on top of me with his whole weight. I felt like I couldn't breathe."

"Did he try to have sex with you?"

V was crying again. "Yes, he tried to force my legs apart and pull down my trousers. I felt him trying to open the zip on his trousers."

"Did you tell him to stop?"

"Yes."

"How many times did you have to tell him to stop before he did?"

"Four, maybe five. I had to shout because it was like he was in a trance, it felt like I wasn't getting through to him."

"But did he stop eventually?"

"Yes, although he was angry. He shouted at me and said something about being bored with hearing about Angus."

"So you went along with what Mr. Hayes was saying about leaving your husband because you were so scared?"

"Yes."

"Not because you had any intention of leaving Mr. Metcalf?"

"God no."

"So I take it you managed to get him to leave?"

"Yes."

"What did you do after he had gone?"

"I didn't know what to do. Angus was in the air so I couldn't contact him and my head was spinning. I was very sick that night and the next day. I couldn't stop being sick and I was so weak I found it hard to stand to go to the bathroom. By the time Angus got home I was in a terrible state. I was running a temperature, I think I was a bit delirious. I didn't have the strength to say anything, let alone tell him what had happened. I was going to, of course, I was going to call the police and everything. But then Mike came back that evening and started saying how we were in love with each other and I was going to leave Angus and go and live with him. I managed to get him to leave again and told Angus everything. It was terrible how upset and angry Angus was, how awful he felt at not having been able to protect me." V had given up in her fight to control her tears, which now streamed down her face. "I feel so terrible about how unhappy I made Angus at the end. How sad and angry. He put me back to bed after we'd agreed that we would call the police in the morning and I must have gone to sleep because the next thing I knew I woke up with a jolt. I could tell the house was empty even lying in bed." She gasped as she spoke, again as if the air could save her, her face contracting.

"What time was this?"

"One thirty."

"What did you do then?"

"I shouted for Angus and then started looking for him, although I knew he wasn't in the house. Then I noticed the computer was on and a file I'd created for the wedding was open with all the names and addresses of everyone we'd invited. I knew then that he must have gone to see Mike."

"The jury will note that there are twenty-three missed calls on Mr. Metcalf's mobile phone from Mrs. Metcalf between 1:47 and 2:31 a.m. I would also like to play the court a recording of the voice mail Mrs. Metcalf left Mr. Metcalf at 2:06 a.m."

Petra signaled to someone and then V's voice burst into the room, her tone shrill and high, her voice clouded with tears. "Gus, I know where you're going, but please don't. You don't know what he's like. Please, please don't. It's not worth it. We'll call the police and they'll deal with it. Please call me. Oh Gus, please."

No one spoke for a minute and a silence fell over the courtroom like a blanket. I held my hands together, but I could feel the shiver begin in my body, as if it had leaped from V to me, as if our communication was so strong it was impossible for our bodies not to respond to each other. I kept my eyes on hers and eventually she looked up briefly, straight into me.

"Did Mr. Metcalf call you back?"

V shook her head and she almost seemed to vibrate. "No. I never spoke to him again."

"When you couldn't get hold of your husband, what did you do?"

V looked back up, but not at me. "I rang Mike. I told him Gus was on his way over and not to answer the door. I told him I was getting in a taxi."

"Which you did?"

"Yes."

"You arrived at Mr. Hayes's house just after two thirty."

V shut her eyes momentarily and her head swayed. She raised her hand and it connected with the eagle. I wanted to leap the barriers and take her in my arms, because I knew what it would be costing her to lie about what we mean to each other. To say that she thought I was going to rape her must have been like her taking a knife to her own soul. I wanted to lift her up and soar into the air and out of all this violence and mess and dread. But I am not Superman, I am only human, and there is a cleverer way to save her. One that is only now becoming clear.

It is obvious that V thinks it is necessary for one of us to remain on the outside, keeping our life ticking over, and that that person has to be her because there is no denying I threw the punch that killed Angus. But she is wrong, she hasn't seen the problem right through to the end and her confusion is written all over her face. I know that tomorrow, when I sit where she has sat today, I have one chance to save her, one chance to make everything all right again.

"Gus was lying on the ground just inside Mike's front door," V said, her voice shaking. "Mike was on top of him, punching and punching him. I ran and pushed Mike off and was screaming for him to stop." Her breath heaved inside her, like it was a gale battering her ribs.

Petra lowered her voice. "I need you to explain to the court how it was that you were found with Mr. Hayes's arms around you when the police and Miss Porter arrived."

V shook her head and another stream of tears ran down her cheek. "I don't remember much of that. Nothing felt real. I remember feeling sure I was going to faint and being sort of pulled upward. But I don't think I even knew it was Mike holding me up."

"How did you feel when you found out Mr. Hayes had killed your husband?" Petra asked, and it was like the whole courtroom held its breath.

V's eyes opened wider, like she could see something denied to the rest of us. "It was like the whole world had fallen in on me. It still feels like that now. When I wake up in the morning it's like I have a wall of concrete on my chest. I'm scared of everything, I find it hard to concentrate or think straight. I miss Angus every single second of every minute of every hour of every day."

And there it was. The admission of what I had already worked out. Those were the words she used to say to me when she was ill before, how she couldn't concentrate or think straight. It was like she was talking directly to me. It wasn't Angus she missed every second of every minute of every hour of every day, it was me.

Petra shook her head. "Were you surprised at the violence Mr. Hayes showed?"

"I never thought anything like this would happen," V said. "But in hindsight I suppose I'm not surprised. It doesn't feel like something Mike isn't capable of."

"So you believe Mr. Hayes to be a violent and dangerous man?"

"I do," V said, looking straight at me as her tears fell silently. "I should have stopped him when I had the chance."

Xander got his chance with V after lunch, although she didn't look as if any sustenance had passed her pale lips.

"Mrs. Metcalf, I am interested in your dismissal of the game you played with Mr. Hayes, this Crave." V looked up at him wearily and her head looked heavy for her neck. "You called it a bit of adolescent fun, even though you were both in your twenties. Is that correct?"

"Yes, I probably shouldn't have used the word adolescent."

"And maybe you shouldn't have dismissed it as a bit of fun. I suggest it meant much more to you than a bit of fun."

V looked at the spot where I knew Suzi to be. "But that's all it was, a bit of fun."

"Sexually charged fun in which you manipulated a stranger and Mr. Hayes to make you aroused."

"It was hardly manipulation. And it aroused us both."

"Did you ever play this game with Mr. Metcalf?"

I had known the question was coming but still my heart lurched like I was on a roller coaster.

"No," V said, and the definiteness of her tone reassured me.

"Why not?"

"Because I didn't want to."

"So you discussed it with him?"

"No, I don't think I did."

"Were you ashamed of it? Embarrassed to talk to him about it?"

"No, absolutely not." V leaned her weight onto the witness box, but then stood straight again. "I didn't want to do anything like that with Angus. Our relationship wasn't like that, it was more than that. That game was just a childish stupid thing. It didn't have a place in the relationship Angus and I had."

The room felt swimmy, as if we had been suddenly transported to the jungle and the humidity was high. But I had to remind myself that she was only doing what she mistakenly thought was the right thing for us.

"That's quite a sudden dismissal of something you had played for many years, something others would find quite hard to comprehend."

Verity looked up and her skin seemed tight across her face, like she had been wrapped in cellophane. "You're making too much of this. No one ever got hurt, or even involved beyond a bit of mild flirtation."

"Except the girl in America," Xander said, and I saw his chest puff out as he spoke.

V looked like she had been slapped. Petra also sat up straighter and I knew V hadn't told her, which proved there were parts of us she was holding back, parts of the Crave she wanted to keep just for us.

"Is it true that you and Mr. Hayes picked up a girl in a bar when you were on holiday two years ago whom you took back to your hotel room and had sex with while Mr. Hayes watched?"

Petra stood. "Objection, My Lord. As far as I'm aware Mrs. Metcalf is not being tried for her sexuality."

"Overruled," said Justice Smithson.

"For the record," Petra said. "It is also no longer a criminal offense to be a sexually active woman."

"Sit down, Ms. Gardner," Justice Smithson said. "You are being ridiculous." He stared at Petra from his stand, his anger clearly radiating off him. Petra's cheeks colored and she opened her mouth, but then sat heavily back into her chair.

"Please answer the question, Mrs. Metcalf," Xander said. "Did you pick up a woman and have sex with her while Mr. Hayes watched?"

"Yes." V jutted out her chin, her jaw set tight.

"And whose idea was it to do that?"

"Mine. I was curious about having sex with a woman but I didn't want to do it without Mike being there."

"Why were you curious, Mrs. Metcalf? Was it something you'd never done before?"

"Yes."

Xander looked down at the papers in his hands. "That's strange be-cause I have statements from an Angela Burrows who says you had a sexual relationship with her for three months in the first year of university."

I looked between Xander and V. I saw V's shoulders rise, but then they dropped again. "Yes," she said.

"Yes what?"

"Yes I had a sexual relationship with Angela."

"Did Mr. Hayes know about it?"

"No."

I can't remember Angela Burrows but next time I am allowed onto a computer I shall look her up.

"So when you asked him to watch you having sex with a woman because you were curious, you were lying?"

"Not exactly. I was curious. I was curious about it in that situation."

"But you chose to lie to get your own way."

"It was hardly a lie."

Xander tipped his head to one side. "We will have to disagree about that, Mrs. Metcalf. Either way, however, it seems fair to say that you and Mr. Hayes were involved in an intricate, highly sexual game that went on for many years and that few other people knew about."

"That's unfair. You're twisting things and making them sound dif-ferent from how they were."

I wanted to tell her to stop looking so angry.

"Could you tell us about the Kitten Club, Mrs. Metcalf," Xander said.

I felt my body pull upward at those words and I saw V do the same. She held her hand to her face and appeared to wobble slightly.

"Mrs. Metcalf, are you all right?" Justice Smithson asked, leaning over his bench.

"I feel a bit faint," V said.

"Can someone get Mrs. Metcalf some water. And a chair," the judge said, and I was aware of movement. I leaned forward, screaming at V in my head and she must have heard because she looked up, her eyes pools of misery. We have another signal, one we learned when we wanted to let the other know that we hadn't told someone anything. Because we had so many secrets, so many pacts and stories that existed between us that it was sometimes dangerous to be in conversation with other people. As soon as I knew she was looking I opened my eyes wide and turned my head to the right so she could be sure that I hadn't discussed this with Xander and she could tell the truth.

"Are you able to continue?" Justice Smithson asked when V had been seated in a chair with water at her side.

"Yes," V said, "I'm sorry."

Xander stepped forward again. "You were about to tell us about the Kitten Club."

"It's a private members club."

"A private members club that specializes in fulfilling sexual fantasies," Xander said. "I believe in layman's terms they organize orgies. Is that correct?"

"It is."

"And you and Mr. Hayes were members?"

"We only went once."

"You paid £500 and you only went once?"

"We realized it wasn't for us when we got there. We didn't even take part the one time we went."

"What made you think you'd enjoy it at all?"

"I don't know."

"It was just the sort of thing you and Mr. Hayes were into then?"

"Well, it turned out not to be."

"But it wasn't out of the question that you would do something like this?"

"I don't see how this is relevant in any way." V turned to look at the judge, but he kept his eyes on the papers in front of him.

Xander ignored her as well. "One more thing about this Kitten

Club," he said, sounding as if the words tasted bad on his tongue. "I believe when you register you have to provide names. They call them code names. And they advise you not to use your real names. Perhaps you could tell the court the names you and Mr. Hayes used."

V looked straight at Xander. "Truth and Lies."

Xander looked at the jury. "Truth and Lies," he repeated, and I thought I heard an intake of breath somewhere.

"It was just a play on my name. It didn't mean anything."

But Xander acted like he hadn't heard her again. "You lied to Mr. Hayes about the ending of your relationship didn't you, choosing to lay all the blame at his door rather than taking any responsibility yourself. You blamed him for his one-night stand, when in fact you were having an affair with Angus Metcalf."

"I've already said I regret that."

Xander turned from the witness box and walked toward the jury. "Would you say you have a face you present to the world and a face you wear in private, Mrs. Metcalf?"

"Objection, My Lord," Petra said.

"Sustained," Justice Smithson replied, which surprised me.

"All right then," Xander said. "Will you please explain to us why on earth you didn't tell your husband that Mr. Hayes came to meet you at work after you received those e-mails on your honeymoon that you said upset you so much? You went for a drink with him and you failed to mention that to your husband."

"It was stupid of me. I was trying to protect both Mike and Angus."

"Or were you perhaps thinking about rekindling your relationship? Perhaps Mr. Hayes isn't as delusional as you keep implying, but actually a pretty good judge of character and motive. Perhaps he was able to see that you were keen to restart what had been a very intense relationship in which you were both clearly very attracted to each other?"

I felt myself getting hard and had to put my hands in my lap.

"That is absolutely not true," V said.

"Which part?"

"All of it."

"So you weren't ever involved in an intense relationship and you weren't ever very attracted to each other?"

V's chin dipped. "No, that's not what I meant. I meant I wasn't thinking about rekindling anything and I do think Mike is delusional." By now, I wasn't even troubled when V said these things because I knew what she was doing and I love her for it. I love that she is trying to preserve our life, I love that we are still working toward the same goal, just in different ways.

"But an easy mistake for Mr. Hayes to make considering your past and the fact that you were again involved in a secret communication?"

"It was hardly a secret communication."

"It was if no one else knew about it." Xander turned and walked back across the room. "Mr. Hayes is very confused by your assertion that he assaulted you the night he came to your house when Mr. Metcalf was away. He says the kiss you shared was entirely consensual and that when you asked him to stop he did. Is that true?"

V's eyes were pleading. "It's true that he stopped when I asked him to, although I had to say no a few times before he got off me. I had to shout at him. And he probably thinks the kiss was consensual because I wanted him to believe that, so I could make him stop."

Xander frowned. "I'm sorry, I don't follow. You kissed him to make him stop."

"I didn't want to make him angry. I was scared. All I was focused on was getting him to leave. I thought he might rape me."

"So let me get this straight. You were so scared of Mr. Hayes you played along with his sexual advances to make him go away, even though you have an intricate, highly sexual history with each other. Then you get him out of your house and you don't immediately call the police, or your parents, or anyone?"

V's eyes were swimming in tears. "I know it sounds strange, but I didn't know what to do. I didn't even know if the police would take me seriously if I did call them."

Xander puffed out his cheeks as if he couldn't get his head around anything V was saying. "Mr. Hayes says that when you went for a drink with him after work you told him Angus was going to be away and he took it as an invitation to come around."

V reached out and grabbed the edge of the stand, her knuckles white. "Oh God, don't be ridiculous. I told Mike that Angus was away because I didn't want him to try to contact me until he got back."

Xander raised an eyebrow. "But you still let him in when he turned up on your doorstep?"

"I told him it wasn't a good idea, but he's much stronger than me."

"But he didn't break down the door or anything to gain entry, did he?"

"No. But I made it clear I didn't want him there. And I tried to shut the door, but he pushed it open so he could come inside."

"But if you'd minded that much you could have shouted at that point, or pushed back. I don't think there is any suggestion you fought each other."

"No, of course we didn't. I thought maybe I could talk some sense into him."

"After you shared a kiss, Mr. Hayes says you talked for quite a while about you leaving Angus and coming to live with him." Xander paused. "Mr. Hayes says you said you wished things had worked out between you."

V's eyes were so filled with tears they looked like they were shaking. "Yes, I did. And every moment made my skin crawl. I've explained why I did all those things. It was to get him to leave."

"It's a strange thing to say to someone though, you must admit. That you wished things had worked out between you, when you were trying to get rid of him and were married to someone else."

"It's not a strange thing to say if you know Mike like I do," V said, and with those words my whole body relaxed, as if it had been held upright by string that had finally been cut. Nobody knows anyone the way we know each other, and now V had admitted it in court, in front of all these people.

"Did you ask Mr. Hayes to help you get out of your marriage? To help you get rid of your husband?" Xander asked.

"No, of course I didn't. I didn't want my marriage to end."

Xander sighed. "Perhaps, Mrs. Metcalf, you could tell us what you did when Mr. Hayes left after the alleged assault?"

"It isn't alleged, he assaulted me." She shook her head and another tear escaped. "After he'd gone all I could do was shower and get into bed and then I started being sick in the night and I couldn't stop. I don't know what happened. It was horrible."

"Perhaps you were feeling like you were heading for another breakdown?"

V looked up, her tears suddenly dried. "A what?"

"A nervous breakdown?"

"What do you mean?"

"Did you take antidepressants for a year after leaving university?"

V looked around the courtroom and a sound like a laugh escaped from her. "Are you serious? Half the country is on antidepressants. It doesn't mean anything."

Xander opened his eyes as wide as they would go and looked at the jury. "So by your estimation six of these good people are currently taking antidepressants. Perhaps you wouldn't mind raising your hand if you are." They all stayed still, a couple even looked quite upset.

He shook his head at V. "Mrs. Metcalf, I have to say, the part of this whole story that I'm finding hardest to get my head around is how you were found by the police in the arms of Mr. Hayes, while your husband lay dying on the floor."

V gasped. "Oh God, I've explained that."

"You've said you don't know how it happened," Xander said. "But that seems unlikely when you remember everything else so well."

"But I don't remember clearly," V said, her voice pleading.

"Perhaps it happened because you and Mr. Hayes are in love, as he says? Perhaps you were comforting each other because you were both shocked and upset that your game had ended in this tragic way?"

"No," V said, but her voice sounded as thin as water.

And that is one of the major flaws in V's plan—nothing she said on the stand today really added up. What I am starting to understand is that quite apart from the fact that we can't be separated, we also must remain true to who we are. We must make sense and nothing makes sense if one of us denies our love.

"Why did you call Mr. Hayes to warn him that your husband was on his way to his house on the night of the murder?" Xander said, and it all felt relentless.

"I wasn't warning Mike. I was trying to protect Angus."

"But if that was true, why on earth didn't you call the police?"

"I don't know. I didn't think of it."

"You didn't think of it." Xander sounded exasperated. "Mrs. Metcalf, we all heard your message. You sounded deeply distressed. Do you really expect us to believe that you didn't consider calling the police?"

"Yes, because it's the truth."

"Or perhaps you were scared to because you realized that your game had gone a bit too far? Perhaps you were worried someone was going to get hurt and you knew you would be implicated?"

V stifled a cry. "No, not at all. I was only worried about Angus at that moment."

"Would you say you're good at ending relationships, Mrs. Metcalf?" Xander asked, turning back to V.

The question was obviously not what V had been expecting. "I don't know. Who is?"

"You like to use others don't you? Like with Mr. Sage and Mr. Hayes."

"God, I was a teenager with Gordon and I've explained the situation with Mike."

"Would you say you're good at your job?"

V looked surprised again. "Yes."

"I believe you're one of the youngest people ever to be taken on by the Calthorpe Centre in a scientific role. Remind us what you're working on again."

"I'm part of a team that is working on the idea of artificial intelligence."

"So, replacing humans with robots?"

"That's a very simplistic way of putting it and, no, of course we're not trying to do that. If anything we're trying to help humans with the programs we hope to create."

Xander raised his eyebrows and turned to the jury. "You must have been very single-minded to have climbed to the top. Very focused. Worked very hard."

"Yes, I have."

Petra stood again. "My Lord, are we now trying Mrs. Metcalf for being a woman with a good job?"

The judge looked over at Petra, his lips pursed. "I am sure that is not what my honorable colleague is implying, is it Mr. Jackson?"

Xander chuckled. "Of course not, My Lord. I am just trying to establish if Mrs. Metcalf is the sort of person to become easily confused, or to not see logical ways out of situations."

"I'm good at my job, yes," V answered, her voice thin.

Xander tapped the rolled-up paper he was holding against his leg. "I don't suppose that either you or Mr. Hayes wanted Mr. Metcalf dead." He looked at the jury. "I think we all can see that neither he nor you are hardened murderers. But I think it is fair to say you are a woman who enjoys game-playing and sex." He let the word hang in the air. "You are clearly clever and adept at solving problems. And I think you are good at getting other people to do your dirty work for you. So when you found yourself attracted once again to Mr. Hayes, you started looking for his help to get out of your marriage."

"No. That is completely not true." I could tell V would be crying again in a minute.

"Come on," Xander said. "It would have been very embarrassing to end that marriage only a couple of months after such a lavish wedding."

"But I didn't want to end the marriage."

"And there is an obvious connection between you and Mr. Hayes. Christ, we can all feel it right here, right now. It's like electricity passing between you." Xander moved his hand as he spoke and I felt the jury looking between us, so they must have seen the shimmering neon string attached to both our hearts. "And it's hardly surprising. You're both very good-looking, intelligent people who have this secret sex game you've played together for years, who've flirted with the idea of orgies and bisexuality. It's hardly a leap of the imagination to see what's happened here."

"Objection," Petra shouted, standing up.

Justice Smithson banged his hand on the table. "Sustained. Mr. Jackson, your questioning is crossing the line."

Xander bowed his head lightly to the judge and then Petra. "I'm sorry," he said, "I got carried away with the atmosphere. No further questions, My Lord."

He walked back to his seat calmly, but the air in the courtroom was anything but. It fizzed and squealed around us, enclosing and disposing of us. V and I were breathing in the same air, our bodies recycling to keep each other alive, as the moments passed in thundering heartbeats.

V stood shakily to exit the witness box and I thought she might stumble but she made it back to our box, where she sat with her head dropped and her back curved away from me.

Xander looked tired when we met in our strange airless debriefing room at the end of the day. I was angry with him for bringing up the Kitten Club without warning me, but he countered with his own anger that, I realized, was just as vibrant as mine.

"Was she lying?" he asked, like a threat. "Did you go more than once?"

"No," I answered. "It was just as she said."

"Shame," Xander said, rubbing his temples like he had a headache.

"I don't even see how it helps anyway. I mean, I did all the same things she did. Petra's bound to ask me about everything."

Xander looked at me disdainfully. "Grow up, Mike. It's totally different for you."

It is morning now and I haven't slept. I have had to go over and over all the things that were said yesterday. Writing it down has helped somewhat. I am sitting on my bunk now, watching the sun break milkily in the fogged sky, and all I know is this: Verity is truth. She is my truth. The only truth. What we know and do is the only thing that matters. It transcends all the petty lies and misrepresentations, all the innuendos and gossip. We rise above it like the eagle does above the mountains. We look down and see a mess but it doesn't touch us. I need to use the truth today to reach a greater truth, a greater place of safety in which V and I can live forever, untouched by all the banality that constitutes this sorry world.

After watching you on the stand yesterday, V, it was like you were giving me permission to lie. You lied for what you thought was our good, but you got it wrong in your confusion, and now I must swoop in like the eagle and guide your hand. I now know what I must do, V.

I know how to save you, my love, my darling, and nothing has ever felt more wonderful.

Y

I am just back from court, but I am compelled to write because the adrenaline is still coursing through my veins. V, all of this has always been for you. I even understand now why I am writing: This will stand as a record of our pure, unending love, binding us together for eternity. We will share and celebrate these words forever and the way we have conspired with our enemies to bring us to the ultimate, craving truth of our love. When you read this, as you surely must, I want you to know that I own every word I uttered today. Every single movement I made in there I made for you, my love.

There was real hate in Petra's eyes when she stood to cross-examine me. Her long thin body vibrated with distaste and her voice was harsh. "Mr. Hayes, I put it to you that you are a fantasist. A dangerous fantasist at that."

"No," I said, "I'm not."

"But then you would hardly admit to it, would you." She put on her glasses and flicked through her notes. "We have of course heard from Mrs. Lasscles, your old headmistress, and I have several school reports and social service referrals in my possession and they all talk about your lack of empathy, your trouble with making friends, your tendency toward violence, and your sexualized language."

I still don't recognize this person, though hazy memories are appearing through the smoke of my mind. I can just about make out chairs flying across rooms and girls crying and adults pinning me to the floor. "I left school a long time ago."

"Not that long," Petra replied. "So you don't deny how you behaved back then?"

"I can't exactly remember. But I think we've established I had a bad childhood. I was an angry kid."

"Would you agree it's fair to say you've never dealt with that anger?" Petra asked, removing her glasses and beginning her walk.

"No. I think I've dealt with it."

"But I mean professionally. You've never seen anyone have you, even though your foster mother and Mrs. Metcalf, doctors even, have advised this."

"No. I've never felt the need."

"But I think we'd all agree that the abuse you suffered would have left deep scars that are almost impossible to eradicate without professional help."

I watched her legs as she walked, willing her to trip and break her neck. "I don't know. I feel fine."

"Do you think the e-mails you sent Mrs. Metcalf after your breakup and then again while she was on her honeymoon were the actions of a rational person?"

"I was very upset, both times."

"Yes, but don't you think they were extreme?"

"I've already said I was very upset when I wrote them. I'm not proud of them at all."

Petra looked at the jury. "I know you all have these in your notes, but perhaps I could read one out to you, dated February 14th, last year." She put her glasses on and opened the papers in front of her. "V, my darling, my love, my everything, please, please write to me. You can't just cut me out of your life like this. How many times can I say sorry? What do I have to do? I will do anything, everything, name your price. I love you, I love you. I crave you, I crave you. Stop this. Stop it you bitch. Fucking stop it, you heartless cow. Don't be this person. Remember who we are. I love you, V, forever and always." Petra looked up as she finished and I could feel the stunned silence of the courtroom like a presence in the air. "There are quite a few e-mails like that," she said.

I nodded, feeling as if there was something pressing on the backs of my eyes. "I'm very ashamed I wrote those things. I didn't mean them. I was desperate."

"They sound more than desperate to me," she said. "They sound dangerous."

"Objection," Xander said.

"Sustained."

Petra shook her head. "Why did you stop writing to Mrs. Metcalf after that e-mail?"

"Because I realized there was no point continuing. I knew I would have to do something big to win her back."

"Which is when you decided to come back to London?"

"Yes."

"How did you feel when you found out she was getting married?"

I squeezed my hands together in my lap. "I was shocked." Xander had told me not to say that the marriage was part of the Crave.

"You didn't feel upset?"

"Yes, I did."

"But you didn't talk to anyone about it? In fact, you concocted an elaborate charade in which you pretended to your work colleagues that you and Verity were still partners."

My skin felt itchy. "It was easier to do that than talk about what had happened."

"Maybe it was easier to pretend to yourself as well?"

"No, I knew the situation."

"You were just determined to reverse it?"

"I knew Verity wanted that as well."

Petra paused for a moment, but then spoke again. "From what I can tell you assumed an awful lot about what Mrs. Metcalf was feeling from a couple of very brief e-mails and meetings when you came back to

London. There are no records of any phone calls between you, no e-mail correspondence apart from the scant few in the files, no long meetings."

"I know Verity very well," I said, keeping my eyes on Petra. "I don't need to spend lots of time with her to know what she is thinking."

"You also clearly don't need to listen to her," Petra said, glancing over at the jury. "She specifically told you she was in love with Angus and not interested in restarting anything with you almost every time you communicated."

"You don't understand," I said, and I knew my voice had risen, so I pinched on the side of my hand in the way Xander had taught me to do.

"Go on then, educate me."

"We have all these secret ways of communicating, which only we understand."

"Oh yes," Petra said, her voice heavy with sarcasm. "You think she doesn't mean the things she says. So, when she says no, she actually means yes, is that it?"

"No. I don't mean—"

"Like when you're forcing yourself on a woman sexually and she's telling you no and you keep going because really no means yes. Is that what you mean?"

"Objection, My Lord," Xander said, standing. "How is this relevant?"

"Yes, Ms. Gardner," Justice Smithson said, "you do seem to be concerning yourself with political point-scoring in this trial."

Petra looked down and her face was a deep red. "Apologies, My Lord, if you feel that way. But I think we can agree that it is relevant, given that Mr. Hayes failed to stop kissing Mrs. Metcalf when she first asked him to on the night of the alleged assault."

The judge waved his assent, but it was obvious he was annoyed.

Xander caught my eye and lowered his shoulders, so I did the same and it made me feel a bit better. "Of course I don't think no means yes," I said. "I stopped when Verity asked me to."

"She had to ask you more than once, I believe. She had to shout. She says you had her pinned to the floor."

"She wanted to kiss me."

"How on earth do you know that?"

"From the way she responded."

"I put it to you that you wanted Mr. Metcalf dead," Petra said, looking straight at me. "I have the medical reports and your injuries were mostly superficial. Mr. Metcalf however sustained a dislocated jaw, a broken nose, cheekbone, and jawbone, a fractured skull, and extensive bleeding on the brain. You hit him very hard numerous times. Much harder than he hit you, much harder than was necessary to stop him punching you."

"I didn't mean to kill him."

"You must have hated him simply because Verity loved him."

"No," I said, shaking my head. "I didn't hate him. I felt sorry for him."

"But he had everything you wanted."

"No, he didn't. He thought he did. But Verity didn't love him."

"But Verity has sat where you are now and told us she loved him."

"She doesn't mean it."

"Oh right, so we're back here. Back to not believing the words that come out of a woman's mouth because they always mean the opposite."

"Objection," Xander said. "Mr. Hayes has never claimed to be talking about all women."

"Sustained," said Justice Smithson. "Ms. Gardner, your point?"

"My point, My Lord," said Petra, walking toward me, "is that you, Mr. Hayes, seem to have established this narrative in which you know Verity better than she even knows herself. Only you know what is best for her or how she should live. Only you understand what she means. Only you hear the things she doesn't say and convince yourself that she has spoken."

"No, you don't understand." The desire to cause Petra physical harm raged inside me.

"And when she broke away from this and was happy in a life that had nothing to do with you, you couldn't bear it and killed Mr. Metcalf in a fit of jealousy and rage, in the way you had been conditioned to behave since childhood."

"That is not true." I could feel the sweat dripping from my brow and the tension in my shoulders, which would result in a mean headache.

"But it is also not true that Mrs. Metcalf wanted to be with you or end her marriage, is it? And it is certainly not true that she ever asked you to help her get rid of Mr. Metcalf."

"You don't understand," I said again and I felt our truth slipping away from me.

"Your childhood sounds terrible," Petra said. "Do you hate your mother, Mr. Hayes?"

I thought of the woman in my wastepaper basket. "No."

"But you refuse to see her?"

"Yes."

"Why is that?"

"Because there's no point."

"Did you read the article in the *Mirror* in which she appeared very contrite and begged to see you?"

It felt like the walls were closing in and I didn't know where we were going. "Yes?"

"So why not see her now?"

"Because she doesn't mean it."

Petra spun to the jury. "There. Another woman who says one thing and means another."

"I didn't mean—" I started to say, but Xander shushed me with his hand.

"I don't think you trust women," Petra said, turning back to me. "Or men for that matter. I think you have constructed your own internal world because that is the only place you feel safe."

"Objection," Xander said. "I didn't realize Ms. Gardner was a psychologist."

"You might do well to save those types of remarks for your closing statement, Ms. Gardner," Justice Smithson said.

"Sorry, My Lord," Petra said. "You're right. Because of course Mr. Hayes is too deeply involved in this fantasy to ever admit to any of it." She walked over to where I was standing, until she was so close I could see her makeup in the creases around her eyes and smell her synthetic floral stench. "I don't even believe you love Mrs. Metcalf," she said, her eyes locked on me.

"Of course I love her," I shouted, the sound deafening in the silent courtroom.

Petra turned her back on me and I wanted to vault the witness box and push her to the ground. "No," she said finally. "You're in love with the idea of being in love. You can't love someone and put them through what you've made Mrs. Metcalf endure."

"But you don't understand," I said, and even though I stopped myself shouting there was a tremor in my voice. "You have no idea."

"What, because I'm a woman?" Petra said as she turned back to face me again.

"No, because you're not me or Verity."

"I would just ask you to do the decent thing and tell the truth about Mrs. Metcalf," she said, looking directly into my eyes. "If you love her like you say you do, then for God's sake let her go and admit that you're lying about her involvement in her husband's murder. Lying about what she feels for you. Lying, in fact, about your whole relationship, which exists only inside your own head."

I held her gaze, her stupid cowlike brown eyes. I shook my head. "No," I said. "I stand by everything I have said. Verity and I are very much in love. We didn't want Angus to die, but there was no way we weren't going to be together."

Petra shook her head and turned away. "No further questions, My Lord."

Xander leaned over his table as he asked the first question. "How did you feel when Mrs. Metcalf ended the relationship last Christmas?"

"Shocked and saddened. But I also understood. I had betrayed her massively and I knew I had to pay for what I'd done."

"That's an interesting phrase. Pay for what you'd done. Is that what Verity said to you?"

"No, but I know the rules."

Xander raised an eyebrow. "What rules?"

It felt like there was too much to say and not enough time. You see, I knew, V, that you were the only person in the room who would understand what I was talking about and, at that moment, I felt nothing but contempt for everyone else. How boring, I thought, not to be us. "Our rules. The rules we live by."

"Is that why you stopped contacting Mrs. Metcalf in February, a month after you returned to New York?"

I could feel my heart beating through my shirt, hard and fast. "Yes. I knew I had to make amends. I knew I couldn't just say sorry, I knew I had to show her how sorry I was. So I set about making plans to come home and buy a house and start creating the sort of life we'd always talked about."

"You must have been pretty shocked then to find out she was engaged," Xander said. He kept his eyes on me as he spoke and I knew he was willing me not to say what I thought.

"I was," I said, keeping my voice steady. "But I also realized how much I had hurt her and it felt like a natural reaction."

He smiled because I had remembered. "Are you saying that you think Angus was a rebound relationship?"

I shrugged, as casually as I could, keeping my mind fixed on all the times we'd played this out, as I'm sure you did, V, with Petra. "I couldn't say, but it seems like a very short amount of time to go from ending a long-term relationship to engagement."

Xander nodded. "And did you attempt to contact Mrs. Metcalf on your return?"

"I e-mailed her to say I was back and I was looking forward to the wedding and meeting Angus and how they should come around sometime."

"So all very friendly?" Xander said. Then he looked at the jury. "See item 12 in your folders."

"Yes, she said we should get together after the wedding. But then I bumped into her, like she said, a couple of weeks before the wedding."

"And how was that?"

I swallowed because it felt like my throat was blocked. I drank from the water in front of me. "It was strange," I said, pausing. "I think it was strange for both of us. It still felt like there was a strong connection between us and it upset me, if I'm honest." Keep to the timeline, Xander had instructed me, remember it as though your life depends on it, which of course it did.

"But you still went to the wedding?"

"Yes, although I wish I hadn't because it was horrid to see Verity marry Angus. It made me realize that I wasn't over her. In fact it made me realize I was still in love with her."

"When was the next time you saw Mrs. Metcalf after the wedding?" Xander asked.

"I went to meet her after work. I felt I had to say a few things to her and she agreed to a drink. I told her I loved her still and I thought she'd made a mistake marrying Angus."

"And what did she say?"

I looked up at that and over at you then, V. Xander had told me not to, but I found I couldn't stop myself. You were staring at me, your face ashen and your eyes black and hard and I knew then that you hadn't yet understood what I was doing. I opened my mouth, but nothing came out.

"Mr. Hayes, you must answer the question," Justice Smithson said.

"She seemed very confused," I said. "She said she loved Angus, but she was distressed and she kept giving me our secret signal."

"Your secret signal?" Xander said. "What's that?"

"When we Craved, her signal to me, when she wanted me to come over and rescue her, was to pull on the silver eagle she wears around her neck." We all looked at you as I said this and the eagle was there, resting gently on your skin. You sweetly put your hand to it, but then dropped it into your lap.

Xander turned back to me. "And is that when Mrs. Metcalf mentioned Angus was going away for a few days?"

"Yes. I took it to mean that she wanted me to come around and we could start sorting all the mess out. But she was away at the weekend, so I went around on the Monday evening and she let me in."

"Mrs. Metcalf says you assaulted her."

My eyes stung with the effort it was taking not to cry. "I think Verity is very confused and that's understandable. It was wrong of us to kiss, but we couldn't help ourselves. And like Verity said, when she asked me to stop I did. We talked for ages afterward about what we were going to do and how she would break it to Angus."

"And you left afterward. She didn't have to shout or ask you to go? She didn't call the police?"

I shook my head. "No. We agreed she would tell Angus the next day and come and live with me."

"But you didn't hear from her the next day?"

"No. I started to get worried that Angus had hurt her in some way or something had happened, so I went around again. I should have left when he told me that she was ill as Verity had made it clear she wanted to be the one to tell him, which would have been the right thing to do. But my impatience got the better of me and I blurted it out. He was very shocked and she was very upset and I left so they could sort it out. I went home and fell asleep and the next thing I knew was when Verity rang me to say Angus was on his way." I realized I had been talking quickly and my breath was coming in short, ragged bursts.

Xander flipped open the pages he was holding. "I also have the medical reports, which show that both you and Mr. Metcalf sustained injuries consistent with a fistfight. Is that your memory of what happened?"

"Yes."

"Who would you say started the fight?"

"Mr. Metcalf. As soon as I opened the door he went for me."

"So he didn't try to speak to you first?"

"No. Not at all."

"Witnesses have testified to the fact that he was standing outside your house shouting for a good ten minutes before you opened the door. Why was that?"

"Because Verity had told me not to let him in."

"Why do you think she said that?"

"She said she didn't want either of us getting hurt."

"Either of you?"

"Yes."

"So what made you open the door then?"

I thought back to those minutes in the kitchen. "It's hard to explain. Lots of people have shouted at me in my life and I wanted him to stop."

"What do you feel about the fact that you killed Mr. Metcalf?"

I looked at my hands and it still felt unreal that they had ended another person's life. "I feel devastated," I said, remembering the word Xander wanted me to use. "Of course I wanted Verity to leave him, but I didn't want anything bad to happen to him."

And that is the truth. Or maybe the real truth is that I didn't care what happened to Angus. I don't think you really cared either, V, although I know you didn't want him dead. I don't think either of us cares what happens to anyone apart from you and I. I don't wish death on others, but at the same time, there are so many pointless people out there, so many disposable lives. Our truth is nothing stranger than that we need no one else, you and I are all there is.

"What was it like when Verity was ill after you left university? When she took antidepressants?"

I could feel your eyes on me, V, and I'm sorry but I had to play the line here, even though we both know it's not what I meant. We both know I loved that time. "It wasn't nice, but we got through it."

"I believe you learned how to meditate in order to help her?"

"Yes, it's a useful skill."

"Would you say you are a naturally calm person, Mr. Hayes?"

"I think so."

"And how about the descriptions others have given of you being a bit of a loner, an outsider, hard to make friends with but very loyal."

I nodded. "I think all that is true. I did have a hard childhood, but I was also very lucky to be taken in by Elaine and Barry, who taught me that there are good people out there. Maybe I did love Verity too much, like her mother said, but also I'm not sure what that means. I do love her. And she loves me."

Xander nodded, and it felt like we were all breathing more heavily. "Mr. Hayes, I am very interested in your take on the game, the Crave, you played with Mrs. Metcalf during your relationship."

"It's hard to explain to outsiders. It was just as Verity said. We'd go to a bar and I'd hang back so a man could approach her and then I'd go over and break it up."

"Mrs. Metcalf testified that it aroused you both, is that true?"

"Yes."

"I believe sometimes you had sex afterward in the bars or clubs where these events took place."

"Yes, we did."

Xander walked toward the jury. "And did you always enjoy these nights?"

"Yes. If Verity was happy then so was I."

"How do you feel now you know that she was lying to you about being curious about having sex with a woman, when in fact she'd had a lesbian relationship already?"

"It doesn't matter," I said, and it doesn't, V.

"And what about the Kitten Club. What did you feel about that?"

After your testimony, V, when Xander and I were talking about whether or not you'd lied about how many times we had been to the Kitten Club, and I had said it had only been once, there was something about the way he said the word *shame* that made me finally understand what all this is about for these idiots who are not us. It unlocked the problem for me, made me see a way out of the mess. Give them what they want and they will all go away.

Yes, V, you and I will have to sacrifice a few years of our lives because this world isn't ready yet to appreciate love in its purest, simplest form. This world deals in violence and lies, deceit and deception. It cannot see purity even when it is placed in front of its nose, choosing instead to turn away and scoff. Well, let them. We don't care, do we, V. We are so much more than that.

That is the reason I did what I did next.

"I enjoyed it," I said. "We both did."

Xander looked up, as if he hadn't heard me correctly and his voice shook slightly when he next spoke. But I recognized the shake, it was one of desire; it was the sound of someone getting what they want. "But I thought Mrs. Metcalf said you only went once? And you didn't take part?"

I kept my voice steady. "We went a few times. And we did take part."

Xander almost smiled. "You took part in orgies? You and Mrs. Metcalf?"

"Yes."

You cried out at this point, V, and the tears gushed from your eyes, the eagle bouncing up and down with your heartbeat.

"Can you tell the court what you did?" Xander asked, almost licking his lips.

Momentarily I lost my nerve; I wanted to stop the pain at that second, I wanted to ignore the greater good and save you. I leaned forward and my eyes locked on yours. "Forgive me, V," I shouted. "It's for the best, I promise. I love you."

You opened your mouth but the only sounds were those of your sobs.

Petra stood up. "This has to stop, My Lord."

"Your defendant cannot address Mrs. Metcalf," Justice Smithson said. "Unless he wants to be found in contempt of court."

Xander walked toward me and my whole body was shaking. The whole room seemed to be shaking. But I drew strength from your continued distress, V, because I knew we were together in our pain: I knew I had more lies to tell about you, and that telling them was the only certain way to protect you, to keep you safe while I was locked away. "Mike, you need to tell the court what sort of hold Mrs. Metcalf had over you."

We hadn't prepared that question and I felt it run into me like a punch. "We are very much in love," I said, and my voice sounded hard and loud.

Xander nodded, conciliatory. "Yes, I don't doubt that. But would you have done anything for her?"

"Absolutely. I still would."

"There's nothing you wouldn't do?"

"Nothing."

The silence throbbed around us. "Even after all this? Even after all she's said about you?"

I nodded. "Verity will have her reasons. It will be okay."

I remembered something else last night, V, something that came to me late as I lay on my bunk turning everything over in my mind. I remembered when we went into that gift shop in Edinburgh, the year we went to the festival. How we were looking through a pile of quotes on wooden plaques and laughing and then you stopped. How you held one up and said it was the first quote you'd ever come across, one which actually meant something worth remembering. I read it over your shoulder that day: *I must be cruel only to be kind / Thus bad begins and worse remains behind.*

"We should remember that, Mikey," you said to me, "Shakespeare is always right." And I didn't understand then why you thought that, but I do now, I absolutely do now.

We must work and bend the truth. Others might see it differently, but, my darling, our kind of cruelty is love by any other name.

Xander snapped shut the folder. "Did Mrs. Metcalf ever ask you to hurt Mr. Metcalf in any way?"

I paused, but only briefly. And, V, I looked straight at you. Remember that. I took a breath deep into my stomach because we had reached the moment I have spent the last weeks debating: What constitutes the truth? Does it exist only in what we say to each other in flimsy puffs of air, often said without real thought? Or is it, as I suspect, more than that? No, surely it is the foundation of all we are. It is in our bones, in our being. It begs to be interpreted in order to reach its true potential.

"She asked me to help her," I said, my heart hammering in my chest and my blood singing in my ears.

Xander stood still for a moment and it was good to see him wrong-footed. I felt him look straight at me but I didn't return his stare because I was never going to take my eyes off you. "When did this happen?"

"When I went to her house on the Monday. After we kissed we spent a lot of time talking about how we were going to handle the situation, like I've said." I stopped for a moment, remembering how the floor had felt underneath me, how we'd sat up, how we'd shivered with desire. "As you know she said that she wished things had worked out between us."

My God, V, you are the most beautiful being ever to have existed, that's what I thought when I looked at you then. I could swim into you and lie still forever. But I knew Xander and all the rest of them would need more. I knew the story needed a more definite climax.

"She told me she wanted to get out of the marriage but that she couldn't do it alone. She asked for my help." The words pricked me as they left my body.

"Mr. Hayes, what did these words mean to you?" Xander asked through my thoughts.

"That she was scared because she hates confrontation. I've always saved her from bad situations and she knew I could help her with this one. Verity didn't want Angus dead, just like I didn't want him dead. But we had to be together. Do you understand that? It is simply impossible that we don't end up together."

I was speaking only to you, V, and you never moved your gaze from mine for one second. You stopped crying. And I knew then that you finally understood what I had done.

Xander, Petra, and Angus's barristers all spent ages summing up, each of them going over and over the same wrong thoughts in the same wrong ways. And then the judge could have had his lines written for him by Xander. He spent a lot of time summarizing the legal issues: How to find me guilty of murder was the most serious charge the jury could bring against me. How to do so they had to be absolutely certain of my intention to kill Angus at the moment I hit him. How they had to be sure I wasn't acting in self-defense. He also reminded them about my upbringing and the mental strain I had been under at the time. He told them that the option to convict me of manslaughter was a realistic expectation.

He did little to hide his revulsion for you, V. He reminded the jury how you had lied, even under oath, about Angela and the Kitten Club, and how you find it hard to remove yourself from unwanted situations, especially ending relationships. He talked for a long time about, as he put it, your extreme and unusual sexual appetites, and how you clearly used your sexuality to exert control over me. I shut my eyes as he spoke to stop myself from screaming out in your defense, but these are the trolls we have to deal with. These are the maggots who would not be fit to feed on our corpses.

In the end we only had to wait twenty-four hours before we were called back in. I was found not guilty of murder but guilty of manslaughter. And you, my love, were found guilty of accessory to manslaughter. I looked over to you when the verdicts were read out and I saw your knees buckle and how your warden had to steady you with her arm. Suzi cried out, but I'm not sure you heard. We had to stay standing to hear Justice Smithson talk about how tragic this case has been and how he believed that neither of us had meant for it to end in Angus's death. He spoke about responsibility and the dangers involved in game-playing and using others.

I remember only one line he said completely clearly: "You, Mr. Hayes, have fallen victim to two emotionally deficient women in your life and I only hope that when you leave prison you choose your future partners with more caution." It took me a while to realize he was talking about you, V, and my mother.

He gave us both eight years, but Xander says we will appeal and it's likely to be cut to about five. With good behavior he reckons we should be out in three to four. It's not that long.

Terry let me watch the news on his TV when I got back from court. We sat together on his fetid bunk and watched Petra stalk down the steps of the courthouse. There were lots of reporters jostling around her and she allowed them to settle before she began to speak.

"In my opinion, the wrong person has been on trial in this case," she said, her anger bristling off her like a force field. "Verity Metcalf appears to have been on trial for her sexuality throughout this sham of a trial, which at times has felt like we were back in seventeenth-century Salem. I did not expect to be standing in a twenty-first-century court-room and hearing words like 'enchanted' and 'beguiled' used about a clever, thoughtful woman. The lies and gossip that have enveloped this case have resulted not only in a dangerous man receiving a reduced sentence, which will see him back on our streets in only a few short years, but in an innocent woman being convicted of a crime she did not commit."

She chose a camera and looked down the lens, out to us. "Anyone who tells you that we have achieved equality should think hard about what has happened here today, should wonder at why none of this even appears unusual or shocking. We in the legal system should all feel ashamed of ourselves today, for justice has not been served."

I felt a coldness rest in my stomach, but Terry shoved me in the ribs. "Fucking women's libbers," he said. "They're all dykes, the lot of them. What they need is a good seeing to by a real man." He laughed hollowly, the sound rattling in his chest. I didn't reply, instead climbing up to my bunk where I notice that the fog has lifted for the night and I can see the stars through my tiny window.

And so we are here, V. Both shut up in our boxes, waiting for the moment we can be together again. Xander forwards me lots of requests from writers and journalists and production companies, all of whom are eager to tell my side of the story, as they put it. He tries to persuade me to talk to them, saying it would be good for me, but really it's just because he's vain and would like to see himself mirrored by a handsome actor. So far I have refused all requests, but I am starting to wonder. News changes quickly and gossip is overtaken. We are bound together by this story, our shared truth, and maybe we need to prolong it. Maybe we need to cement it forever on screens and in books so that we are always bound together by words.

Thank you for dropping the assault charges. I know of course that you never really meant it to go to court, it was simply another part of the Crave, another way to take us close to the edge before pulling back. And you were right to plead no contest to Angus's family's ridiculous civil action about the will. I recognized what they were when I saw them in court. But it doesn't matter; we wouldn't have ever touched a penny of his money anyway, would we, my love.

V, I know you like instant gratification and I know you will be finding the thought of spending even three years without me very hard, which is why I write to you every day. Long letters about our glorious future.

I especially like to talk to you about our home. The garden will be spectacular this spring, but it will be perfect when we return. Anna told me that all gardens need three years to properly settle and become the spaces they are meant to be. I lie on my bunk and think of this and it is like we planned it. You will be amazed at the cleverness of the planting and I can see you there, sitting among the swaying flowers as I cook supper on the barbecue. We can lie on the hot stones and look up at the clouds and you can teach me again to see pictures. We will make love in every room of the house and I will show you the numbers of the women in the cupboard in the kitchen, which I have decided we can't paint over. We will tell each other their stories, we will give them their proper endings.

We will get on airplanes, V, and lie on deserted beaches where the breeze kisses our skin. We will drink cocktails in strange hotel rooms where no one knows our names and swim in seas deeper than our imagination. We will hold each other tight every night, our bodies wrapping around each other, our heads resting against each other. We will sleep peacefully, our breaths in unison, warm and deep. And I won't wake in the night and want to uncoil your brain because I will know what is there. You will put your hand on my chest and feel my heartbeat and I will kiss every inch of your body. We, my darling, are creatures of perfection held in a state of waiting, our anticipation making our reunion all the better in the end.

V, we have managed what all other lovers yearn for but fail to do. We have eclipsed the world and exist only within our hearts. We have almost reached a state of perfection, a state in which our communication is all that matters. I shut my eyes and think about the wonderful days and weeks and months and years of togetherness stretching before us, in sickness and in health, forsaking all others, till death do us part, forever and ever, amen.

Oh God, V, you made me wait, but I have finally received a reply to all the letters I have written. It was a postcard on which you had written three words in capital letters: YOU ARE NOT.

I turned the card over and on the front was a photograph of an eagle, soaring high in the sky over snowcapped mountains. I laid the card on my bunk, its four corners in perfect line with each other, and then sat cross-legged in front of it. I stayed very still like that for a long time, just savoring the moment.

I shut my eyes because I had to process everything. I had to allow the eagle to soar into my brain and show me the way, just as you always intended. My darling, I know what others will think you mean with these words, but I also know you would never be crass and obvious. I love how you used our three-word code and the way you make me work, that nothing is straightforward with you. I know what you really mean. But I don't need you to tell me that I am not guilty.

The Crave I know is over. We don't need it anymore. We are beyond that now. Beyond anything outside of ourselves. But for old times' sake, I crossed out your three words and replaced them with the ones that will always mean something just to us: I CRAVE YOU. I readdressed it and put it into the prison mail system, so you should receive it tomorrow.

You, V, are the only person who has ever known what I need to survive in this world. I know Elaine and Barry, even my mother, tried their best, but you are the only person who has ever seen deep inside me, who has touched my soul.

We are humans, flailing and mistaken, but that doesn't matter. Because we love, we can forgive. We know the truth. We know what love is: the kindest and the cruelest emotion.

I am coming for you, V. I am coming.

ACKNOWLEDGMENTS

The first draft of this book was written in a mad spurt of anger at the continued injustices perpetrated against women in our so-called civilized society. So thank you to my husband, Jamie, and my son, Oscar, for putting up with this male-centered anger (when neither of them is the type of man I am angry with). And thank you to my daughters, Violet and Edith, for at least pretending to be interested as I instruct them against the patriarchy at any given opportunity.

Thanks also to the people who always read early versions of my books, this one included—my mum and dad, Lizzie, Emily, Polly, and Dolly. The encouragement and pushing is much appreciated.

Thanks to Sarah Thorne, for letting me watch her in court and for her invaluable legal advice.

Huge thanks to my agent, Lizzy Kremer, who is most definitely the best asset any writer could hope for, with her forensic eye and measured, thoughtful, calm advice, which is always, always right.

And finally thank you to my two editors, Selina Walker in the UK and Daphne Durham in the United States, who have both read and edited this book in a way I could have only dreamt of, with lightness and wisdom.

A Note About the Author

Araminta Hall is the author of *Everything and Nothing*. She has
an MA in creative writing and authorship from the University of
Sussex and teaches creative writing at New Writing South in
Brighton, where she lives with her husband and three children.
Our Kind of Cruelty is her first book published in the United States.